F
JOI   Join in

C.2

JOIN IN

JOIN IN

MULTIETHNIC SHORT STORIES

BY

OUTSTANDING WRITERS

FOR

YOUNG ADULTS

EDITED BY

DONALD R. GALLO

Delacorte Press

Published by Delacorte Press
Bantam Doubleday Dell Publishing Group, Inc.
1540 Broadway, New York, New York 10036

A portion of this book's royalties, earmarked for research in young adult literature,
will go to the Assembly on Literature for Adolescents
of the National Council of Teachers of English (ALAN).

Library of Congress Cataloging in Publication Data

Join in : multiethnic short stories by outstanding writers for young adults
/ edited by Donald R. Gallo.
p.   cm.
Summary: Seventeen authors, at the invitation of the editor, wrote these stories
especially for this collection featuring teenagers in America from various ethnic
backgrounds.
ISBN 0-385-31080-3
1. Short stories, American. [1. Short stories.] I. Gallo, Donald R.
PZ5.J8806   1993
[Fic]—dc20   92-43169
CIP
AC

Manufactured in the United States of America

November 1993

1   3   5   7   9   10   8   6   4   2

BVG

FOR JACKIE CRONIN . . .
whose persistent provocations
prompted me to start this collection

CONTENTS

DILEMMAS

CONNECTIONS

CONFRONTATIONS

INTRODUCTION

Since the founding of America, our country has been composed of diverse ethnic groups. The nation's diversity has become even more evident recently, with its highest rates of immigration in nearly a hundred years, especially of Hispanic and Asian peoples. The increasing variety of cultural groups in our public schools, along with a renewed interest in (and controversy over) the content of the literature that students are required to read, has revealed the need for a greater variety of ethnic characters and cultural issues in the books available to students, especially those in the middle grades and in junior and senior high school.

A century ago, most people seemed comfortable with the concept of America as a melting pot—a giant geographical caldron in which immigrants shed their individual ethnic identities for the larger identity of being *an American.* But many people today are not as willing to ignore their ethnic roots—they want to be both American and ethnic. They understandably want to be recognized for their individuality. Thus, in place of a melting pot, many people have come to see America as a bowl of flavorful stew or a colorful garden salad, in which numerous distinctive ingredients each contribute to the combined flavor that, as a result, is more satisfying than any single ingredient could be alone.

American literature in recent years has been infused with a number of significant novels about Asian teenagers, while good books featuring African American characters have continued to be published. Still, only a handful of novels focus on Puerto Rican, Mexican, and other Latino young people—members of ethnic groups that together, according to authoritative predictions, will soon constitute the largest minority group in the United States. And although publishers have been making a strong effort to find authentic stories that feature Native American adolescents, there are still very few books about contemporary American Indian teenagers, and almost none about Arab Americans. In addition, prior to this book, there has been only one collection of short fiction by a variety of young adult authors that has attempted to fill the need for more ethnic stories for teenage readers.

Taking one small step in an attempt to address this deficiency, I invited a number of authors from different ethnic backgrounds to write a story featuring American teenagers from specific cultural groups. These writers were told that their stories need not focus on racial issues (though some do, inevitably) and that white characters need not be excluded from their stories. I was hoping for realistic stories about normal teenagers involved in typical teenage conflicts, though I did not want white characters with black or brown faces painted on them. What I looked for—and what you will read in this collection—was good stories about *people*, mainly teenagers, who also happen to be Black, or Vietnamese, or Puerto Rican, or Native American. The ethnic background of the characters, nevertheless, plays a significant role in what happens in each story. Lensey Namioka's "Fox Hunt," for example, is a story about the growing attraction between a high school boy and a girl who steps off the school bus behind him one day—a typical teenage love story in most ways. But the main reason they are involved is because of an old Chinese legend, and this ethnic element makes the story different from the typical boy-meets-girl romance. Or in Kleya Forté-Escamilla's "Coming of Age," both teenage characters are forced to face harsh realities in their individual worlds largely because of attitudes that their Mexican culture has fostered.

In order to assure authenticity in the presentation of ethnic backgrounds and issues, I began my search for new stories by contacting well-known writers of novels for young adults who themselves are members of the same ethnic group they write about. The task was not an easy one, mainly because there are relatively few well-known ethnic writers in the business to begin with. In addition, several of the most popular writers regrettably had no time to write something new for this collection because they had too many other writing and speaking obligations.

Those Black, Asian, and Latino writers who did respond, did so enthusiastically. Four of those writers were, in fact, themselves immigrants to America at a young age: Kleya Forté-Escamilla having been born in Mexico, Minfong Ho in Burma, Lensey Namioka in China, and Maureen Crane Wartski in Japan.

But their contributions alone would not have produced as balanced a collection as I had hoped for, and so I sought stories from other writers who are not people of color—but who have created sensitive and insightful novels featuring teenage characters from different ethnic backgrounds. Some people question whether Caucasian authors can write authentic stories that feature people from other ethnic groups. As readers, we assume that if an author is African American, the ethnic elements in his or her story about Black characters are authentic. But a reader is more skeptical about the story's authenticity when a Caucasian writes about Black, or Hispanic, or Vietnamese characters. Understandably so. The proof is in the reading. You will have to judge for yourself.

In almost all the stories written by white authors for this collection, the author has had an intimate connection with the ethnic group she or he has chosen to write about. Although Elsa Marston is of Anglo-Saxon ancestry, for example, she has lived in Lebanon, is married to a Lebanese man, and has researched Lebanese history and culture for the nonfiction books she has written. So she knows Lebanon and Lebanese people as intimately as she can without being Lebanese herself.

There is also another important consideration to keep in mind when judging stories with characters whose ethnic background differs from that of the author. For most of the stories in this collection, if a white writer had not written about characters from a particular ethnic group, there would be no story to represent that ethnic group. Linda Crew, an Anglo whose 1989 novel *Children of the River* won numerous awards because of its poignant description of the life of Cambodian refugees, said this regarding her own writing about Cambodians:

> These people have stories to tell, but they are currently too busy to write, and their command of the English language isn't good enough yet to enable them to tell their own stories effectively enough. So I felt I had to tell their stories until they could do so themselves.

In spite of my efforts to find capable writers who understand teenagers from different ethnic groups within America's borders, there are still many ethnic groups that do not appear in this collection and that still remain underrepresented in American literature. Among them are Native Hawaiians and other Polynesians, Koreans, West Indians, Asian Indians, Egyptians, Costa Ricans, Nigerians, Argentinians, Filipinos, Eskimos, Hmungs,

Indonesians, Pakistanis, Colombians, Nicaraguans, and Salish Indians from the Northwest Coast, as well as numerous other Native American peoples. I hope that writers from those and other ethnic groups in America will soon emerge to tell stories about teenagers that can be included in collections that one day will follow this one.

The destructive Los Angeles race riots in the spring of 1992 and the murderous attempts at "ethnic cleansing" currently taking place in various parts of the world are striking evidence of the need for tolerance and understanding of the differences among us. After a jury acquitted the Los Angeles police officers who had publicly beaten Rodney King after a traffic violation, and after the destruction of nearly ten thousand businesses, property damage of nearly one billion dollars, the arrests of nearly seventeen thousand people, and the deaths of dozens of human beings, a tearful Rodney King on May 1, 1992, in the middle of the rioting pleaded on television for calm and restraint when he said: "Can we all get along?"

Getting along. Can we stop hating each other? Can we stop fighting with each other? Can we start understanding one another? It is my hope, and the hope of the authors represented here, that this collection of short stories might help just a little toward that end.

In the pages that follow, you will read stories about friendships and prejudice, expectations and disappointments, happiness and pain, connections and confrontations. The characters are Vietnamese, Puerto Rican, Cambodian, Japanese, Cuban, Lebanese, Chinese, Black, Laotian, Chicano, and Pueblo Indian. But most of all, they are American teenagers—interested in having friends, playing in a musical group, getting a driver's license, studying for the SATs, dealing with adult authority figures, falling in love, playing baseball, wanting to be treated fairly, and being accepted.

They are all part of the delicious mix that is America. Come, join in.

Expectations

On the Number Two subway train heading uptown, it's business as usual for most passengers. But for three high school dudes with money in their pockets, there's nothing more important than checking out the honeys. But then what?

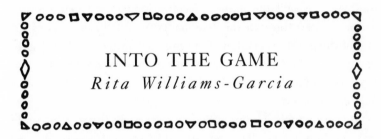

INTO THE GAME
Rita Williams-Garcia

G-chuk-a-chuk. G-chuk-a-chuk. We made one pathetic sight. Three lonesome guys on payday, getting jerked all the way uptown by the Number Two train. *G-chuk-a-chuk. G-chuk-a-chuk.* That shouldn't have been. Not when we had freshly clipped shape-ups (courtesy of the Nu Bush Cutters) and money in our pockets. *G-chuk-a-chuk. G-chuk-a-chuk.* There we sat, staring at subway ads when there were two Brooklyn College girls in smelling range, licking their lip gloss, dying to be talked to.

What we must have looked like. My mouth was hanging open. Manny was staring off, remembering a girl who was never his. Dupree was hunched over so low, his head was under his seat. My man was gone. His head was bobbing and his lips were twitching, though nothing came out, unless you want to count "FFFFFICA!" as conversation.

His spit landed on one of the Brooklyn College girls' arms. She and her girlfriend leaped up and fled into the next car. The bad news was, we could have gotten something going. Asked them for the time. Where they from. How's the college scene. I was building up to it, too. Not that they would have given three high school dudes any play, especially the way we looked. I caught our reflections in the window facing us. Frightening! Our eyes seemed glassy, and our faces long and pointed. I couldn't blame them for bolting.

With the seats now vacant, I stretched my legs out, only to discover I wasn't the only one going for comfort. This Korean woman broke through the straphangers and threw herself into one of the empty seats, her shopping bags into the other. I guess her corns were killing her a lot more than we could intimidate her. She had us figured right: three of the weakest dudes to shoot out of the Bronx.

At that moment Dupree decided to turn up the volume on his "psycho hoodie" act. He vaulted out of his seat, raised his arms like a DC Comics action figure, and yelled "Mutha FICA!" then collapsed into his seat.

Most of the riders took it as business as usual on the Number Two, though some were genuinely scared. "It's okay!" I called out. "He just found out he's a taxpayer." I looked down on Dupree, who between nodding, mumbling, and getting jerked Seventh Avenue style, looked like a whacked-out holyman. "Yo," I said. "You gotta give some to get some, so get off that riff."

DuDu didn't want to hear that. He wanted back everything he claimed the federal government withheld from him, starting with the money from his first paycheck. Me and Manny let him get his stuff off because we knew he'd wind down. Wasn't nothing wrong with him. He was just trying to bug those people out. I figured we'd get off at 125th Street, catch a flick, and have some laughs, and DuDu would be DuDu again.

The day had fallen apart around noon in the mailroom. We had torn open our first pay envelopes knowing that minimum wage checks could only be but so respectable, even with overtime. Me and Manny got exactly what we anticipated. Deductions for latenesses, a pinch here and there for Social Security and taxes. DuDu, however, didn't take it so well. When he saw the difference between the net of what was, and the gross of what could have been, a chunk of it going to FICA, he started bugging. He got into a beef with the lady at the check-cashing place because he thought she was laughing at his digit. "I could be running for Mr. Benz," he told her. "I don't need this." Mr. Benz was a tenth grader and a local kingpin, tagged for his twin Mercedes. Me and Manny laughed at DuDu because he had forgotten one thing: He, like Manny and me, was one of the weakest dudes to shoot out of the Bronx. Instead of working in the neighborhood like everyone else, we had taken mailroom jobs in an office downtown. An office with a dress code. Now that was weak.

The doors opened at Chambers Street, and a herd of pinstripe suits charged in. DuDu shouted like a train conductor, "Step lively and watch your pockets! Watch your pockets! FICA's in your pocket!"

People either turned our way or tried hard not to notice us. A concerned mother gripped her child's shoulders, and the Korean woman guarded her shopping bags. My eyes stayed on the tops of my sneakers. Manny was too dejected to care what anyone thought. Dupree put his headphones on and shoved a tape into his Walkman. He started "Ja-fakin'" righteously off-key to a reggae beat: "FICA's in my pocket ripping out my heart . . . Oh FICA! . . . Everybody say FICA."

People were now studying crack posters and glancing at us while the train ripped wildly up Seventh Avenue. Instead of steeling his butt to his seat, DuDu surrendered to the rocking and jerking, so every lurch forward gave him the power to jump out of his seat.

It wasn't supposed to be this way. The three of us bumping knees on a payday. This was supposed to be the summer for getting girls. Not just dreaming about them. Looking at them. Lying about them. But talking to them. Taking them out. Being put through changes that only girls can put you through.

At least last year, when we were three no-muscles-rippling, no-car-cruising, lint-pocketed tenth graders, we had three solid reasons for leaving girls alone. Now things were different. The tide was turning in our favor. We had jobs and the use of Manny's mother's boyfriend's car, not to mention we had filled out respectably.

What we didn't have was a spectacular rap to get the door open. For girls, good talk rated highly with juicy kissing—so I'd heard. Since Manny had been liking Up The Block Carmen since eighth grade, he was elected to get us into the game. Me and DuDu were counting on Manny because Carmen had nice-looking cousins. Unfortunately, Manny'd always choke around Carmen. The best he could do was "Yo, Carmen, w'sup? Yeah . . . cool . . . aw'ight . . . peace," then tell us, "Me and Carmen got that silent love going on." It must have been deaf, dumb, and stupid love because Carmen got tired of waiting for Manny to kick it and settled for some jerk from Bronx Science. To this day Manny gets sick when he sees them up the block. And that's what's so pathetic: Manny believed silent love was working.

Dupree had the same problem in reverse. Count on DuDu to take everything to the extreme. Like that time we crashed this block party in Washington Heights. The music was thumpin', the people were peaceful, and the card tables were decked with six-foot heroes. We were having a good time, coolin' on a hot July afternoon in our Bermuda shorts, checking out the honeys. Courage was building that night. In our hearts we knew we'd be slow-walking some girls to their front doors. Then Dupree (can't take him nowhere) wanted to stand out. He grabbed about twenty-thirty napkins from a table and rolled them up into this blunt sausage. He went around the side of the brownstone and put the rolled napkins in his shorts so it hung just right. With his confidence in check, he joined the party, grabbed a girl, and started dancing. Everybody's checking him out, and we're yellin' "Go, DuDu!" I mean, he was looking good, and me and Manny were going "That's my man," until DuDu went wild, forgot what was what, and started jumping and spinning like he was on MTV. Even the girl he was with stepped back. When he took that final jump, everything, I mean everything, jumped. We left no dust in the wind when we jetted. And for all that hype and humiliation he didn't get off one word to the girl he was dancing with.

Yet deep down I know, if I had a chance to get close to a girl, tell her things she would and would not want to hear . . . I'd choke. Say the wrong thing and embarrass myself. I don't understand it. I know I got a smoker deep inside me, but it never surfaces. Get me around some girls, and I end up fronting like I'm the iceman, when I'm really dying because girls are . . . vicious. The "finies" don't even look at you, let alone hear you talking. The "okeydokeys" got attitude 'cause they know they're number two. And the "uglies" want to hurt you to brag that they did.

Damn. I must be bugging. I can hear the train huffing "jerk— you jerk—you jerk—you jerk—you jerk . . ."

I saw Manny, Dupree, then myself through the door's reflection. Curley, Moe, and Slow Moe. Inhaling the same breath for ten years too many. Sooner or later, one of us had to get into the game. Even if it meant cutting the others loose.

The train stopped at Penn Station. The people pushing to get out battled with those pushing to get in. Three girls managed to slingshot through a hole—the little one forced the hole open—as they made their way to the back. These girls had conquered Thirty-fourth Street. Each had huge pink Conway bags and brown Macy's bags. They were comparing and exchanging loot, being as loud as they pleased, attracting attention. Especially ours.

"The one in the green," I said to Manny. "Nice hair."

"The one in the granny shades," Manny said. "A heart-breaker." He grinned. "I like that in a girl."

"Sucker." Manny was destined to get dumped hard by the first girl who listened.

"That leaves DuDu with Troll Baby," Manny said.

She was tearing tags off of clothes. Troll Baby didn't look bad. In fact, she was kinda cute underneath all that wild hair. She was just short. Really short. Muscular and serious. Look at her rip those tags! Now, why couldn't I go for her? Why did I have to make the finest one My Girl?

Dupree was fidgeting with his Walkman. He hadn't noticed the girls.

It was probably their first payday as well. "They're beautiful and employed," I said.

"Working queens," Manny agreed.

"It could happen," I said. "Flick. Pizza. Phone numbers."

"You asking them?"

The silence lasted too long. Manny bailed me out saying, "They're probably hooked up. As fine as they is."

I went back to staring at subway ads, the ones that promise to relieve pain. My eyes were glassy with daydreaming: I had My Girl pinned against her front door. . . . Her mom's yelling for her to come in. . . . Her green top presses against my shirt. . . . My hands slide from shoulders to hips. . . . I lean in for that kiss. . . .

The crashing of coins hitting tin yanked me into consciousness. I caught myself with my mouth open and closed it quick. It was a blind man making his way down the car, shaking his can twice between a drag, step drag. I wanted the train to throw him off balance and send his can flying for pulling My Girl from my lips. No such luck. The blind man had things under control, drag stepping, can shaking and chanting while the train rocked. "I have no one in this world. . . . Please help me please. . . . Please help me please. . . . I have no one in this world. . . ."

I slapped DuDu on the shoulder, and he looked up at me all

evil as if he was the one who just got jerked. I was getting tired
of his act. "Toss him a dollar," I said.

DuDu chirped like a girl who does not curse. "Give who a
dollar? FICA's got my dollar."

"Mine, too," Manny said, letting the blind man go past.

I looked over at the girls, wishing they'd put us out of our
misery and get off the train so we could stop thinking we had a
chance. My Girl, the one with the nice hair and green top,
reached into her purse. Even her fingers were long and perfect.
Or they looked that way because she was far away. I swear. Girls
look so good when they're out of reach. I watched her peach-
colored nails digging around for change. As she reached for the
blind man's can, I could see she wasn't wearing any bracelet,
though she did have a gold chain around her neck. That was
when I noticed a splotch on her neck that was either a monster
hickey or a birthmark. I must have been doing some heavy X-ray
staring because the tables suddenly turned, and she was now
staring at me.

Shades and Troll Baby were also staring. I was praying DuDu
was FICA free. The last thing we needed was a relapse. Not
when we were on the verge of making contact. Me and Manny
tried to play it off, faking like movie extras, talking and signaling
to look like we belonged in this scene. It was past pathetic.

The girls went back to their pink bags.

"The pain," I said putting my hand over my heart.

Manny didn't smile like I thought we would. Instead he said
loud enough, "One of us should go over there and check them
out. See if they're worth it. See if they wanna hang out."

Even Manny was getting tired of bumping knees with the
fellas—though he wasn't man enough to go over there.

Then as if she'd heard him, Manny's girl, Shades, pulled down
her dark granny glasses about an inch, looked us up (never
down), then reported something to My Girl. DuDu's girl cut her
off, protesting and shaking her Brillo pad head "no way."

Who asked you? me and Manny were thinking.

"Go. Ask them," Manny said.

"Ask who what?" Dupree was now back among the conscious. He spotted the girls at the opposite end. "Now, she's a winner," DuDu said, smiling at Troll Baby. "Want me to do it? I'll do it." When he said it, we recognized that napkin-rolling light bulb clicking on in his eyes.

"Hold him back," I told Manny, who was thinking the same thing. We started getting loud, laughing, and trying to restrain DuDu from humiliating us. Me and Manny were laughing so hard, paying the other riders no mind. They probably thought we were fighting for real. In between bopping DuDu upside the head, we kept checking out the girls. My Girl and Shades kept stealing glances our way but not overdoing it. Troll Baby did all she could to keep My Girl and Shades from giggling.

Then the connecting door slid open, and a young cop stepped into the car. He marched slowly, his footsteps coming down too hard as he scanned the train for something or someone. He stood directly across from us, clearly issuing a warning with his hawking eyes: Chill out. His police hat seemed slightly tilted, ready to fall off his narrow, eggplant-shaped head. Instead of looking ominous he looked stupid. Stupid looking or not, his hand stayed near his nightstick.

Me and Manny eased up, sharing the same premonition, while DuDu kept saying, "I'll do it. I'll do it."

G-chuk-a-chuk. G-chuk-a-chuk. "Jerk — you   jerk — you jerk . . ."

I caught our reflections. Damn, we looked stupid. One of us had to get up. One of us had to stride down to those lovelies and say "Yo . . ." Cop or no cop. It wouldn't be Manny, and it couldn't be DuDu.

The train pulled into 116th Street. *Get in the game,* I thought. *Let those girls shoot you down, roll their eyes, and act like you're a fly buzzing round their golden hoops.* They could rip me apart or be as kind as they look. I didn't care. If a cop was going to stand over me, then I was going to at least stand up. Go over there. Rap my heart out.

I pulled myself up.

The girls had their bags by the handle and stormed out of the train the same way they came in.

I tapped Manny and DuDu. "Let's go."

"This ain't our—"

"Go!" I yelled, grabbing one of them by the shirt. The conductor announced the next stop. The doors were preparing to close. We made a dash for the door, bulldozing the cop, who wasn't expecting us to bolt. The cop's hat fell on the platform. Dupree scooped it up and tossed it into the car. He yelled to the cop, "Peace, man. I'm a taxpayer!" and we beat it up the stairs howling like animals. Oh, man, we couldn't stop laughing, especially DuDu who hadn't cracked a smile all day.

"Where they at?" I asked boldly—as if I knew what to say when we found them.

They were walking slowly down the street. We stood at the top of the steps unable to move as they walked away. Not because we were punks but because they could walk that walk and control us, even at a distance. My Girl had on sandals. Manny's wore flats. Dupree's had on hikers. Hikers! We could have stood there and watched them until they disappeared. They chatted, and took bite-size steps, and tossed their heads like movie extras trying to look like they belonged in this scene.

I looked at Manny and DuDu. The girls weren't too far away. And the way I figured, big feet and long strides being what they are, and bite-size steps being what they are, it would take ten– twenty steps to catch them. One to get in the game.

Rita Williams-Garcia

While riding the F Train in New York City one day, Rita Williams-Garcia found herself sitting near three teenage boys who were discussing their day. "They were of color, hulking, wore way-out haircuts, and laughed too loud, which made the other passengers fear for their lives," she says. That image stuck with her, and later, when she was invited to write a story for this collection, "Into the Game" was the result. "Real kids frighten me and make me laugh," she states.

Williams-Garcia is an African American born to Southerners who migrated to New York City in the 1940s. The name Garcia was added to Williams, she says, "as a wedding gift from my husband's Puerto Rican father."

Before she found success writing novels for young adults, Ms. Williams-Garcia pursued a career as a dancer and worked as an administrator in a marketing and media company. It is therefore only natural that dancing is what the main character does best in Rita Williams-Garcia's first novel, *Blue Tights*, the story of a teenage girl who joins an African dance group, begins a relationship with the Muslim drummer, and becomes more aware of her Black heritage.

Her second novel, *Fast Talk on a Slow Track*, won a Parents' Choice Award and was named a Best Book for Young Adults by the American Library Association in 1992. It's the story of a slick, competitive high school valedictorian who encounters failure for the first time.

Her next book will focus on a fourteen-year-old mother, pregnant again, who is sent by her mother to live with relatives in Georgia. The tentative title of this soon-to-be-published novel is *Like Sisters on the Homefront*.

Ms. Williams-Garcia is currently pursuing a master's degree in creative writing at Queens College in New York.

◻◊○○▲○○◊○◻

There was talk about a mysterious fox spirit among Andy Liang's ancestors. But that couldn't be true—could it?

FOX HUNT
L e n s e y   N a m i o k a

Andy Liang watched the kids from his school bus walk home with their friends. He could hear them talking together and laughing. He always got off the bus alone and walked home by himself.

But this time it was different. A girl got off the bus just behind him and started walking in the same direction. He wondered why he hadn't seen her before. She was also Asian American, which made it all the more surprising that he hadn't noticed her earlier.

As he tried to get a better look, she went into the neighborhood convenience store and disappeared behind a shelf of canned soup. He peered into the store, hoping for another glimpse of her. All he saw were some of the kids from the bus getting bags of potato chips and soft drinks.

Andy sighed. He was used to being a loner, and usually it didn't bother him—not much, anyway. But today the loneliness was heavy. He overheard the other kids talking, and he knew they were planning to study together for the PSAT. From the looks of the snacks, they were expecting a long session.

Andy would be practicing for the test, too, but he would be

doing it by himself. *I'm better off doing it alone, anyway,* he thought. *Studying with somebody else would just slow me down.*

The truth was that none of the others had invited him to study with them. *So all right,* he said to himself, *they think I'm a grind. What's wrong with that? I'll be getting better scores on the PSAT than any of them, even if there's nobody to coach me.*

He finally found the girl standing in front of a case of barbecued chicken. She was staring so hungrily at the chickens that his own mouth began watering, and he would have bought a piece on the spot if he had the money. But with the change in his pocket, he had to be satisfied with a candy bar.

Leaving the store, he reached his street and passed the corner house with the moody German shepherd. As usual, it snapped at him, and he automatically retreated to the far side of the sidewalk. Although the dog was on a chain, Andy didn't like the way it looked at him. Besides, a chain could always break.

Today, the dog not only snapped, it began to bark furiously and strained against its chain. Andy jumped back and bumped against the girl he had seen earlier. Somehow she had appeared behind him without making any noise.

He apologized. "I didn't mean to crash into you. That dog always growls at me, but today he's really barking like crazy."

The girl shivered. "The dog doesn't seem to like me very much, either." Before he had a chance to say anything more, she turned and walked away.

Again Andy sighed. He hadn't even had a chance to find out what her name was or where she lived. Was she Chinese American, as he was? What grade was she in? At least she went on the same school bus, so there was a chance of seeing her again.

But he didn't have much hope that she would be interested in him. Girls didn't go for the quiet, studious type. Last year, one of the girls in his geometry class had asked him to give her some help after school. That went pretty well, and for a while he thought they might have something going. But after she passed the geometry test, she didn't look at him again.

Maybe if he studied less and went in for sports, girls would get interested in him. But then his grades might slip, and his parents would never let him hear the end of it. He had to keep his grades up, study hard, be the dutiful son.

His brother had managed to get a math score of 800 on the PSAT, and now he was at Yale with a full scholarship. Andy had to try and do as well.

More than once he had asked his parents why it was so important to get into a good college. "Lots of people get rich in this country without going to college at all," he told them.

His father would draw himself up stiffly. "The Liangs belonged to the mandarin class in China. I've told you again and again that to become a mandarin, one had to pass the official examinations. Only outstanding scholars passed, and only they had the qualifications to govern the country."

Andy's father always got worked up about the subject. He might be only a minor clerk in America, he said, but he was descended from a family of high-ranking officials in China.

Another thing Andy noticed was that when his father went on at length about the illustrious Liang family, his mother always listened with a faint smile. She seemed to be amused for some reason.

But that didn't stop her from also putting pressure on Andy to study hard. Every night, she would ask him whether he had done his homework, and she double-checked his papers to make sure everything was correct.

Normally Andy didn't mind doing his homework. He liked the satisfaction of a job well done when he finished a hard problem in math. But lately, all the extra work preparing for the exam was beginning to get him down. His mind wandered, and he began to daydream. He had visions of becoming a snake charmer, making a balloon trip over the Andes, or practicing kung fu in Shaolin

Temple. He saw himself in the English countryside, riding a galloping horse in a fox hunt.

He tried to stop wasting time on these stupid daydreams. Maybe his mind wouldn't wander if he had someone to study with. But nobody wanted to study with him. Nobody wanted to spend time with a nerd.

Next day, the girl got off the bus again with Andy, and this time, instead of going into the convenience store, she began to walk with him. When they reached the yard with the German shepherd, they both automatically backed away from the fence.

Andy and the girl looked at each other and grinned. He was encouraged. "I'm Andy Liang. Are you new in the neighborhood?"

"We moved here last week," she replied. "My name is Leona Hu. But Leona is a silly name, and my friends call me Lee."

She was inviting him to call her Lee and including him among her friends! Andy could hardly believe his luck. An attractive girl was actually ready to be friends. He was grateful to the German shepherd.

The girl had big almond-shaped eyes. Andy had overheard Americans saying that Chinese had slanty eyes, although his own eyes did not slant. Lee's eyes, on the other hand, definitely slanted upward at the corners.

Her hair had a slightly reddish tint, instead of being blue-black like his own. She wasn't exactly beautiful, but with her hair and her slanting eyes, she looked exotic and fascinating.

When they came to his house, Andy wished he could keep Lee talking with him. But she smiled at him briefly and went on. He had to stop himself from running after her to find out where she lived. He didn't want her to think that he was pestering her.

Was she going to take the PSAT this year? If she was, maybe they could study together!

At dinner that night, his father went on as usual about how important it was to do well on the PSAT. "We immigrants start at the bottom here in America, and the only way we can pull ourselves up is to get a good education. Never forget that you're descended from illustrious ancestors, Andy."

Again, Andy noticed his mother's faint smile. Later, he went into the kitchen where he found her washing the dishes. "Why do you always smile when Father gives me his pep talk about education? Don't you agree with him?"

"Oh, I agree with him about the importance of education," his mother said. "I'm just amused by all that talk about *illustrious ancestors.*"

"You mean Father wasn't telling the truth about Liangs being mandarins?" asked Andy. He took up a bunch of chopsticks and began to wipe them dry. Usually, his mother refused his help with the chores. She wanted him to spend all his time on his homework.

But tonight she didn't immediately send him upstairs to his desk. She rinsed a rice bowl and put it in the dish rack. "Well, the Liangs haven't always been mandarins," she said finally. "They used to be quite poor, until one of them achieved success by passing the official examinations and raising the status of the whole Liang family."

"Hey, that's great!" Andy liked the idea of a poor boy making good. It was more interesting than coming from a long line of decadent aristocrats. "Tell me more about this ancestor."

"His name was Fujin Liang," replied his mother. "Or I should say Liang Fujin, since in China, last names come first." Again she smiled faintly. "Very well. You should really be studying, but it's good for you to know about your ancestors."

Liang Fujin lived with his widowed mother in a small thatched cottage and earned money by looking after a neighbor's water buffalo. His mother added to their meager income by weaving and selling cotton cloth. It was a hard struggle to put rice in their bowls.

But Fujin's mother was ambitious for him. She knew he was smart, and she decided that he should try for the official examinations. In theory, any poor boy could take the examinations, and if he passed, he could raise his family to mandarin status. But rich boys could afford tutors to help them study. For Fujin, even buying a book was a luxury.

He was so eager to learn that he crouched under the window of the nearby school and tried to eavesdrop on the lessons. Whenever he saved enough money to buy books, he would read them while seated on the back of the water buffalo. Once he was so absorbed that he walked the buffalo into a rice paddy. But he managed to read the precious books until he knew them all by heart.

Through hard work he grew up to be a fine scholar. His mother thought he was finally ready to take the examinations, but he himself wasn't so confident. The other competitors were the sons of rich families, who could afford the very best tutors.

He continued to study late every night, until his head began to nod. So he tied the end of his pigtail to a nail in the ceiling, and whenever his head fell forward, the pigtail jerked him awake.

One night, while he was struggling to stay awake over his book, he heard a soft voice behind him. "A fine, hardworking young man like you deserves to pass the examination."

Fujin whirled around and saw a beautiful girl standing behind him. Somehow she had appeared without making any noise. She had huge, bewitching eyes that slanted sharply. Could he be dreaming?

"Let me help you," continued the girl. "I can act as a tutor and coach you."

"And that was how your ancestor, Liang Fujin, got the coaching he needed to pass the examinations," said Andy's mother.

Andy blinked. "But . . . but who was this mysterious girl? And how come she was such a great scholar? I thought women didn't get much education in the old days."

His mother laughed. "Nobody in the Liang family would say. But I'll give you a hint. When the girl lifted her skirt to sit down, Fujin caught a flash of something swishing. It looked like a long, bushy tail!"

It took Andy a moment to get it. Then he remembered the Chinese stories his mother used to tell him, stories about the *huli jing*, or fox spirit. The mischievous fox, or *huli*, often appeared in the form of a beautiful girl and played tricks on people. But in some of the stories, the fox fell in love with a handsome young man and did him a great service. She expected a reward for her service, of course, and the reward was marriage.

"So my ancestor passed the examinations because he was coached by a fox?" asked Andy.

"That story is a lie!" cried Andy's father, stomping into the kitchen. "It was made up by malicious neighbors who were jealous of the Liangs!"

Andy's mother shrugged and began to pack the dishes away. His father continued. "Liang Fujin passed the examinations because he was smart and worked hard! Don't you forget it, Andy! So now you can go up to your room and start working!"

His father was right, of course. Fox spirits belonged in fairy tales. He, Andy Liang, would have to study for the PSAT the hard way.

Andy was delighted when Lee told him that she was also planning to take the PSAT. She agreed that it would be a good idea to study together. He was eager to begin that very evening. "How about coming over to my house? I'm sure my parents would love to meet you."

Actually, he wasn't sure how delighted his parents would be. He suspected that they would be glad to see him with a Chinese American girl, but they'd probably think that a girl—any girl—would distract him from his studies.

He was half sorry and half relieved when she said, "I'm going to be busy tonight. Maybe we can go to the public library tomorrow afternoon and get some sample tests and study guides."

That night he had a dream about fox hunting. Only this time, he found himself running on the ground trying to get away from the mounted horsemen and howling dogs. There was somebody running with him—another fox, with reddish hair and a bushy tail. It flashed a look at him with its slanting eyes.

Andy and Lee began studying sample PSAT tests at the library. Working with someone else certainly made studying less of a drudgery. Andy felt relaxed with Lee. He didn't suffer the paralyzing shyness with her that seized him when he was with other girls.

She was really good at finding out what his weaknesses were. English grammar was his worst subject, and Lee fed him the right questions so that the fuzzy points of grammar got cleared up. As the days went by, Andy became confident that he was going to do really well on the PSAT. At this rate, he might get a scholarship to some famous university.

He began to worry that the help was one-sided. *He* was getting first-rate coaching, but what was Lee getting out of this? "You're helping me so much," he told her. "But I don't see how I'm helping you at all."

She smiled at him. "I'll get my reward someday."

Something about her glance looked familiar. Where had he seen it before?

They had an extralong study session the day before the exam. When they passed the corner house on their way home, the

German shepherd went into a frenzy of barking and scrabbled to climb the Cyclone fence. Both the chain and the fence held, fortunately. Lee looked shaken and backed away from the fence.

At Andy's house she recovered her color. "Well, good luck on the exam tomorrow." She looked at him for a moment with her slanting eyes, and then she was gone.

Again, he thought he remembered that look from somewhere. All during supper, he was tantalized by the memory, which was just out of reach.

That night he dreamed about fox hunting again. It was more vivid than usual, and he could see the scarlet coats of the riders chasing him. The howling of the dogs sounded just like the German shepherd. Again, he was running with another fox. It had huge slanting eyes, bright with mischief.

He woke up, and as he sat in his bed, he finally remembered where he had seen those huge, slanting eyes. They were Lee's eyes.

Next day Andy met Lee at the entrance to the examination hall. He suddenly realized that if he said her name in the Chinese order, it would be Hu Lee, which sounded the same as *huli*, or fox.

She smiled. "So you know?"

Andy found his voice. "Why did you pick me, particularly?"

Her smile widened. "We foxes hunt out our own kind."

That was when Andy knew why the German shepherd always snapped at him. He himself must be part fox. His ancestor, Liang Fujin, had accepted help from the fox spirit after all, and she had collected her reward.

Lensey Namioka

Born in Beijing, China, Lensey Namioka emigrated to America with her family when she was nine years old. Her husband was raised in Himeji, Japan. Together they have traveled all over the world and now live in Seattle, Washington.

Although she is Chinese American, her most popular books for young adults are those in the series about two young samurai warriors, Matsuzo and Zenta, in feudal Japan, the first of which was _White Serpent Castle._ That novel received the Washington State Governor's Award. It was followed by _The Samurai and the Long-Nosed Devils, Valley of the Cherry Trees, Village of the Vampire Cat,_ and _Island of Ogres,_ the last two of which were American Library Association Best Books for Young Adults. _Village of the Vampire Cat_ was also nominated for an Edgar Award. The newest book in that series is _The Coming of the Bear._

Lensey Namioka is also the author of _Who's Hu?,_ a humorous story about a Chinese teenager, and _The Phantom of Tiger Mountain,_ a mystery-suspense story set in China before the Mongol invasion.

The idea for "Fox Hunt" came from the stories Lensey Namioka heard as a child in China about the _huli jing,_ or fox spirit. "I thought it would be fun to write a story about the fox spirit in America," she says.

Her most recent book is _Yang the Youngest and His Terrible Ear,_ a contemporary story for middle-grade readers about an immigrant Chinese family living in Seattle. Her next book for young adults, titled _April and the Dragon Lady,_ explores intergenerational conflicts within a Chinese American family.

◻◐○○▲○○◑◻

Paul had never been so close to an Anglo girl before. Now what was he going to do with her?

EAGLE CLOUD AND FAWN
Barbara Beasley Murphy

"What happened yesterday has nothing to do with what you will do today," I told the girl.

She was sitting at a round table, and I was her waiter for breakfast at the new Hotel Santa Fe.

"Why not?" she said with a little smile.

"Because."

"What happened yesterday has everything to do with what *I'm* going to do this morning and this afternoon," she said.

The dining room was full, and I looked for somebody to come and join her at the table. She was too young to be traveling alone. The girl had light hair and light eyes. When she smiled at me, her eyes closed as if she were smelling perfume.

"What did you do yesterday?" I said, standing behind the chair across from her.

"I went to the Museum of Fine Arts, the cathedral, and the galleries." Her guidebooks were spread out on the table, and her hands, which were tan, moved them about constantly. "Today's got to be the Folk Art, the Indian Arts and Crafts, and—"

"No, it doesn't," I said, shaking my head to let my dark hair move smoothly over my shoulders.

Peeking over her guidebook, she watched it. Her eyes took in my long hair, my face and shoulders and chest. I'm six feet, one hundred eighty pounds. She was thinking about me, I could tell. Yesterday when I first waited on her, she didn't think about me. But I was making sure today was different.

"Why do you say it doesn't have to be one of those places?" she said.

"Because I . . ." I said, bending near her to catch her fragrance and to let her sense my strength. "Because I don't want to go there. There are more important places and things to see."

Her eyes widened, her mouth narrowed, and a dimple appeared in her shiny cheek. She took a breath and started to scoot her chair back. "I thought you were working here. Aren't you? You were yesterday."

"What I did yesterday—" I said, and she giggled before I finished the sentence. The sunlight had just fallen on this side of the building. Like an arrow, it pointed at this girl, making her sparkle. My last day of work was supposed to be tomorrow. Friday. This coming weekend was Indian Market, and the next week, I'd start at the American Institute of Indian Arts.

"I was working yesterday," I said. "And I worked a little while this morning, and I'm quitting now."

I untied the white apron around my waist and laid it on my arm. Two other people I was waiting on at another table stared at me.

"Why are you doing that?" the girl said with a laugh. She had closed her eyes again. Her eyelids were like rose petals.

"So _I_ can have a vacation like you!" I said.

"Huh!" she went. "Well, I'm not only here on vacation. . . ."

I walked over to the hostess and told her I suddenly had to leave. "Something's come up," I said, trying not to smile.

The hostess, Jean, frowned so hard that grooves appeared between her eyes. "Bad guy! You're fraternizing with our hotel guests, aren't you?" she demanded to know.

"That's not what I call it, Jean."

"I have to report you, Paul."

"Okay."

I went back to the pretty girl's table, and as I passed it, I said, "Come on!" And she did. Even though she didn't know my name and I didn't know hers.

You want to know why I did this, but I can't tell you. I never picked up a non-Indian girl before. Hardly ever even talked to one. I didn't want to know one until I saw this girl. This girl with the beautiful eyes, in the yellow jumpsuit, I wanted to talk to.

My friends know some Anglo girls, some Black girls, a lot of Hispanic girls. Not me. I don't have a girl. Louisa, my friend at St. Catherine's last year, moved away to Kansas. I don't answer her letters. Some things don't last.

So this Anglo girl and I found ourselves on the Paseo at nine A.M. on a sunshiny day in August. I was wearing new expensive running shoes, jeans, and a gray ribbed T-shirt from Eddie Bauer on Lincoln Avenue. First thing I'd ever got there. I had some money from winning an art prize at my graduation in May. It didn't have any strings attached to it, because it memorialized a guy who'd died young and had been a great kid. I could spend it on anything I wanted.

The Anglo girl was short and curvy, and she came up midchest on me. She had one of those perfectly arranged, perfectly laid-out small faces like in a magazine.

She turned her pretty face to me now and said, "Are we walking or driving?"

"What's your name first?" I said. "Then we'll decide."

"What's yours first?" she said.

"Paul. Eagle Cloud," I said, surprised at myself for telling her that name.

"Eagle Cloud's your Native American—I mean, First American name?"

I nodded.

"Mine's Stephanie Levine, but when I still wanted to be an actress, I called myself Fawn Bliss."

"Fawn. That's a good name," I said, and she touched my hand. I moved closer to hear her breathing. She was panting a little. I attributed this to the altitude. She wasn't used to it yet. And when I was closer, I saw the freckles sprinkling her nose. They were so delicate that unless you were right up on her, you wouldn't see them.

"Well now. Walking or driving?" she said.

"I bet you're a planner," I said.

"Uh-huh. Everybody in New York's got a Filofax."

"I got my truck," I said. "If you want to see the Indian lands, we'll go by pickup."

Fawn nodded but did not look up into my eyes in her usual bold way. I wondered if she was scared or as excited as I was. The day spread out before us like a land I'd never entered. I was a tourist, too.

We took the highway north. By then, Fawn had told me she was in New Mexico for the first time.

"Where's your family?" I said. "Didn't they want to come with you?"

"Uh . . . I'm from Riverdale—in the Bronx . . . New York City," she said, her voice going up and making it sound like a question.

Why didn't she answer what I'd asked? She'd said she was seventeen. I thought that was too young to travel alone. I was eighteen, a guy, and I'd never been out of state alone. I looked over and caught a sorrowful, blank stare in her eyes. She took a deep, deep, deep breath, stuffing something she didn't want to reveal. I wanted to find out what it was.

Driving the old truck my dad and I shared, I was quiet. This was carpool day for him, so I got the pickup. Driving, I like to be quiet, and I was hoping she'd do the talking. We passed Camel

Rock, the entrance to Tesuque Bingo, and the road to Tesuque Pueblo on the left.

"What's a *poo-eh-blow*?" Fawn asked.

"What's a pueblo!" I burst out.

"Yes. Is that a *poo-eh-blow*?" She pointed to an adobe house with a flat roof.

"I live in a pueblo," I said.

"Can I see it? Why don't you answer my question?" she said grouchily, but with a little laugh afterward.

"Because you don't answer mine," I said.

Another big breath stuffer. Then she started asking a whole lot of fast questions, about Indians and pueblos, which she was finally pronouncing like I did.

"I'm going to show you San Ildefonso," I said. "It's only fifteen minutes from here. Then you'll know for sure what a pueblo is."

"Good! That's great! I love learning something new, Eagle Cloud."

It was funny hearing my Indian name said by her.

We were headed toward Los Alamos. "I don't want to go *there!*" she yelled. "I don't want to see those bombs."

"We're not going there. Here, we're turning. San Ildefonso Pueblo."

"Oh, good. I'm relieved," she said as the pickup bounced over the cattle guard, down the dirt road into the plaza. It was bigger than a football field and earthen, too.

"Once you pass the cattle guard, you're in the Indian world, not the white world anymore."

"Good!" she said again. "Look! All your houses are flat-topped."

I pointed out the huge old cottonwood tree and the much older, round adobe kiva. Each one stood alone. The kiva was over five hundred years old, I told her.

"I want to go up those stairs outside of it. And can we go down the ladder poking out the top, too? I want to see inside it."

"Tourists aren't allowed," I said. "It's sacred to the Indian people."

"What about friends?" she said, sounding a little hurt. "What happens inside there?" Her face was flushed with curiosity.

"We have ceremonials, prepare for dances. We sleep there sometimes. Why did you come to our state?" I said, full of burning questions myself.

"I was accepted at St. John's College in Santa Fe. So I'm going there, starting next week," she said smoothly, but I caught the tremor in her voice. Things didn't sound that smooth. It made me shiver.

"Where are the stores? Sidewalks? Where do you give the dances? What are they about?"

"The dances are in the plaza, right here. They're like . . . prayers."

"And what is that *huge*, flat-topped mountain sitting almost in the middle of everything? You've got a museum, but no stores," she said, reading the signs. "And who are the tribal police? What do they do? And there's your church. I know, the conquistadores were here."

I told her about Black Mesa, the flat-topped mountain. "The sacred water serpent lives there. Underneath, a giant is sleeping."

She smiled and closed her eyes. "I'm trying to imagine them, Eagle Eyes," she said.

"Cloud. Eagle Cloud."

She laughed and kept her eyes shut.

"Our house is not far from the plaza," I said.

We turned north and then west up the drive to my house. It's a five-room house in the middle of a field. Woods run in back of it down to the Rio Grande. I wished I had cleaned up the porch for her, but I didn't know she was coming. Nobody was home. My folks are divorced, and I'm with Dad. My sister's with Mom in San Juan Pueblo.

Inside, Fawn peered into the living room. "You've got TV. What are those?" she said, pointing to the ceiling. Brushing against her warm back, I walked into the room and she followed.

"Dad hung the Indian baskets made by our ancestors there."

"Oh . . ." She breathed, picking up a framed photograph and putting it close to her eyes. "Is this you?"

"In my antelope costume. For the dance on our feast day," I said. "I was nine."

"You were an antelope *dancer*?" I nodded, and she continued to gaze at the picture. "I do modern dance. I think I'd like to do this," she said dreamily.

"Only boys are chosen for it." I grinned at the thought of her as the antelope dancer.

"Were there other animals?"

"Yes. Buffalo and deer dancers. It was eight degrees above zero."

"Brrr! I like getting to know you. . . . I feel like I'm in a story. Everything's so different."

She was the sparkliest, noisiest, nosiest girl I'd ever met, so I showed her the paintings I was planning to take to Indian Market.

"You did these?" She caught her breath. "Little old you?"

"Yes." I couldn't help smiling, she had such an admiring look in her eyes.

I was entering one of the paintings in the judging. She pointed at it. "What is that large figure rising into the sky?" she said in an awed voice.

"The small person down here is the drummer. This is the drummer spirit helping him. The drummer carries the heavy drum all day, carries the rhythm, the heartbeat of the dance."

"The *heartbeat* of the dance. Oh, my! Will I ever get to see a dance?" Fawn said in a flirty way.

I started to say *I hope so* or *yes,* but all I said was "I don't know."

"Could it—could it ever be, that I have a spirit over me like the drummer does?" she asked in a serious voice as we left the house.

"Do you need one?" I said. Her face turned deep red. She took my hand. It was moist and hot, and she clung to me.

At home I'd grabbed fruit, tortillas, and drinks for our lunch. I took her high up to Tsankawi where our ancient ones lived long ago. Up there you can see almost all of New Mexico and the mountains of Colorado, too. Climbing the stick ladders, scurrying over the narrow paths cut deep into the earth by the ancients' feet, and seeing the ruins of the cliff dwellings and houses, Fawn was breathless.

"Oh, this is amazing!" she said, her eyes shining.

We sat on the rim of a towering sandstone cliff to eat. The birds were hungry, too, and trying to find the little nuts trapped in the piñon cones nearby.

"Fawn, do you always travel by yourself to faraway places? I didn't think New Yorkers let their pretty daughters do that," I said.

A shadow came over her face. We sat against two rocks opposite each other, our bare feet touching. The breeze whipped my hair and ruffled hers. Behind her, the sky was as pale as drinking water in a gourd. We could have been floating in air. We were above the trees and birds, with white clouds billowing over and beneath us. Far-away mountains framed the distance.

"My mother and father did not come with me, Eagle Cloud, because I wouldn't let them," she said. Her muscles hardened as if there had been a struggle over this. Not understanding, I waited, hoping she'd explain.

"I needed to be free of them. They want me to live like *them.* It happens that my grandfather—a really nice man—was—was

shot in front of his apartment house. He was waiting for my
grandmother to come down and go to the Shakespeare in the
Park with me. We were going to celebrate my graduation that
night. Instead we sadly prepared for his funeral the next day."

"That's awful! Was he robbed?"

"I think he couldn't hear when the mugger said 'Give me your
wallet.' When he was alone, Grandpa Abe always turned down
his hearing aid," she said with tears rising in her eyes. "We don't
know what really happened, but nothing was taken from him.
Except . . ."

". . . his life," I said, feeling the puzzling sadness of it. I'd
never been told anything like this before and didn't know what to
do.

"And so my grandfather, who had always helped people, who
was active in causes, left me a lot of money. With no strings
attached. Now I'm free," she said with tears falling.

"Free from what?" I said. Indians talk about freedom from
oppression. "What does that mean in your heart?" I wanted to
know, moving toward her. I knelt on the ground, pulled her into
my arms, and squeezed her shoulder with my hand. She laid her
head on my shoulder, sighing. We stayed that way, melting together like colors on a canvas.

"It was eight weeks ago tonight that I lost my Grandpa Abe,"
she said.

"Only eight weeks," I echoed, feeling her hurt, feeling sorry
for an Anglo for the first time.

Her cheek was wet. I bent down to kiss her. A piece of my
hair got in the way of our mouths, and she pushed it away,
making my heart pound.

"So that's why I'm here alone. Grandma Hattie wanted to
come with me, but I said no. To be *me* now, I have to be strong
and not afraid. My mom's so angry the money was left to me, not
her. It's made my father crazy. I heard them talking at night, all

night. I wanted to go far away. I need to be on my own. I want to find my own way."

"I think you were a little bit scared when I asked you to come with me. I sensed it, didn't I?"

Her smile began to come back, making my heart warm again. "I was a little bit shy, I confess. But I didn't listen to it. You were brave or bold, and I like that."

I folded her small body into mine and asked the spirits to protect her.

Early Saturday, Fawn came to the Indian Market. It was held on the plaza in Santa Fe. She met my father, who did not say much. He probably didn't approve. She marveled at the crowds and was there when the official brought me a blue ribbon, first prize for painting. She was so excited. I could tell she was really impressed I'd won a blue ribbon.

"Little old me," I said.

"Yes!" she said. "I want to buy that painting."

I was asking a thousand dollars for it and wouldn't let her spend the money. I sold it to another New Yorker for nine fifty.

"But I had the money!" she said.

"I'm going to paint one for you. One that shows the spirit that's with you, over your shoulder, high in the sky."

Fawn smiled the smile that touched my heart. I wanted to hold her again, but now I was kind of afraid. "I'm going to give it to you for your dorm. You can put it on the wall."

"Oh, I will! I will," she said.

Dad and I closed the booth on Sunday. I ate dinner at my mother's and then went back to San Ildefonso. Suddenly I missed my mother there. Nothing in San I looked the same to me. I was seeing things through Fawn's eyes. Yet I didn't understand her that well, and I wanted my own sense of what I was seeing back. It was uncomfortable, scary. I thought about calling Louisa in Kansas to see if we were still friends.

And then like summer clouds billowing up and covering the sky, new thoughts rolled over the old feelings. What if, after all, Eagle Cloud and little Fawn really liked each other?

I ran through the woods to the river. The Rio Grande, golden with mud, was slowly swirling between its banks. I stretched out on the sand and looked into the water. Puffy clouds were reflected on its silky surface as if the sky were rolling down on top of me.

What kind of spirit would watch over a person like Fawn?

The ripples made a form like a man. Like a very tall man. And like a skyscraper, too. I'd never seen one myself, but of course, I knew what they were like.

A *grandfather* skyscraper, I thought, breathing hard. I stayed until the river turned dark and the sky blossomed with stars. Fawn! She was dancing in my mind.

If I wouldn't sell her a painting, I thought, I must really like her. If I'm making one and giving it to her, I must really like her.

Half hoping I didn't, I knew I did.

I knew I ought to be getting ready for art school tomorrow, too, but I was floating on my thoughts like a nightbird in the sky. San Ildefonso, it occurred to me, was the place where all creative thoughts came from. Suddenly sorry my own favorite grandpa wasn't alive to hear the story of Fawn and me, I jumped up and started running.

What I had to do tomorrow had nothing to do with what I was doing tonight. I was going to create the spirit for Fawn. I was painting the painting tonight.

Barbara Beasley Murphy

A mixture of Irish, English, French, and German ancestry, Barbara Beasley Murphy has always been interested in relationships between people from different backgrounds. Her first book, *Home Free,* was about a friendship between an Anglo boy and a Black boy in the American South during the civil rights struggle. In *One Another,* she explored the blossoming romance that develops between a French exchange student and an American girl. In *Annie at the Ranch,* an animal rescuer meets a Native American boy when she goes to New Mexico to help her veterinarian aunt. And her newest novel, *The Antelope Dancer,* concerns the kidnapping of a family from the San Ildefonso Pueblo.

Murphy has based the character of Paul in "Eagle Cloud and Fawn" on Gary Alan Roybal, a real-life nineteen-year-old artist from San Ildefonso. Gary Alan's mother once said: "Every time I cross the cattle guard to go to work, I tell myself I'm in the White world." Murphy, wondering what it would be like for a Pueblo boy to bring an Anglo into his world, an outsider, especially someone he cared about, began to explore that idea. At the same time, she also considered the debate taking place among today's Native Americans in the Southwest over how much they should become part of the American mainstream and how much of their Indian culture and values might be lost in the process. "I hoped to catch some of this conflict and fervor in my story of Paul," she says.

Barbara Beasley Murphy is also the author of *No Place to Run* and the very popular Ace series, written with Judie Wolkoff, starting with *Ace Hits the Big Time,* a story that was also made into a School Break Special for CBS television. In the next Ace book, Ace, in search of his roots, will accompany his father to New Mexico.

◻◗◗◗▲◗◗◗◗◻

Rodney Suyama hopes to be the first Asian rapper to make it to the big time. All he needs is a new name, a catchy act, and maybe a little talent.

NEXT MONTH . . . HOLLYWOOD!
Jean Davies Okimoto

"This is your last chance, Rodney," I said to myself as I looked at the poster on the wall across from my locker. FRANKLIN HIGH TALENT NIGHT . . . the red letters were enormous, with sparkly stuff sprinkled on them . . . SIGN UP BY MAY 19TH!

I've always wanted to be in Talent Night. I knew the exact second they put that poster up and the exact dates you could sign up. I also knew this was May 19 and I had fifteen minutes to get to the activity office before it closed.

Technically, it's very easy to be in Talent Night. They don't have auditions—all you do is sign up. But wanting to be in it and actually signing up to do your talent in front of the whole school are completely different things. My sophomore year, I froze outside the door of the activity office. I got a little farther my junior year; two steps inside the office before I bolted.

"Get a grip," I said to myself as I paced back and forth outside the door. "Your career in the entertainment business will be history if you don't even start it." Finally, with two minutes left, like the two-minute warning in a football game, I went into the activity office and by some miracle signed my name . . . Rodney Suyama.

My ambition is to be the first big-time Asian rapper, a serious rap artist in the great tradition of Young MC. Totally nineties—relevant, hopeful, upbeat, maybe a few lines about the earth—stuff like that. I have a lot of original raps I've worked on for years, but I just haven't known what to call myself. A rap artist needs to have the right name. When I signed up, I just put my own name and decided I'd worry about my rap name later. As everyone would agree, the name *Rodney Suyama* doesn't cut it for a rap name.

Actually, I should mention that I'm not all Asian—I'm half Asian and half white—my exact heritage is half Japanese American and half Polish American. But like a lot of biracial kids who are half white, I think of myself as the half that's not white. Besides, most people assume my sister Suzanne and I are totally Asian (we think our mom's genes blew our dad's out of the water). You could also say Dad himself got blown out of the water, as we've only seen him once since he moved to the East Coast. After he and Mom split up, we also dropped him from our hyphenated name. Mom led the charge. No longer was she Helen Suyama-Delenko. Whack! Off went the Delenko . . . back to good old Helen Suyama. Suzanne was next. Chop! Down with Delenko . . . Suddenly she was just plain Suzanne Suyama. Although *plain* is not a word you'd use to describe Suzanne. My sister looks like someone in a Nordstrom catalog, which is where she basically lives—not in the catalog but in the store. I was the last to dump Delenko; maybe it's harder for a guy to erase his dad. But Suzanne didn't seem to bat a false eyelash; the way her name looked seemed to be all that mattered to her.

"It's true, what they say," Mom would mutter when Suzanne went out with another *GQ* guy in a Beamer. "Hippies beget yuppies. Of course, I wasn't exactly a hippie, and let's hope your sister is only temporarily stuck in the eighties." Then she would give me . . . The Look. No words, but that look is a command. *Don't* You *Dare Go Eighties On Me, Rodney.*

Believe me, an eighties person is the last thing I want to be. Right on the edge of what's new is the place for me. My rap's gonna be something that's totally out there. I've been practicing for Talent Night every second since I signed up. This is no small thing at our house. All my mom says is, "Don't embarrass me, Rodney." Now *that* is a joke. In April, Mom and her friend, Elaine Shanahan, had a booth at the University District Street Fair. Elaine, who is a potter, has wild red hair and wears only black clothes but is a nice person even if she is a little weird. She and Mom teach art at an alternative school, but that's Mom's day job to pay the rent. Mostly, she wants to do her art. It doesn't seem to faze her that there isn't a big demand for aluminum slug sculpture. Her sculptures are enormous, too, a hundred times bigger than real slugs (slimy snails with no shells that crawl around the bushes in the Northwest).

I was walking through the fair with my two best friends, James Robinson and David Woo. James wants to be a film director—his heroes are James Singleton, Robert Townsend, and Spike Lee. He worships those guys. Besides their movies, his favorite is *The Seven Samurai.* James has seen it thirty-eight times. Every time we go to the video store and we're looking around trying to pick a movie, James grabs *The Seven Samurai.* "How 'bout this one?" he says, like he's never seen it before.

So that day, there we were on the Ave. We have on shades, we're strolling by the booths, chomping hot dogs, makin' jokes. Then I hear it: The Voice. My mother has trapped a customer. She leans out of her booth holding a giant aluminum slug. Except if you didn't know it was supposed to be a slug, you would say it was a bunch of aluminum cans hooked together that landed in a Cuisinart and got run over by a moving van.

"The Pepsi generation signified all that is young and beautiful, carefree . . . Pepsodent smiles and prosperous America; this Pepsi can has been transformed into a slimy, spineless lowly creature, which greedily destroys gardens. A metaphor for the destruction of the garden of earth. 'Slug' can also mean a bullet, signifying the violence that is destroying our culture." The Voice is intense, high pitched. Mom is on a roll.

David notices first. "That your mother, Suyama?"

"Yeah," I choke.

"That stuff's art, man?" asks James.

"Yeah, she thinks she's Yoko Ono . . . ha-ha." I laugh, faking a little merriment, praying to be beamed up to some planet.

And when I tell her about Talent Night, *she* says, "Don't embarrass me, Rodney." Suzanne is worse.

"An Asian guy just can't be a rapper, Rodney."

"Why the hell not?"

"You gotta be Black; they're the only guys that are cool rappers."

"Yeah, what about Vanilla Ice?"

"Personally, I think he's a cheap imitation," Suzanne says in a snobby voice.

"I could call myself 'Lemon Ice.' "

"Like dog pee in the snow."

Support is not a concept known to my sister, at least not when it comes to me. But thank goodness my girlfriend is in favor of my music career. Ivy is very enthusiastic about my being a rapper. Well, actually, that's not exactly true (not about her supporting me), the part about her being my girlfriend.

I've been sitting next to Ivy Ramos all semester in language arts. She always talks to me, and we've gotten to be good friends. I walk her to her locker after class, we hang around and talk, stuff like that. Ivy's dad is Filipino and her Mom is Black (Filipino American and African American if you want to get technical), and Ivy is very pretty; actually, she's beautiful. And nice, too. Not snobby like a lot of beautiful girls I could name, such as Suzanne Suyama.

Ivy was the main squeeze of the famous Lavell Tyler, who is the greatest running back to ever play at Franklin, who has a full scholarship to the U and will probably be the most famous running back to ever play for the Huskies. Guys like Lavell Tyler don't breathe the same air as guys like me. All semester Ivy told me about her and Lavell, and I ate it up. I even got into pretending I'm the great Lavell with a girl like Ivy. Then last month it all changed.

She came into class, looking like someone had died. Blowing her nose, sniffing, her beautiful dark eyes practically swollen shut from crying.

"Ivy . . . what's wrong?" I whispered.

"That bitch"—*sniff, sniff*—"that bitch"—*sniff*—"bitch"—*sniff* —she mumbled, dabbing her eyes.

After class, she sat there while everyone else left. "Rodney, stay with me."

Music, that was what those words were. I cemented my butt to the chair.

When the class had emptied out, Ivy slowly stood up. "Take me to Burger King, willya, Rodney? I can't face that lunchroom."

As we walked out of the building, I put my arm around her. Ivy leaned her head into my shoulder, still making little sniffing sounds.

At Burger King the whole story came out. She and four other girls from her family psychology class had gone to John Muir, the elementary school near Franklin, to observe kindergarten kids for some kind of child development thing. On the way back she saw none other than Lavell Tyler in the front seat of Deleisha Johnson's car kissing Deleisha Johnson.

"I felt like a total fool! There he was in broad daylight, kissing that girl. That bitch!"

"That's terrible," I said sympathetically.

"Then, when I saw him before class and let him have it—he had the *nerve* to tell me to be understanding and that he just wanted to see us *both*! I told him what he could do with that idea!"

"So you broke up?" I tried not to sound too cheerful.

"Of course! No way am I putting up with that boy's crap! I want a guy who'll be reliable—you hear what I'm sayin', Rodney?"

Reliable Rodney, that's what they call me. From then on Ivy and I were inseparable. I walked her to class, carried her stuff, picked her up at her job. Although we never really defined our relationship, we were more than friends, although I don't think she thought of me exactly as her boyfriend. Whatever it was, I was the first guy on the spot after Lavell, and it was probably a rebound thing. But so what? Who cares? I got to be with her. And little by little it did get a bit more physical. . . . I'd put my arm around her, we'd give each other back rubs . . . nothing too heavy, but nice . . . very nice.

But my mother, even though she liked Ivy, got crazy. Every other word was *safe sex.* How was school today, Rodney . . . remember, have safe sex. . . . Pass the rice . . . remember, Rodney, safe sex. . . . The phone's for you, Rodney . . . remember, safe sex.

"I know all about safe sex, Mom."

"Oh—well, that's a relief."

"It's when a dog humps your leg."

That shut her up for a while. But one thing about my physical relationship with Ivy was that she got closest to me when Lavell was in sight. As soon as she'd see him coming down the hall, she'd grab my hand and walk along holding it, looking into my eyes and smiling as if we were the only two people in the world. In fact, the one time we did kiss was when we were walking by the track after school. The track team was working out and Lavell was warming up, stretching on the grass, his muscles bulging all over the place. As we got opposite him, Ivy stopped, slipped her lovely brown arms around my neck, lifted her face, and brushed my mouth with her sweet soft lips. Then she slowly pulled away, took my hand, and led me down the sidewalk because I was dazed and could hardly walk. Did I mind that this was probably for the benefit of Lavell Tyler? No, I did not. I'm not a proud person, and I would take Ivy on any terms, any terms whatsoever.

Ivy wanted to help me find a good rapper name because we both agreed that Rodney Suyama didn't have the right sound. It was her idea to go to Baskin-Robbins. We were going to write down all the names of the flavors that would be good for an Asian rapper, but there weren't that many, just Lemon Surprise and Banana Delight, so we left and went to the park.

"How 'bout Almond Joy?" Ivy wondered.

"A candy bar?"

"Cause your eyes are almond-shaped?"

"Almond Joy is *chocolate* on the outside," I reminded her, as we walked behind the tennis courts and sat under a tree.

"Oh, right. How 'bout Golden Raisin . . . or Lemon Drop . . . or Golden Wheat?"

"Isn't that a cereal? How come we gotta name me a food?"

"We don't have to. Hey, how 'bout Havana Banana?"

"I dunno—sounds like I'm Latino. Besides, banana used to have a bad connotation, like you weren't really Asian. Remember?" I lay back on the grass and folded my arms behind my head, looking at the sky for some inspiration.

"Yeah . . . Asian on the outside and white on the inside." Ivy chewed on a blade of grass. "I'm telling you, Rodney, if I got worried about stuff like that, it'd make me crazy. Like, I wouldn't be cool enough to be Black since I'm half Filipino, or vice versa." She sighed, "I can't be bothered with that. Now what d'ya think, how 'bout DJ Lemon Drop?"

"I like Havana Banana better—but probably people would think I was a wannabe Latino." I thought about this for a minute. "Actually, being Latino would be cooler than being half Japanese and half Polish." But then I had an idea. "Ivy, why not somethin' with *happa*?"

"*Happa?* Like people who are half Asian?"

"Sure. *Happa*'s anybody who's half Asian—I think it came from Hawaii, from *happa haole*."

"*Happa haole* means half white, right?"

"Yeah. What d'ya think? MC Happa? Or DJ Happa?"

Ivy smiled. "Happa Poppa?"

"I don't think so." Then I sat up. "I know—I've got it! Ice Happa."

"That's not bad, Rodney. Not bad at all."

"Okay, Ice Happa it is."

On Saturday Ivy and I were at the mall at Southcenter. "You know, Rodney, maybe it would be good if you could rap in front of an audience so you could have some practice before the real Talent Night." She was almost becoming my manager, she was so into it. Ivy had to buy some underwear, so we split up and I hung around The Bon's main floor while she took the escalator. I was leaning against a counter, imagining Ivy in her underwear, doing some pretty deep daydreaming. I kind of lost touch with what was going on; probably the lady had been saying "excuse me" trying to get me to move so she could see the stuff in the case I was leaning on, but I didn't hear anything. Finally, I felt this little shove and I looked over, and there was this totally pissed lady who glared at me and snarled, "Why don't you go back to Japan!" Then she stomped off. I froze and just stared at her disappearing into the crowd.

Back at my house, Ivy and I were sitting in the kitchen having pizza with Mom, and I told them both about that lady.

"What did you do after she said that?" Mom's eyes bored into me.

"Yeah, what d'ya say, Rodney?" Ivy chimed in.

"I said, 'My family's been here for four generations—why don't *you* go back under your rock, you blue-headed old bag.'"

"Rodney!" Mom was shocked, but she also laughed.

"Did you really say that?" Ivy was skeptical.

"No." I sighed. "She stomped off before I knew what happened. But I'm gonna do this great rap about bashing." Then I had an idea. "Ivy, why don't you be in the act with me?"

"I can't do a beat box. I'd just end up spitting on the mike. Besides, I thought you had a drum machine."

"I do. I do." I was getting excited. "See—what you could do is be like that pink Energizer rabbit on TV. I'll be doing the rap and you'll go back and forth with this bass drum, wearing a pink rabbit outfit—"

"Rodney, I did not raise you to want to put a young woman in a bunny suit!"

"Not a bunny, that rabbit, that rabbit on TV."

"I have pink sweats, and I could make some cute pink ears—" Ivy was getting interested.

"Yeah, and you'll go back and forth—and on the drum on one side there'll be the Rising Sun, the Japanese flag, and you'll hit it with a big steel mallet—"

"An anvil," Mom chimed in.

"Right, then when you turn around and come back across the stage, the other side of the drum will have the picture of the earth with a rainbow around it, and you'll hit that with a regular bass drum mallet."

Ivy got excited. "Then you'll be doing the rap the whole time while I'm this visual thing!"

"Visual . . . political . . . this is quite an idea, Rodney." Mom feels like she failed with Suzanne, and I'm the last hope for her politics.

"We just gotta perform in front of people before Talent Night," Ivy said, "because we have *got* to be good."

"You can." Mom jumped up and went through the pile of mail by the kitchen phone. "Look, this came yesterday—I'm glad I didn't throw it out." She handed us this flyer. AN EVENING OF COMMUNITY MUSIC AT NWAAT it said on the front.

NWAAT is the Northwest Asian American Theater; Mom

sometimes goes to plays there. "It's a musical talent show kind of thing. Anyone can be in it, and there's still time to sign up," she said, pointing to the entry form.

Ivy and I practiced every night for the next two weeks in my garage until we had the whole thing down. She even moved exactly that robot way the rabbit does on TV. But that was where the comparison left off—Ivy did not look goofy like that rabbit. In her pink sweats she looked sexy. Very sexy. "This week NWAAT, next week FRANKLIN, next month HOLLYWOOD . . . then LONDON! . . . TOKYO . . . THE WORLD!" Ivy had big plans for us.

The night of the NWAAT show, we were scheduled to be the fourth act. There wasn't enough room backstage for the performers, so we all sat in the front row of the theater. Ivy had her coat on over her rabbit outfit. The first three acts were kids we knew from school. The emcee was Phillip Omori, who is a local weather guy on TV. He came out on the stage and announced the first act.

"We are proud to present a very talented member of the Asian community, Eric Lew, who will play Max Reger's Cello Suite Number One."

His parents probably gave him a cello in his crib—the guy was unbelievable. The audience must have clapped for five minutes. Then the emcee came back.

"Ladies and gentlemen, our next performer is Julie Muramoto, who will play Paganini's Caprice Number Twenty-four."

Julie, a kind of a Kristi Yamaguchi look-alike, got up there with her violin and blew everybody away. She was amazing, like some symphony person.

"Maybe we didn't read the flyer right," I whispered to Ivy, who was fiddling with her bunny ears in her lap. "Maybe it's supposed to only be classical stuff."

"Shhh," she hissed. "We're gonna be great. Chill, Rodney."

They clapped for Julie Muramoto for at least five minutes, too.

"Next we have Marlene Santos singing an aria from Verdi's *La Forza del Destino,* 'Pace, pace, mio dio,'" said the weather guy. "Ms. Santos will be accompanied by Martin Wong on the piano."

The audience went wild when that girl finished singing. Then she and Martin Wong bowed and she left the stage, while he stood by the piano. The emcee got up and announced that Martin Wong would play Chopin's "Revolutionary" étude.

When the audience finally got through clapping for Martin Wong, which seemed like a bazillion years later, the emcee got up on the stage and said, "Ladies and gentlemen, we are happy to present Ice Happa."

Ivy and I went up on the stage. My drum box was backstage, and I plugged it in and brought it out and pushed back the piano. The lights dimmed. I started to rap:

Don't be a dope / when we gotta have hope / here's the word, you nerds / don't thrash, don't bash, get along

Ivy came out in the rabbit suit, banging the drum with the Rising Sun on it. There was a big murmur from the audience when they saw her, and Ivy strutted along, her head held high. She got to the edge of the stage and turned, starting back across with the rainbow earth thing facing the audience. I kept rappin'.

Don't mess the earth / you gotta love this planet / don't break it, we can make it / get along
Don't blame, it's a shame / be a friend, we can mend . . .

Then Ivy tripped over the cord to my drum box. *Splat!* She landed on her butt, knocking the mike over. The bass drum flew through the air and hit me in the stomach. *Bam!* Ice Happa lies flattened with the rabbit. The audience goes berserk, they laugh like hell, they are rolling in the aisles. The curtain closes.

On the way to the parking lot, Ivy and I are mobbed by people. The Franklin kids beg us to do the act for Talent Night.

"You were hilarious, Rodney," said Marlene Santos.

"I didn't quite get the rabbit part," Eric Lew said, "but you were funny."

"That was the funniest thing I've ever seen," said Julie Muramoto. "Great act, you two."

In the parking lot, Ivy and I sat in the car.

"Damn."

"What's the matter, Rodney?"

"I was supposed to be cool."

"So? No one has to know that."

"Yeah, but we know."

"At Talent Night, I'll trip on purpose."

"Damn, I really wanted to be cool."

"We'll change your name, too." Ivy was already thinking ahead.

"To what?"

"Butterscotch Nut."

"Damn."

Then Ivy snuggled next to me. "It's good makin' people laugh, Rodney. I like goin' out with an entertainer."

Then she started to kiss me, but she stopped all of a sudden. "You keep bein' reliable, you hear what I'm sayin', Rodney?"

"Uh-huh."

Then I kissed her, and we stayed in the car in the dark parking lot for a long time.

Lavell Tyler was nowhere in sight.

Jean Davies Okimoto

Author of ten books that range from picture books to adult nonfiction, Jean Davies Okimoto is a psychotherapist of white European ancestry who is married to a Japanese American psychiatrist. Together they have a biracial family, with her two Caucasian daughters and his two Asian American sons. The inspiration for "Next Month . . . Hollywood!" was provided by one of her stepsons—who has many Black friends and a strong affinity for African American culture and music—when he performed a rap as part of a college skit.

Okimoto's most recent books include *A Place for Grace*, a picture book featuring a hearing dog and her hearing-impaired owner, and *Molly by Any Other Name*, the story of an Asian girl, adopted by a white American family, who wants to find her birth mother. Rodney, in "Next Month . . . Hollywood!" incidentally, is the cousin of Roland Hirada, one of the characters in *Molly*. That novel was an International Reading Association Reader's Choice Book.

Her other popular titles include a middle-grade novel, *Take a Chance, Gramps!*, a Pacific Northwest Booksellers Readers Choice Book which has been nominated for the Mark Twain Award, and *Jason's Women*, an American Library Association Best Book for Young Adults. *My Mother Is Not Married to My Father* and its sequel, *It's Just Too Much*, were recently published in Japan.

Jean Okimoto is also the founder of the Mayor's Reading Awards in Seattle, which recognizes fifth graders who have shown the most improvement in reading. The program focuses on chapter one, special education, and bilingual students.

◻◗◗◦▲◦◖◗◗◻

Friendships

It had been necessary for Lucinda's family to leave their home in Cuba. But she has been so lonely in New Jersey.

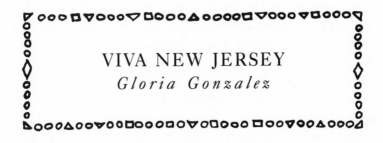

VIVA NEW JERSEY
Gloria Gonzalez

As far as dogs go, it wasn't much of a prize—a hairy mongrel with clumps of bubble gum wadded on its belly. Pieces of multicolored hard candies were matted in its fur. The leash around its neck was fashioned from a cloth belt, the kind usually seen attached to old bathrobes. The dog's paws were clogged with mud from yesterday's rain, and you could see where the animal had gnawed at the irritated skin around the swollen pads.

The dog was tied to an anemic tree high above the cliffs overlooking the Hudson River and the majestic New York City skyline.

Lucinda traveled the route each day on her way to the high school, along the New Jersey side of the river. The short walk saddened her, despite its panoramic vista of bridges and skyscrapers, for the river reminded her of the perilous journey six months earlier, when she and her family had escaped from Cuba in a makeshift boat with seven others.

They had spent two freezing nights adrift in the ocean, uncertain of their destination, till a U.S. Coast Guard cutter towed them to the shores of Key West.

From there they wound their way north, staying temporarily

with friends in Miami and finally settling in West New York, New Jersey, the most densely populated town in the United States. Barely a square mile, high above the Palisades, the town boasted a population of 85,000. Most of the community was housed in mammoth apartment buildings that seemed to reach into the clouds. The few private homes had cement lawns and paved driveways where there should have been backyards.

Lucinda longed for the spacious front porch where she'd sat at night with her friends while her grandmother bustled about the house, humming her Spanish songs. Lucinda would ride her bike to school and sometimes not see a soul for miles, just wild flowers amid a forest of greenery.

Now it was cement and cars and trucks and motorcycles and clanging fire engines that seemed to be in constant motion, shattering the air with their menacing roar.

Lucinda longed painfully for her grandmother. The old woman had refused to leave her house in Cuba, despite the family's pleas, so she had remained behind, promising to see them again one day.

The teenager, tall and slight of build with long dark hair that reached down her spine, was uncomfortable among her new classmates, most of whom she towered over. Even though the majority of them spoke Spanish and came from Cuba, Argentina, and Costa Rica, they were not like any of her friends back home. These "American" girls wore heavy makeup to school, dressed in jeans and high heels, and talked about rock singers and TV stars that she knew nothing of. They all seemed to be busy, rushing through the school corridors, huddling in laughing groups, mingling freely with boys, and chatting openly with teachers as if they were personal friends.

It was all too confusing.

Things weren't much better at home. Her parents had found jobs almost immediately and were often away from the tiny, cramped apartment. Her brother quickly made friends and was picked for the school baseball team, traveling to nearby towns to compete.

All Lucinda had were her memories—and now this dog, whom she untied from the tree. The animal was frightened and growled at her when she approached, but she spoke softly and offered a soothing hand, which he tried to attack. Lucinda persisted, and the dog, perhaps grateful to be freed from the mud puddles, allowed her to lead him away.

She didn't know what she was going to do with him now that she had him. Pets were not allowed in her building, and her family could be evicted. She couldn't worry about that now. Her main concern was to get him out of the cold.

Even though it was April and supposedly spring, the weather had yet to top fifty degrees. At night she slept under two blankets, wearing warm socks over her cold feet. Another night outdoors, and the dog could freeze to death.

Lucinda reached her building and comforted the dog, "I'm not going to hurt you." She took off her jacket and wrapped it quickly around the animal, hoping to disguise it as a bundle under her arm. "Don't make any noise," she begged.

She waited till a woman with a baby stroller exited the building and quickly dashed inside, unseen. She opted not to take the elevator, fearful of running into someone, and instead lugged the dog and her schoolbag up the eight flights of stairs.

Lucinda quickly unlocked the apartment door and plopped the dog on her bed. The animal instantly shook its hair free and ran in circles atop her blanket.

"Don't get too comfortable," Lucinda cautioned. "You can't stay."

She dashed to the kitchen and returned moments later with a bowl of water and a plate of leftover chicken and yellow rice.

The dog bolted from the bed and began attacking the food before she even placed it on the floor. The girl sat on the edge of the bed and watched contentedly as he devoured the meal.

"How long has it been since you've eaten?"

The dog swallowed the food hungrily, not bothering to chew, and quickly lapped up the water.

It was then, with the dog's head lowered to the bowl, that Lucinda spotted the small piece of paper wedged beneath the belt around its neck. She slid it out carefully and saw the word that someone had scrawled with a pencil.

"Chauncey. Is that your name?"

The dog leaped to her side and nuzzled its nose against her arm.

"It's a crazy name, but I think I like it." She smiled. Outside the window, eight stories below, two fire engines pierced the afternoon with wailing sirens. Lucinda didn't seem to notice as she stroked the animal gently.

Working quickly, before her parents were due to arrive, she filled the bathtub with water and soap detergent and scrubbed the animal clean. The dog didn't enjoy it—he kept trying to jump out—so Lucinda began humming a Spanish song her grandmother used to sing to her when she was little. It didn't work. Chauncey still fought to get free.

Once the animal was bathed, Lucinda attacked the clumps of hair with a scissor and picked out the sticky globs of candy.

"My God, you're white!" Lucinda discovered. While using her brother's hair blower, she ran a quick comb through the fur, which now was silvery and tan with faint traces of black. "You're beautiful." The girl beamed.

The dog seemed to agree. It picked up its head proudly and flicked its long ears with pride.

Lucinda hugged him close. "I'll find you a good home. I promise," she told the animal.

Knowing that her parents would arrive any moment, Lucinda gathered up the dog, covering him with her coat, and carried him down nine flights to the basement. She crept quietly past the superintendent's apartment and deposited the animal in a tiny room behind the bank of washing machines.

The room, the size of a small closet, contained all the electrical levers that supplied power to the apartments and the elevator.

Chauncey looked about, confused. He jumped up as if he knew he was about to be abandoned again. His white hairy paw came dangerously close to hitting the protruding, red master switch near the door.

Lucinda knelt to the animal. "I'll be back. Promise."

She closed the door behind her, praying the dog wouldn't bark, and hurried away. An outline of a plan was taking shape in her mind.

Ashley.

The girl sat in front of her in English and always went out of her way to say hi. She didn't seem to hang out with the other kids, and whenever they passed in the corridor, she was alone. But what really made her even more appealing was that she lived in a real house. Just a block away. Lucinda had seen her once going in. Maybe Ashley would take Chauncey.

Lucinda's parents arrived from work, and she quickly helped her mother prepare the scrumptious fried bananas. Her father had stopped at a restaurant on his way home and brought a *cantina* of food—white rice, black beans, avocado salad, and meat stew. Each food was placed in its own metal container and clipped together like a small pyramid. The local restaurant would have delivered the food to the house each day, if the family desired, but Lucinda's father always liked to stop by and check the menu. The restaurant also made fried bananas, but Lucinda's mother didn't think they were as tasty as her own. One of the nice surprises of moving to New Jersey was discovering that the Latin restaurants supplied *cantina* service.

"How was school today?" her mother asked.

"Okay," Lucinda replied.

The dinner conversation drifted, as it always did, to Mama's problems at work with the supervisor and Papa's frustration with his job. Every day he had to ride two buses and a subway to get to work, which he saw as wasted hours.

"You get an education, go to college," Lucinda's father sermonized for the thousandth time, "and you can work anywhere you like—even in your own house, if you want. Like a doctor! And if it is far away, you hire someone like me, with no education, to drive you."

Lucinda had grown up hearing the lecture. Perhaps she would have been a good student anyway, for she certainly took to it with enthusiasm. She had discovered books at a young age. School only heightened her love of reading, for its library supplied her with an endless source of material. She excelled in her studies and won top honors in English class. She was so proficient at learning the English language that she served as a tutor to kids in lower grades.

Despite her father's wishes, Lucinda had no intention of becoming a doctor or lawyer. She wasn't sure what she would do—the future seemed far too distant to address it—but she knew somehow it would involve music and dance and magnificent costumes and glittering shoes and plumes in her hair.

They were talking about her brother's upcoming basketball game when suddenly all the lights in the apartment went out.

"*Qué pasó!*" her father exclaimed.

Agitated voices could be heard from the outside hallway. A neighbor banged on the door, shouting, "Call the fire department! Someone's trapped in the elevator!"

Groups of tenants mingled outside their apartments, some carrying candles and flashlights. The building had been pitched into darkness.

"We'll get you out!" someone shouted to the woman caught between floors.

Lucinda cried: "Chauncey!"

He must've hit the master switch. She could hear the distant wail of the fire engines and knew it was only a matter of minutes before they checked the room where the dog was hidden.

"I'll be right back!" Lucinda yelled to her mother as she raced out the door. Groping onto the banister, she felt her way down the flights of steps as people with candles hurried to escape.

The rescuers reached the basement before she did. Two firemen were huddled in the doorway checking the power supply. Lucinda looked frantically for the dog, but he was gone.

She raced out into the nippy night, through the throng of people crowded on the sidewalk, and searched for the dog. She was afraid to look in the street, expecting to see his lifeless body, the victim of a car.

Lucinda looked up at the sound of her name. Her mother was calling to her from the window.

"Come home! What are you doing?"

The girl shouted, "In a minute!" The crowd swelled about her as she quickly darted away.

Lucinda didn't plan it, but she found herself in front of Ashley's house minutes later. She was on the sidewalk, with the rest of her neighbors, gazing up the block at the commotion in front of Lucinda's building.

"Hi," Lucinda stammered.

Ashley took a moment to place the face and then returned the smile. "Hi."

Lucinda looked about nervously, wondering if any of the adults belonged to Ashley's family. She didn't have a moment to waste.

"What happens," she blurted out, "when a dog runs away? Do the police catch it?"

The blond, chubby teenager, with light green eyes and glasses with pink frames, shrugged. "Probably. If they do, they only take it to the pound."

"What's that?" It sounded bad, whatever it was.

"A shelter. Where they keep animals. If nobody claims 'em, they kill 'em."

Lucinda started to cry. She couldn't help it. It came upon her suddenly. Greatly embarrassed, she turned quickly and hurried away.

"Wait up!" The blonde hurried after her. "Hey!"

Lucinda stopped, too ashamed to meet her eyes.

"Did you lose your dog?" Ashley's voice sounded concerned.

Lucinda nodded.

"Well, let's go find him," Ashley prodded.

They searched the surrounding neighborhood and checked underneath all the cars parked in the area in case he was hiding. They searched basements and rooftops. When all else failed, they walked to the park along the river, where Lucinda pointed out the tree where she had found him.

The girls decided to sit on a nearby bench in case Chauncey reappeared, though they realized there was little hope.

Lucinda knew her mother would be frantically worried.

"She probably has the police looking for me," she told Ashley.

"You've only been gone an hour."

"It's the first time I've left the house, except to go to school, since we moved here," she revealed.

It was a beautiful night, despite the cold tingling breeze that swept up from the river. The New York skyline was ablaze with golden windows silhouetted against dark, boxlike steel structures. You could make out the red traffic lights along the narrow streets. A long, thin barge sailed down the river like a rubbery snake.

Lucinda learned that Ashley's mother was a lawyer, often away from home for long periods, and her father operated a small business in New York's Chinatown, which kept him busy seven days a week. An only child, she spent her time studying and writing letters.

"Who do you write to?" Lucinda asked.

"My grandmother, mostly. She lives in Nevada. I spend the summers with her."

Lucinda told her how lucky she was to be able to see her grandmother. She felt dangerously close to tears again and quickly changed the subject. "I never see you with any friends in school. Why?"

Ashley shrugged. "Guess I'm not the friendly type. Most of the girls are only interested in boys and dates. I intend to be a famous writer one day, so there's a lot of books I have to read. Just so I know what's been done."

It made sense.

"What are you going to be?"

Lucinda admitted she had no ambition. No particular desire. But maybe, if she had her choice, if she could be anything she wanted, it would probably be a dancer.

"My grandmother used to take me to her friend's house who used to be a famous ballerina in Cuba. She'd let me try on her costumes, and she'd play the records and teach me the steps. It hurt my feet something awful. Hers used to bleed when she first started, but she said it got easier after the first year."

Ashley told her, "You have the body for it. I bet you'd make a wonderful dancer."

When it became apparent that Chauncey would never return, the girls walked home together.

Despite all that had happened, Lucinda found herself sad to have the evening end. For the first time since leaving her homeland, she felt somewhat at peace with herself. She now had someone to talk to. Someone who understood. Someone who carried her own pain.

"Wanna have lunch tomorrow?" Ashley asked her. "I usually run home and eat in front of the television. I'm a great cook. My first book is going to be filled with exotic recipes of all the countries I plan to visit. And if you want," she gushed excitedly, "after school we can go to the library. You can get out a book on how to be a ballerina."

Lucinda agreed immediately, "That would be wonderful!"

The girls parted on the sidewalk, and Lucinda raced home where her irate father and weeping mother confronted her angrily.

"Where have you been! I was only going to wait five more minutes and then I was calling the police! Where were you?"

Before she could stammer a reply, the lights went out.

"Not again!" her mother shrieked.

Lucinda's heart throbbed with excitement.

Chauncey was back!

She ran out of the apartment, unmindful of the darkness, with her mother's screams in the air: "Come back here!"

This time Lucinda made it to the basement before the firemen, and she led her pal safely out the building. She reached Ashley's doorstep just as the first fire engine turned the corner.

Gloria   Gonzalez

Born and raised in New York City, Gloria Gonzalez spoke Spanish at home, her father having been born in the Canary Islands off the coast of Spain. She began her writing career as an investigative reporter for various New Jersey newspapers before turning her attention to playwriting.

Her plays have been produced throughout the United States as well as in Europe and on television. *Curtains* was named one of the Best Short Plays of 1976. And *Cafe Con Leche* has been running in repertory at Repertorial Español in New York City since 1984.

Her first novel for teenagers was *The Glad Man.* In it, two young people befriend an old man who lives with his dog in an old bus at the city dump and change his life forever by writing a letter to their local newspaper about him. She has also written mystery novels, including *A Deadly Rhyme,* which is about a girl who finds that events predicted in an old poem start to come true.

Gaucho, first written as a television script produced on CBS Television in 1970, is her most popular novel for young adults. It depicts the life of a New York teenager who is desperate to earn enough money to buy a plane ticket for his mother and himself so that they can return to their native Puerto Rico. In the process of trying to make some quick money, he gets himself into a lot of trouble.

After living for many years in West New York, New Jersey, where "Viva New Jersey" takes place, Gloria Gonzalez and her family recently moved to Las Vegas, Nevada. She recently published *The Thirteenth Apostle,* a mystery novel for adults, and is currently at work on a novel for teenagers titled *Amen, Chino.*

◻◊○○▲○◌◊○◻

Jeff and Bull think they see championship potential in Ngo Huynh, but it seems that this Vietnamese student can't maintain his concentration for very long. Will Ngo Huynh live up to his name?

NO WIN PHUONG
Alden R. Carter

Ngo Huynh Phuong. Mr. Keneally wrote the name on the board. "Kids, I want you to welcome a new classmate. He is Vietnamese, and you pronounce his name '*No Win Fong.*' Did I come close?" He smiled at the lanky kid standing near his desk.

"Close enough," the kid said.

"Good. Now, class, it's been explained to me that Vietnamese family names come first and given names last. So if the Bull over here were Vietnamese, he would be Larsen Peter, not Peter Larsen." I stood and made a bow just to make sure everyone remembered me, although at six feet and two-oh-five, I'm pretty hard to forget. "Thank you, Bull," Mr. Keneally said. "You can sit down. So, class, you call our new friend Phuong, not Ngo." He smiled at the kid. "Right?" Phuong nodded without changing expression.

Mr. Keneally rattled on, telling us that Phuong's dad had been teaching at the University of Wisconsin medical school for the last few years and had recently taken a job at the clinic here in Shipley. Phuong had two older sisters and a little brother. And a mother, too, I guess, although I didn't hear much about her, since Jeff poked me about then. "Will you look at that kid?" he whispered. "I thought all Vietnamese were short."

I measured Phuong against Mr. Keneally's six-two or -three. "They must come in all sizes. He's five-ten, maybe a little better."

"And look at those arms."

I looked at Phuong's long, sinewy arms and big hands. "Big hooks, too," I said.

"You bet. That guy's our new pitcher."

"How do you know he even plays?"

"God, don't you watch the news, Bull? All those Asian kids are killer baseball players. Betcha he can hit, too." Jeff rubbed his hands. "This is the guy we've been waiting for."

Phuong took a seat on the far side of the room, and Mr. Keneally told us to get out our algebra books. I glanced at Jeff. He was already busy juggling the lineup card.

Jeff's an optimist. I guess you've got to be when you're not only the captain but the best pitcher, shortstop, and hitter on a team that's just a tad short of other talent. Take me, for example. I'm a good catcher and I can hit a lick, but people in the stands have been known to knock off a large soda and a bag of peanuts, take a leisurely trip to the can, and be back in their seats in the time it takes me to run out a routine grounder. And that's with Jeff screaming at me all the way down the line.

At lunch, we tried to get seats next to Phuong, but three girls beat us to it. In a town where we don't see minorities very often, Phuong was exotic and you could already see the girls maneuvering for a chance at him. Phuong seemed embarrassed by the attention. He smiled and answered their questions, but his voice was so soft that we couldn't hear him. Fifteen minutes before the end of the hour, he excused himself, dumped his tray, and headed for the door.

"This is our chance," Jeff said. "Come on."

"I'm not done eating yet."

"Move it, Bull! You weigh too much already."

"Don't either," I said. But I followed along, balancing my tray in one hand while I tried to eat my pie.

Jeff glared at me. "God, you're slow. Give me that." He grabbed my tray, and I was able to slam-dunk the rest of my pie before we headed up the hall to the classroom wing. Phuong was nowhere in sight.

We didn't find him until it was nearly time for fifth period. He was standing in the biology room talking to Ms. Heaton. She glanced up, saw us, and clutched at her heart. "My lord, I'm having hallucinations. Bull Catcher and Captain Jock coming early to class." She turned to Phuong. "Are they really there?"

Phuong studied us without cracking a smile. "They seem to be."

"Are you sure? All the formaldehyde fumes around here can do strange things to your head."

Jeff grunted sourly, but I grinned at her. "We're here, Ms. H. Just thought we'd make your day."

"And you have, Bull. You definitely have. See that lab table? It's got to go to the art room, and you two look like just the guys to get it there." She gave us the dazzling smile that along with some pretty amazing chest development make her the favorite teacher of every boy in junior high. The girls hate her.

Jeff grouched at her. "Why do they need a lab table in the art room?"

She shrugged. "Lord knows. I just follow directions. *Di-rec-shuns.* They're sort of like orders. Like, don't smash the door-jamb on your way out." She gave us that dazzling smile again. I melted, Jeff grumped. She went back to talking to Phuong while we wrestled the table through the door and lugged it down the hall to the art room.

One of the school counselors grabbed Phuong right after biol-ogy, so we weren't able to catch him until after the last bell. He was headed for the door with about eight books under his long arm. "Crap," Jeff said, as he dug frantically for the extra glove in the bottom of his locker. "You don't suppose he's some kind of brain, do you?"

I grinned. "Don't you watch the news? All those Asian kids are killer students."

"Don't make jokes—this is important. You know what they say, 'On the seventh day—' "

"God made baseball. Ya, you've said that before."

"It's true. Come on, we've got to get this kid's priorities straight."

He jogged to catch up. Phuong glanced at him coolly. "Phuong, I'm Jeff Hanson." He stuck out a hand. "Saw you around today. How do you like Wisconsin?"

Phuong raised his eyebrows a millimeter. "It's all right. I've been in Madison for the last three years."

"Oh, ya. Right. Well, I meant central Wisconsin."

"It's okay."

"Good. Glad to hear you're enjoying it. . . . So it must be tough starting at a new school in the spring."

"I can handle it."

"Well, good. So . . ." Jeff hesitated. "So anyway, how'd you like to play some ball?"

Phuong stared at Jeff, and I noticed for the first time how dark and cold his eyes were. For a long second, I thought he was going to tell Jeff to buzz off, but then he said quietly, "Which kind?"

"Well, baseball, of course. We're getting geared up for summer league. Practice starts in three weeks. So, uh—what do you say?"

"I imagine I could give it a try."

"That's great. I think you're just the guy we've been looking for." Jeff waved a hand at me. "Oh, by the way, this is the Bull.

He's my catcher, and he's a good one. Can't run worth a damn, but he makes a real good target."

"Hi," I said. Phuong said hi back.

"Bull, scrounge us some gear from Keneally, would ya? We'll be at the field." He draped an arm around Phuong and almost dragged him toward the outside door.

I got the storeroom key from Mr. Keneally, who's officially our coach but doesn't do much except show up at the games, where he spends most of his time swatting mosquitoes. Jeff's the one who really calls the shots, and that's fine with Mr. Keneally.

Outdoors it was your typical early April day in Wisconsin—cold and dreary. But the snow was gone, and the ball field had dried out pretty well. I slung the equipment bag over my shoulder and headed for the field.

Jeff and Phuong were flipping a ball back and forth while Jeff talked nonstop. "You see, the problem is that I'm the only guy on the team who can pitch, but I'm also the best shortstop, and I can't play two positions. Anyway, what we need is another pitcher. When I saw those long arms of yours, I said, 'Whoa, talk about power. That kid's got it.' Now if you can play some short, too, and hit a lick now and then, we are going to be in fat city." He scooped up a low throw from Phuong. "So what do you think of the plan?"

"In theory or in practice?"

Jeff hesitated. "Well, in both, I guess. Hey, you speak pretty good English."

"I don't see why not—I was born in Los Angeles. And by the way, I haven't played much baseball."

"No problem. I can tell you've got the skills. We'll just smooth out the rough spots. Bull, you ready?"

"Just about." I buckled my left shin guard, pulled my mask down, and squatted behind the plate. "Let 'er rip."

For a couple of minutes, it looked like Jeff had picked us a winner. Phuong wound up, and I could see that he'd played enough baseball to get the motion down. And speed? Ya, he had that all right. His first pitch came in like a BB and hit so hard that my palm stung through the padding of my mitt. His fastball had a natural tail to it, dropping just short of the plate and making it a little hard to judge. When I muffed his third pitch, it caromed off my right shin guard, and I began wishing that I'd taken time to put on my nut cup. I mean, Jeff's fastball is bad enough, but one of this guy's could make a steer out of the ol' Bull real quick. Jeff yelled, "Come on, Bull! The rest of you is slow, but those hands are supposed to be like lightning."

I grinned, jogged after the ball, and flipped it back to Phuong. "It's got a nasty bite to it, partner. Give me another right down the middle."

While Phuong hurled and I tried to keep my Bullhood intact, Jeff stood on the first-base line, grinning as if he'd discovered the reincarnation of Nolan Ryan. But then Phuong lost it. His next pitch sailed about four feet over my head, buzzing like an angry hornet. The one after that hit three feet short of the plate, splattering me with dirt. For ten minutes, I leaped and dove for his pitches, but Phuong never came close to the plate again. He still had enough stuff to throw the ball through a barn wall—but only if he were aiming at a pretty good-size barn.

Jeff stood with his arms hanging and his mouth gaping, as his dreams of a summer-league championship went through nuclear meltdown right before his eyes. Finally, he set his jaw and marched to the mound. "Look, you're way overthrowing, Phuong. At the start, you just let the motion do it for you. Now you're forcing the ball. Let me show you." He snatched the ball from Phuong and sent five fastballs blazing across the plate to thunk into my mitt. He turned to Phuong. "That's how you do it. Nice and easy. Now try it again."

Phuong got the next couple of pitches close to the plate, but then everything went haywire again. I signaled for time and started jogging to the mound. But my lack of speed got me again, and Jeff was already laying it on Phuong by the time I got there. "Damn it, Phuong! Stop trying to blow a hole in the backstop. Just pick your spot and let the motion flow. The follow-through will give you the speed." Jeff pushed him away from the rubber and pantomimed a half-dozen deliveries. He let the ball go on the last one, and it zinged across the plate to rattle the chain-link backstop. Jeff wrenched the glove from his hand and shoved it into Phuong's stomach. "Now try it again."

Phuong's hands didn't move. He fixed a cold stare on Jeff. "No, thanks. I've learned all that I want to from this experiment."

"This isn't some science class! This is baseball. Now, come on, try to get one across the plate."

Phuong gave him a thin smile. "As I said, no thanks. I'll let you know if I'm interested in trying baseball again." He sauntered off to pick up his stack of books, leaving Jeff in a sort of paralyzed shock.

Jeff couldn't believe that anyone could walk away from baseball, and I had to give him a hard nudge to break the paralysis. We returned the gear to the storeroom and started for home. For a while Jeff slumped along in silence, then he did some groaning, followed that with some cursing and five minutes of incoherent bitching, and finally fell to muttering to himself. He was still in that stage when we parted at the corner of Hayes and Grant.

I wanted that championship, too, but I could shrug off the disappointment of losing Phuong. Not Jeff. To him, winning that championship would mark a fitting finale to all the years our gang had played ball together. Next year, we'd be in high school, and only Jeff would make the varsity the first season. I'd settle in for a year or two as JV catcher, while Billy Collins, our center fielder, scrapped for a place in the outfield. But the rest of the guys just wouldn't have the size, speed, talent, or ambition to make it. This was our last chance as a team, and Jeff was damned if he'd let it slip past.

I guess I make Jeff sound like some kind of muscle-headed jock. He's not. For all the razzing Ms. Heaton gives us, he's a decent student. And he's a nice guy and a good leader. Sure he gets pushy sometimes. Winning, particularly at baseball, makes a lot of difference to him. But it doesn't mean everything. Back when we were in grade school, junior high kids were always asking him to join their teams. But he'd never do it. Instead, he stuck with us, even though that meant losing nearly every time we played kids two or three years older. When I got big early, I followed his example, sticking with our gang even when I could hit a ball farther than anyone in school.

By now, our gang has played together for three or four summers. None of us has Jeff's talent, but we all know that we're a whole lot better with him leading us. So we let it slide when he gets ornery and forgets that winning isn't everything. And despite the fact that I'm slow and nobody can play short or pitch worth a damn except Jeff, we're not that far away from being a pretty good ball club. With Phuong throwing like he had those first few minutes, we'd have a real shot at taking the league championship.

But Phuong wasn't interested in trying again. Jeff approached him at lunch the next day and again the day after that. But even though Jeff apologized for getting grouchy, Phuong just shook him off. When Jeff came back to our table after failing the third time, he snapped at me: "You ask him, Bull."

"What difference would that make? He doesn't want to play. Leave him alone."

"He's just holding out."

"For what? A bigger signing bonus?"

"I don't know what he wants. But he's got to play."

"No, he doesn't. Only you've *got* to play. Most of the rest of us have another life now and then."

Jeff glared at me, and I grinned back. He took a deep breath. "Look, Bull, if we can get Phuong straightened out, we can win that championship. Without him, my arm's going to fall off before we make it to the quarter finals. Now maybe I didn't play this right. Maybe I broke some Oriental custom, and now the guy's not going to play until I do something to show I'm really sorry. Just go find out what he wants. If I've got to walk over hot coals or let him stick bamboo slivers under my toenails, no problem. Just as long as it gets him to pitch."

"Uh, Jeff, don't you think it's just possible he doesn't want to pitch?"

"No! Nobody with a fastball like that doesn't want to pitch. It's got to be something else."

"I doubt it," I said, but—as usual—I did what I was told. Phuong glanced up from his book when I sat down across from him. "Biology?" I asked. He nodded and went back to studying a diagram. "Uh, Jeff really wants you to give us another chance. He said you can even stick bamboo slivers under his toenails if that'll help."

Phuong's head jerked up, and if his eyes had been cold before, this time they were black ice. He stared at me for a long moment and then leaned back in his chair. "Doesn't that strike you as a racist stereotype, Bull? Something out of the Rambo movies, where Stallone's always blasting evil little yellow men?"

Poleaxed. Yep, the ol' Bull had gotten one right between the eyes. And he deserved it. I gave him a rueful grin. "Ya, I guess it does. Hey, I'm sorry, Phuong. Jeff was just trying to make a joke."

"But you repeated it. And I thought you were the one with brains."

"Not this time, I guess." I shrugged. "I'm sorry. I got taken stupid." I hesitated. "I'll tell Jeff. I'm sure he didn't mean anything by it, either."

Phuong studied me for another long moment and then nodded. "Fair enough. But it's still no on the baseball."

"Phuong, I don't get it. The other day I could see by your

motion that you'd done some pitching. Why don't you want to do any now?"

"All the pitching I ever did was in my backyard in Madison. I don't like teams."

"Why not?"

He hesitated, and for a second I thought he was going to tell me something. But he decided against it. "Because I don't. Period. Now excuse me." He leaned forward, hunching over the biology text again.

"Okay," I said, got up, and went back to our table to give the bad news to Jeff.

Jeff stewed for a week, while the spring warmed, the ball field dried out, and the grass started showing signs that it had survived another winter of subarctic cold. Time for some serious practice. But no matter how Jeff shuffled and reshuffled the lineup card, we just didn't stack up as a championship team. We needed Phuong, and Phuong didn't need us.

Phuong stayed to himself around school—not unfriendly, just quiet. The girls got frustrated trying to get his interest, and he usually sat by himself in the cafeteria, a book open beside his tray. We'd found out quick enough that he was one heck of a student—a speed merchant at algebra and an ace at biology. But when it came to phys ed, he was a disaster. That was weird, because you could see that he had a ton of talent. It just never came together for very long. He'd make a couple of great plays in a volleyball or a basketball game, then mess up every time after that. It made Jeff mad as hell, particularly when Coach Renkins developed the habit of sticking Phuong on our team.

Somewhere along the line, Jeff's frustration took over. He started getting on Phuong, yelling at him and trying to shame him into getting all that talent going at once. I didn't like it, and most of the other guys didn't either. But Jeff's always been our leader, so no one stood up for Phuong. When I tried to get Jeff to

ease up, he got mad. "I don't settle for second best! I use everything I've got, and I do it for the team. The trouble with Phuong
is that he just doesn't give a damn about teams. Everything's an
experiment to him. He tries something, does it well, and then he
lets his mind wander. To hell with the team; Phuong's off looking
for another experiment. And that makes him a selfish jerk."

"That's not really your business, you know. He's got a right to
be any way he wants to be."

"Not when Renkins keeps putting him on my team!"

A couple of days later, we had phys ed outside for the first
time that spring. Some juniors from the high school down the
street were on the volleyball courts, just itching for a chance to
stomp some kids a couple years younger. And Jeff, of course,
wasn't about to back away from a challenge. We gathered around
him. "Look, we can take these jerks. We'll lull 'em a little, then
rotate the tallest guys to the net and really stick it to 'em." He
glanced at me and Phuong. "And, Phuong, for God's sake, keep
your head in the game."

It worked—almost. With Jeff serving, Phuong and I came to
the net and started putting some lethal spikes on the juniors. We
were within a point of winning when Phuong messed up. Jeff set
up the final point a foot above the net, but instead of spiking it,
Phuong swung wildly and missed completely. It was just like
he'd suddenly forgotten how to play the game. The juniors came
roaring back, and we never got another chance at the serve.
When they laid down the winning point right in front of Phuong,
Jeff was mad enough to chew razor blades. While the juniors
cheered and high-fived, he grabbed the ball and whipped it at
Phuong. For once, his aim was off, and the ball went bouncing
across the blacktop. Their stares locked—Jeff's blazing, Phuong's
freezing—and I took a step forward to get between them. "Cool
it, Jeff," I said. He glared at me, then stalked off toward the
locker room.

He was still mad when we stopped by our lockers on the way

to lunch. Phuong came past, his usual stack of books under an arm. Jeff glared after him. "God, just look at him. Study, study, read, read. His eyeballs are gonna fall out."

I shrugged. "Maybe he enjoys it. I think I saw you with a book once."

"Knock off the jokes, Bull. You haven't been funny in weeks."

The ol' Bull takes some pride in the wisdom he subtly disguises as wit, so I shot back, "You haven't had a sense of humor in weeks. Not since Phuong decided that being Jeff Hanson's pitching machine wasn't the ticket to fame, glory, and happiness. Yours, especially."

Jeff's face got red. "Is that what you really think?"

"That's what I think," I snapped, and walked away.

In the cafeteria, I sat down a couple of places from Phuong. He glanced up and then went back to reading. I chewed my food, for once not tasting it. I was pissed at Jeff, pissed at Phuong, and not real happy with myself for letting the whole thing get to me.

Jeff slapped his tray down on the table across from Phuong and sat down so hard that the dishes jumped. Conversation around us died, as kids turned to see what was happening. Jeff ignored them. He leaned in toward Phuong. "Hey, what's with you, man? Can't you keep your mind on anything? I set up that ball perfectly, and you blew it. So we lose again, just because you can't remember to concentrate for one damned second. *No win* —that's a good name for you. Just when we're about to put the other team away, you space out and we get creamed. Aren't you good at anything, Phuong?"

Phuong leveled that cool stare at Jeff. "I'm good at some things. Better than you, I imagine."

"Ya, like what? And don't give me any garbage about math or science. I mean sports and games."

Phuong studied him for a long moment. "I'll play a game with you. I'll stare you down."

Jeff snickered. "What are we going to do? Sit here looking at each other until somebody falls asleep?"

"No, we stare. No blinking allowed. The first one who blinks, loses."

"Well, no problem, friend. I've got more willpower in my little finger than you've got in your whole body."

"We'll see," Phuong said. He reached into a pocket and pulled out a bag of sunflower seeds. "Ready?"

"Ready." Jeff leaned on his elbows and stared into Phuong's eyes. Phuong popped a seed between his front teeth and chewed the kernel slowly.

I kept time, while maybe two dozen kids gathered around. It wasn't much of a spectator sport for the first couple of minutes, but by the time the second hand on the wall clock hit three minutes, I could see sweat starting to glisten on Jeff's forehead. Phuong seemed unfazed by the passing seconds, his dark, cold eyes never breaking with Jeff's burning blue stare.

At four minutes, Jeff's eyelids were twitching, and I could see him starting to breathe a little faster with the effort of not blinking. Phuong popped another sunflower seed. "Soon," he said softly, "we'll start seeing who's got willpower." That made Jeff mad, and he stared even harder.

Two more minutes edged slowly off the clock. Jeff's eyes filmed, then started to tear. Phuong's eyes began to well too. He smiled slightly. "The hardest part is letting a tear fall without blinking. I don't think you can do it. You'll crack first. Just like one of these seeds."

Jeff sucked in a breath through clenched teeth. "Not a chance, *No Win*. You're going to lose again."

Phuong cracked a seed between his teeth and smiled. "Just wait and see."

Minute seven must have been torture, but minute eight was agony. Jeff fought with everything he had, teardrops hanging on the lower eyelashes of both eyes. A tear slid slowly down

Phuong's cheek. He didn't blink, only reached for another sunflower seed.

At eight minutes forty-three seconds, Jeff cracked. He
dropped his face into his palms and rubbed his eyes furiously.
Phuong sighed, straightened, and daubed at his eyes with a nap-
kin. Jeff got up and stomped out, not looking back.

The crowd of spectators drifted off. "You won," I said to
Phuong.

"Yes, I won," Phuong said. He didn't seem very happy about
it.

"Jeff will want to try again tomorrow. He'll practice in front of
the mirror tonight." Phuong shrugged. I hesitated, then asked,
"What's the deal, Phuong? How come you can't concentrate like
that on volleyball or baseball?"

He looked at me, and his eyes weren't cold but pained. "I
concentrate too hard, that's the problem. When I start learning
something, I do okay for a while. Then I start wanting to win,
and I concentrate so hard, I mess up." He paused. "Then I make
like I didn't care to begin with. That way people can't see how
bad I feel."

I knew exactly what he meant. More than once, I'd stood at
the plate with the crowd noise and the chatter from the benches
pressing in on me and the whole game weighing me down like a
load of bricks. And the pitcher winds up, and the ball comes in
big and fat, but I'm so tight that I can't get the bat off my
shoulder to save my butt. Then it's strike three and I'm out of
there, walking back to the bench with my head hanging, trying
not to show just how bad I feel about letting the team down. It
took me a lot of called third strikes before I learned that I'm
better off going up there with nothing on my mind except trying
to see the ball leave the pitcher's hand. But how could I explain
to Phuong that sometimes it doesn't pay to think too much? I
tried: "But that's, uh, kind of a matter of practice. You know—

getting comfortable with something. Then you don't have to concentrate so hard."

He shook his head. "I used to spend hours in the backyard throwing a baseball through a tire. I can put a fastball just about anywhere I want to, anytime I want to. Just as long as nobody's watching. That's why I'm no good in a real game. I care too much about winning."

I hesitated. "Is this something about trying to . . . you know, make it in a white world?"

He stared at me, then slowly shook his head. "Sometimes I can't believe you hicks. It's not a white world. It isn't even close. Yellow people, brown people, black people—we aren't minorities; we've got you outnumbered. Why don't you worry about making it in *our* world?"

I hunched my shoulders and stared at my hands. "I'm sorry. I never thought about it like that before." I looked at him. "You're good to have around, Phuong. I'm sorry Jeff's being such a jerk. He's not a bad guy most of the time. It's just . . . Oh, hell, I don't understand it anymore. It's more than winning, it's about the team. He really believes in belonging to a team, in working together to do something." I shrugged. "And you don't, so I guess we're all stuck."

Then he floored me. "Oh, I believe in teamwork, all right. It's just that I'm no damned good at it. I'd love to be part of a team, but nobody ever puts up with me very long." He shrugged. "So I go my own way. I don't have any other choice." He picked up his tray. "I think you'd better go look after your buddy. But do me a favor, huh? Don't tell him what I told you. I don't need any more of his crap."

"Well, maybe if you explained things to him. Told him that you just need some extra time to get comfortable—"

Phuong shook his head. "Not a chance. I'm No Win Phuong. I'm stuck with that."

I found Jeff down on the ball field. He was sitting in the first-base coaching box, throwing pebbles at the rubber at the center of the pitcher's mound. He glanced up. "Hiya, Bull."

"How you doing?"

He shrugged. "Okay, I guess." I sat down beside him, picked up a pebble, and tossed it at the pitcher's mound. It bounced high off the rubber. Jeff snorted. "Hell, I've been trying to do that for fifteen minutes, and you get it on the first shot. This is definitely not my day for competitive sports."

"You don't have a lot riding on this one."

"No. We don't have any ego thing."

"Ya, I already know I'm better," I said, hoping to get a rise out of him.

But he was thinking about something else. "You know, I'm not sure I could stare down Phuong if I tried every day for a year. God, he wasn't even sweating."

"But you're going to try anyway."

He shrugged again. "Maybe, I'm not sure. . . . God, what I wouldn't do to harness all that guy's willpower and talent. Those eyes would scare half the batters so bad, they'd piss in their pants and never take a swing. But what can I do? Phuong just doesn't care enough."

By now, I knew different, but I couldn't think how to tell him. Finally, I said, "Jeff, I think you might try asking him one more time. But take it slow and easy. Don't expect him to be a star right off the bat."

"He'd never do it. He hates my guts, and I probably deserve it."

"I'm not sure, Jeff. I think you might be surprised."

At lunch the next day, Jeff sat down across from Phuong again. Neither of them said a word all through the meal. Talk had gotten around about the staring contest, and I could feel the kids at the nearby tables getting ready to crowd in to watch. Jeff timed it so that they both finished eating at the same time, then he leaned down and pulled his two gloves out of a paper bag at his feet. He tossed one on the table in front of Phuong. "We've still got fifteen minutes. Let's go play some catch." He got up and walked toward the kitchen to dump his tray.

Phuong looked at me. "Do it!" I mouthed at him. He hesitated another second, then got up and followed Jeff toward the door and the spring afternoon.

They threw the ball back and forth until it was time for fifth period, then did it again for nearly an hour after school. That was their routine for the next three days. They didn't talk, just tossed the ball back and forth. I watched from the sidelines, chewing on a blade of new grass and doing as much homework as I felt like. On Friday, Jeff said only one line: "Want to pitch some?"

Phuong shrugged. "I imagine I could give it a try."

Jeff shouted, "Bull, get some gear on! And try to hurry, Bull— we've only got four hours until dark." I bestirred myself but didn't make any rush of it. Let 'em sweat.

Phuong was fine for ten minutes, then lost it. But Jeff didn't say a word, and after I'd dodged a few nut-busters and scalp-shavers, Phuong got it back. He was fine from then on until we quit for the day.

The next Monday, the team had its first official practice. Mr. Keneally showed up for about ten minutes, just to be polite, then left so we could get down to business. My job was to get Phuong ready, while Jeff concentrated on knocking the rest of the team into shape by the end of the school year. I worked Phuong's pitch count up until he was throwing the equivalent of three or four innings every day. He had his wild streaks, but you could see him getting more comfortable and more fluid all the time. It developed that he could cut the fastball to give us a second-out pitch, and he started experimenting with a little lollipop change-

up that was going to drive hitters nuts once he got it under
control. And then there was my suggestion for a fourth pitch: the
Ryne Duren. But I'm getting ahead of myself.

Every afternoon, we'd work in the bullpen during fielding
practice and through most of batting practice before knocking off
to get in a few swings against Jeff. As usual, Jeff came in tight and
fast on me, but I could see him cutting his speed against Phuong.
When I groused once, he grinned. "Temper, temper, Bull. You're
just sore because I struck you out and then let Phuong hit a
couple of easy ones." He slapped me on the arm. "Come on.
We'll worry about his hitting and fielding later. Right now, all I'm
worried about is his pitching. And that's your department." I
gave a bad-tempered grunt, picked up my gear, and lugged it
over to the bullpen, where Phuong was itching to work a little
more on his change-up. (I mean, hell—Jeff could throw me one
of those lollipop pitches once in a while.)

The next Wednesday, Jeff had the guys chasing fungoes in the
outfield, so Phuong and I moved from the bullpen onto the field.
And I swear Phuong could have drilled a Dixie cup. Jeff and the
other guys drifted in to watch. After a few minutes, Billy Collins
—who's got more guts than sense—picked up a bat and headed
for the batter's box. Jeff stopped him. "Not yet. Phuong's not
ready, and neither are you. Wait a few days."

He was right. The next day, I needed a net to catch Phuong.
Finally, after about twelve sprawls in the dirt, a half kilometer of
chasing wild pitches, and three or four good dings on the shins, I
signaled for time and trudged out to the mound without the
vaguest idea of what I was going to say. Jeff, who'd been watching us between hitting fungoes, tossed the bat to one of the other
guys and joined us. Phuong stood there steaming, so mad that he
wouldn't even look at us. Jeff said quietly, "You just haven't got it
today, Phuong. That'll happen. Come on, we'll hit some
fungoes." Phuong didn't move. Jeff hesitated, then reached out

and gently took the ball out of Phuong's glove. "Tomorrow you'll have your control back. Don't worry about it now."

"He's right," I said. "It happens to every pitcher. Even Jeff."

Phuong stared for a long moment into the distance. Then he sighed. "Ya, okay. Tomorrow." He turned to follow Jeff, while I went to shed my gear and to examine the bruises on my legs.

As soon as I'd finished warming up Phuong the next day, Jeff yelled, "Positions, everybody!" He waved to us. "You, too."

I stood and tipped my mask back. Somehow I'd expected this. I grinned at Phuong. "I guess you're throwing batting practice, partner. Ready?"

He gave me half a smile. "I imagine I could give it a try."

"Okay," I said. "One is a fastball, two is a cut fastball, three is a change, and four is the Ryne Duren."

This time he grinned. "Gonna use number four, huh?"

"Yep, and you know who's going to see it first."

For those of you who may not have heard of Ryne Duren, the great Yankee reliever of the fifties, let me give you two clues about pitch number four. First, Duren was fast as hell. Second, most batters firmly believed that he was at least two-thirds blind. You guess the rest.

Jeff picked up a bat and stepped into the box. I said out of the corner of my mouth, "You'd better hope he's not wild."

"Don't I know it," he said. He took a couple of practice swings, then shouted to Phuong, "Okay, hotshot, let's see what you've got."

"Get ready to duck," I said. I waggled one finger, and Phuong nodded.

Phuong's fastball came in belt high, and I swear it hummed when it dropped just before it crossed the plate. Jeff's swing was two seconds late and a foot high. Or thereabouts. "Jeez, does that fastball have a bite," he muttered. "Not bad!" he yelled. "But I've got you timed, sucker!" He didn't—not by a long shot—and it took him five more swings before he managed to send a weak bouncer to first. He stepped out while the guys fired the ball around the horn. "Nasty," he said. "*Real* nasty." He grinned like a wolf, and I knew that he was thinking about some unsuspecting sheep in a certain summer baseball league.

"Give him some time," I said. "He's not ready for the real thing yet." Jeff nodded and stepped back in. I let him see another fastball, then waggled four fingers. Phuong nodded, wound up, and sent the Ryne Duren screaming two feet over Jeff's head. Naturally, Jeff bailed out with an audible yelp of terror. From his backside, he stared first at me and then at Phuong, who was doubled over laughing on the mound.

I grinned. "That's our new pitch. We call it the Ryne Duren. Like it?"

"Why you son of a—"

"Tut, tut," I said. "Temper, temper."

Phuong started the season in right field. Jeff pitched, bringing Phuong in for two or three innings late in a game if we had a decent lead. Phuong gave up a few runs on walks and wild pitches, but Jeff let him work through his problems, and you could see him getting better with every inning. He made his first start in the middle of June and lasted four innings. He finished his second start for his first win, although that was largely thanks to some superb catching and two homers by yours truly. (Ya, Jeff and a couple of the other guys had pretty good games, too.)

Four days later, we played the defending champs in a game Jeff had been dreaming about all winter. His arm was fresh, so I figured he'd take the load, but he paused before stepping into the box at batting practice. "How's Phuong look?"

"Okay," I said, "but I haven't let him uncork one yet."

"Well, now's the time." He took a couple of practice cuts.

I waved to Phuong. "Let him see the real thing, partner."

Phuong nodded and blazed a fastball across the plate well

ahead of Jeff's swing. Jeff winced, tightened his stance, and came up empty a second time. He stepped out and stared for a long moment at Phuong, who gave him a slight smile. "You working a ladder on me, Bull?"

"Step at a time," I said. "The next one's coming in belt high."

"And it's going right back where it came from—Phuong needs his fielding practice."

I grinned and set up belt high, dead center with the plate. Phuong wound up, and the ball came in like a white bolt out of the background of green trees and blue sky. And even knowing where it was going, Jeff couldn't catch up to it. "Where do you want the next one?" I asked.

"I don't. He's ready, and those bums have seen enough."

I looked over at the opposing bench, where several guys had stopped talking and were staring nervously at Phuong. I stood and stretched. "So you're going to let him pitch?"

"Yep. You see any reason why not?"

"No, except I figured you wanted this game so bad that you wouldn't trust him."

Jeff gazed for a long moment at the mound, where Phuong had knelt to adjust a shoelace, and then he said quietly, "He's better than I am. That's what counts. And by the way, it hurts like hell to admit it."

"Well, you said it, all those Asian kids are killer baseball players."

"I don't know about all, but this one is. Just as long as he doesn't start thinking too much."

"You figured that out, huh?"

"Ya, I figured out a lot of things about him. And me, too, I guess. . . . Come on, we've got a ball game to win. Tell Phuong to relax and pitch his own game. I've got to tell Ned that he's playing right."

"Can we throw a Ryne Duren?"

"If there's nobody on, you can throw it the first time that fat first baseman comes up. He hit two homers on us last time, and it might get him thinking. Otherwise, stick to the fastball."

"Gotcha."

For the first five innings, Phuong was something to behold. Except for the single Ryne Duren—which produced a satisfying chalkiness on one fat first baseman's face—I called nothing but fastballs. Except for one blooper to right, the champs didn't hit diddly. But in the sixth, with us ahead three-zip, their lead-off man bounced a single into center, and their next batter stepped into a Phuong fastball while trying to bunt. (Luckily, it took him on the thigh and he managed to stagger down to first.) That was enough to shake up Phuong. His next pitch was a yard outside, and I retrieved it just in time to see their lead-off guy sliding into third.

I called time and jogged out toward the mound. Jeff started in from short, but I waved him back. On our bench, Mr. Keneally roused himself long enough to give me an inquisitive look. I let him have a reassuring grin.

Phuong was glaring at his shoes, glove on hip. Before I could say anything, he muttered, "It's going to happen again."

"Bull crap," I snapped, jolting him into looking at me. I grinned and drawled it out slow: "Bullll crappp. I'm going to put up my mitt, and you're going to hit it. That's all I'm going to do, and that's all you have to worry about."

"And you seriously think that's going to work?"

"Guaranteed, partner. We're just gonna play catch."

He took a deep breath, still not believing me. "Okay. Just a game of catch."

I gave him a swat on the butt and jogged back to the plate. I grinned at the next batter. "Seen any good emergency rooms lately? My boy's gone just a tad wild." He didn't think it was funny. Nor did the next guy or the guy after him, as Phuong struck out the side.

The last three innings were a breeze. Every now and then, I'd glance out at Jeff, who was nervously kicking the dirt at short between hitters. I knew that he was dying to call time for a quick visit to the mound, but he managed to control himself. In the ninth, Ned muffed a fly ball in right to give the champs a runner at second, but Phuong didn't so much as bat an eye. He mowed down the last three batters like they were little kids swinging sponge bats.

With the final strikeout, Jeff's self-control broke and he charged for the mound. When I got there a minute or two later— my speed hasn't improved any since spring—Jeff was thumping Phuong on the back and yelling: "No Win Phuong! That's what everybody's going to call you now, because nobody's ever gonna win against you again."

About that time, all the other guys got to the mound, and there was a lot of backslapping and high-fiving. In the middle of it all, Phuong just grinned. And for once his eyes weren't a bit cold. I winked at him. "You've got yourself a team," I said, and handed him the ball. "Have 'em autograph it."

For a second, I thought he was actually going to cry, but then he grinned and flipped it back to me. "Not this time. This one's yours, partner."

Alden R. Carter

"I'm afraid my ethnic roots were peeled and tossed into the stew pot two or three generations ago," says Alden Carter. He and his wife recently calculated that their children are five-sixteenths English, one-fourth Lithuanian, one-eighth Irish, one-eighth Swedish, one-sixteenth Dutch, and one-eighth unknown (but probably English or French). He concludes: "Quite simply, we are white Americans from central Wisconsin. Nothing more." Having no readily definable ethnic heritage to pass on to their children, Carter's family now celebrates *every* festival day on the calendar, no matter whose culture it honors.

All of Mr. Carter's first four novels—*Growing Season; Wart, Son of Toad; Sheila's Dying;* and *Up Country*—were selected as Best Books for Young Adults by the American Library Association. His most recent novel for teenagers, *RoboDad,* was named Best Young Adult Novel of 1990 by the Society of Midland Authors. He is also the author of twenty nonfiction books on a wide variety of scientific and historical subjects. His most recent nonfiction titles are *Battle of the Ironclads: The Monitor and the Merrimack* and *China Past—China Future,* an overview of Chinese history and culture.

The idea for "No Win Phuong" came to Carter while he was doing research on Vietnamese names as part of another writing project, teaching his athletic nine-year-old son some rudimentary baseball skills, and thinking about the nature of teamwork. "For some time," he says, "I had been musing on the concept of team sports and the problem of acceptance for those who are awkward in expressing a desperate desire to participate." As a teenage player, he confesses, "I, like Phuong, often squandered what ability I had by thinking too much and reacting too late." Perfect background for this story.

◻◗◦◦▲◦◦◗◻

Being ignored was bad enough. But the racial slurs hurt even more. Where would Lien find the strength to deal with those?

A DAUGHTER OF THE SEA
Maureen Crane Wartski

"Hey, Mr. Manning, can't we go fishing? It'd be a lot more fun than collecting creepy crawlies."

Lien didn't pretend to laugh with the rest of the group as Curt Hanson clowned around. She didn't feel like laughing. In fact, she wished she'd never come on this Saturday outing with her high school Biology Club.

During the long ride from Brockton to Orleans on the Cape, she'd been totally ignored. Except for the club adviser, Mr. Manning, no one had even spoken to her. It was as if Lien Huan didn't exist.

A strong sea-wind whipped Lien's long black hair as she climbed out of the van and walked some distance from the others to look at the sea. A September storm had lashed Cape Cod the previous night, and the sea beyond the dunes was still fretful. As she watched white-frothed waves pummel the shore, Lien could almost hear Grandpa relating his favorite sea story.

"On the morning that terrible voyage began," she imagined him saying, "the sea was like a raging demon. 'Come, sons and daughters of the sea,' it roared at us, 'do you dare to start the longest journey of your lives?'"

"Lien?" Mr. Manning's voice broke into her thoughts. "Lien, you're far away. Are you woolgathering?"

Low, so that Mr. Manning couldn't hear, Curt Hanson snickered, "That's what happens to slopes when they eat too much dog meat."

Lien's hands closed into fists before she remembered that Curt outweighed her by about a hundred pounds. Besides, fighting just made for more trouble. It was because her older brother had started getting into fights and running with a gang that the Huan family had moved to Brockton.

But there were troubles here in Brockton, too, and big-mouthed Curt Hanson was only one of them. There was the GOOKS, GET OUT sign that had been spray-painted on the steps of the house that Ma and Papa rented along with Uncle Dac and Aunty Hong. Rotten eggs had been smeared all over the driveway a week after they moved in, and the windows of the convenience store that the family had bought had been smashed many times over. And then there were the Huans' neighbors—most of them indifferent, a few friendly, many definitely hostile.

School was no different. The teachers tried—Mr. Manning, especially, went out of his way to be helpful—but Lien had found that only the Asian kids were friendly. It was Ahn Doh, one of the Vietnamese girls she'd met, who had convinced her to join the Biology Club. Because she was interested in biology and liked Mr. Manning, Lien had agreed.

But Ahn hadn't come on today's field trip, and without her, Lien felt very much alone. She skimmed her eyes over the other students who made up the Biology Club. She didn't know Mitch Kennedy or Naomi Barnett, but fair-haired, freckled Shani Moore was in Lien's freshman biology class, and Debby Olivera sat across from her in English. Besides a perfunctory "hi," neither of the girls had bothered to talk to Lien.

And then there was Curt Hanson. Lien sighed. Unfortunately for her, Curt was in her homeroom, and each morning he went out of his way to antagonize her. Even more unfortunately Curt, who wasn't even a member of the Biology Club, today had tagged along with his friend Mitch.

Perhaps Mr. Manning had heard Curt's obnoxious comments? But apparently he hadn't because he was saying, "All right, today we're going to catalog organisms that live in the tide pools. Low tide is an hour from now, so until then we can do our bit for ecology and pick up six-pack holders and anything that could hurt wildlife. We'll break into two groups."

Please, please let me be in Mr. Manning's group—but he was saying, "Naomi and Debby, you're with me. Shani, Lien, and Mitch, you're a team. You, too, Curt."

"Why can't we pick our own teams?" Curt protested.

Mr. Manning ignored this. "We'll go left, you go right. We'll meet back at the van in an hour. Have fun."

"Yeah, right," Curt muttered as the teacher walked away. "Some fun when we're stuck with Miss Saigon."

She didn't have to stand here listening to his insults. Turning on her heel, Lien started down the dunes. She was halfway down when Curt came barreling down and nearly knocked her over. "Why don't you watch where you're going?" she cried.

Like a rattlesnake poised to strike, he wheeled to face her. "No," he snarled, "*you* watch out."

"This is a free country," Lien wanted to retort, but the look in Curt's pale blue eyes silenced her.

"You gooks come here to *our* country and take all the jobs. You stink up everything. You people make me sick, so just get out of my face."

Something inside Lien hardened into ice. She couldn't move or speak as Mitch said uncertainly, "Hey, Curt, lighten up."

No one else said anything. Not looking at any of them, Lien walked stiff-legged down the sand dunes onto the beach. Her heart was pounding like a jackhammer, her legs were rubbery, and angry tears made her eyes feel as though they were full of grit.

Since leaving Boston, Lien had become used to unshed tears. You didn't waste time crying in the Huan family because there was no time *to* waste. For Lien, there was school, and there was the store. Everyone in the family worked in the store. Even Grandpa would putter around and smoke his pipe and wait on the Vietnamese customers. Whenever anyone would listen to him, he'd tell stories about his fishing days and relate how he had sailed his boat across the South China Sea.

Once, only once, Lien had complained to her mother about school. "*Thoi-dii*—stop, and think what you are saying," Ma had said in her practical way. "Life in America is good. You don't know what real hardship is, fortunately."

Maybe not, Lien thought now as she walked along the deserted beach, but over and over she'd heard the story of how her family had left Vietnam on Grandpa's rickety old fishing boat. The Huans had almost starved on that horrendous journey, but somehow they had kept alive, and by some miracle Grandpa had managed to evade pirates and survive storms till they made landfall in Hong Kong.

Lien had been born in a Hong Kong refugee camp. She had been just a baby when the family came to America. Papa had owned a small store in Vietnam before the Communists came, but the family had been nearly penniless when they finally reached America.

For a while they'd depended on the charity of the church that had sponsored them and set them up in a small Boston apartment—but not for long. The Huans had worked hard: Papa and Uncle Dac in a factory, Ma and Aunty Hong at cleaning people's houses, Grandpa in a restaurant washing dishes.

"*Cho, cho.*" Grandpa always chuckled when he told Lien this story. "Wait and be patient, I told them all. We are tired and sad now, but that will change. For sons and daughters of the sea, there are always new horizons."

But sometimes patience didn't help. Lien wiped her eyes with the back of her hand and looked back over her shoulder. Noting that her so-called team had stopped to examine something on the beach, she looked toward the sea again.

That was when she saw the fish. It lay sleek and dark like a large exclamation point in the breakers not far from shore. As Lien watched, it began to swim about. A shark in a feeding frenzy? she wondered, nervously.

Now the fish was swimming closer to shore, and something about the way it moved made Lien catch her lower lip in her teeth. She wished she knew more about fish, wished that Grandpa were there. He would surely know what was happening.

She turned and shouted to the others in her group. Curt and Mitch didn't look up, but Shani Moore did. When she saw Lien waving, she said something to the others and came running over.

"There's a big fish in the water!" Lien called out to her.

"What fish?" Shani began, then caught her breath. "Oh," she gasped. "Wow. What is it? Do you know?"

Lien shook her head. "A shark?"

The boys had now come up, and Curt scoffed, "That's no shark—it's a whale. My father knows all about fish. He told me whales are so stupid, they swim up onshore and die."

"It's a pilot whale," Mitch corrected. "I saw a show about them on TV last year. They sometimes get confused and beach themselves."

"It *looks* confused—like it's swimming in circles," Shani said. "Can't we do something to help it?"

"*Nada*—zip." Curt, Lien realized, was enjoying being the voice of authority. "Once that sucker beaches, it'll die."

"I'll get Mr. Manning." Mitch took off down the beach and returned a short while later with the rest of the group and the club adviser, who mused, "One pilot whale all alone—looks like a very young calf, from the size of it. It must have become disoriented and wandered away from its pod during last night's storm. Now it doesn't know how to get back to the open sea."

"Can't we get it turned around?" Lien asked. Curt snorted in disgust, but Mr. Manning nodded.

"We can try," he said. "Listen up, now. Lien, you and Shani go to the nearest house and call the police. Tell them that you've found a pilot whale in the shallows and ask them to contact the New England Aquarium and also the Center for Coastal Studies in Provincetown. Have you got that? The rest of us will try to keep the whale from beaching."

As Lien climbed the dunes, she couldn't keep the image of the lost young whale out of her mind. Once again she wished that Grandpa were with them.

"What can your grandfather do?" Shani wondered, and Lien realized she'd spoken her last thought aloud.

"He used to be a fisherman," she explained. "He's always talking about fish."

"My grandmother's a talker, too," Shani volunteered. "She lives with us. It drives my mom crazy, but I like it when she tells stories about when she was a girl in Ireland."

"My grandpa lives with us, too. Sometimes he calls me 'daughter of the sea'—" Lien stopped short. Shani didn't care about Grandpa or his stories. Perhaps she'd laugh—but instead, Shani looked surprised.

"I guess grandparents are all alike, huh? I never knew Cambodians before—"

"Vietnamese," Lien corrected. She couldn't help adding, "What do you mean, you don't know us? We're all over school."

"I mean, I don't *know* you," Shani explained. "I've seen you around school, sure, but you always stick with your own friends—"

She broke off as a patrol car drove slowly down the road.

Shani flagged it down and explained what had happened. "I'll get on it right away," the policeman promised. Then he added, "I remember one winter storm when thirty whales got beached."

"What happened to them?" Lien asked uneasily.

"I think volunteers managed to save some," the policeman said, vaguely.

Perhaps Curt was right after all, Lien thought as she and Shani hurried back toward the beach. Perhaps—

"Lien, look!" Shani exclaimed.

Lien's heart sank. They had reached the sea again, and in the short time that they had been away, the tide had ebbed considerably. The lost whale was now struggling in much shallower water. Mr. Manning, together with Mitch, Debby, and Naomi, was standing waist deep in the surf and apparently attempting to turn the creature around.

Curt sat on a pile of rocks, massaging his ankle. "I sprained it," he complained when Shani asked him what was the matter. Then he added sullenly, "I'm not even a member of your stupid club, and anyway, it's a waste of time. Once a whale starts to strand, it's history."

Ignoring Curt, Shani waded into the water. Lien followed. Though the September sun was warm, the sea was so cold on her bare legs that she cried out with shock. Then she gasped again as the whale smacked the water with its tail and doused her with spume.

"Turn him around—turn him!" Mr. Manning was shouting. "Lien, Shani, grab hold of him! Try to push him toward the open sea!"

Determinedly, Lien waded up to her waist, then stopped. She didn't want to touch, let alone take hold of, the big, slimy creature. As she hesitated, it turned in the water and rubbed against her.

The sleek, dark skin wasn't slippery! It felt like wet suede cloth. And it was making soft, squealing noises—scared noises.

Without further thought, Lien grabbed as much of the whale as she could and tried to help the others point it toward the open sea.

"Turn, willya?" Mitch was pleading. "Don't you want to join your friends?"

For a second it seemed as if the whale had gotten the message, and they all cheered as it began to swim toward the open sea. But a few minutes later it turned around and once more headed for the shore.

"Why does he keep *doing* that?" Lien asked as they splashed toward it.

Wiping away the salt spray from his eyes, Mr. Manning explained that no one really knew why pilot whales beach themselves. "Their guidance system might get disoriented by a storm or by some kind of geomagnetic field sent out by submerged rocks," he said. "Anyway, this little guy has double trouble. Pilot whales are social creatures who live in a pod—a community of whales. They depend on each other for help and company. Junior probably couldn't even survive without his friends."

"Then even if we get 'Junior' back into the sea, he'll die," Shani said unhappily.

"He'll certainly die if he's beached. Whales are mammals, but they're made to float in the water. On dry land, Junior's internal organs would very likely be crushed by his own weight." Mr. Manning added, "But don't give up hope, crew. The New England Aquarium has saved whales like our Junior before this. We just have to keep him from beaching himself until they get here."

He broke off as the whale's tail whapped down on the water, practically drowning its would-be rescuers. "One more time, group!" Mr. Manning ordered. "Let's try to get him turned around!"

Lien dug her toes into the sand and grabbed hold of the young whale's flipper. "You *have* to try!" she shouted at him. "You're a son of the sea, darn it."

Junior tried to dive in the shallow water. The others let go, but Lien stayed with him. "Brave whale, big whale, go back to the sea," she commanded.

Her words ended in a shriek as Junior shook loose and knocked her off her feet into the water. Lien came up, sputtering, and saw the young whale heading for shore once again.

Lien lost track of time. Over and over, they caught and pointed Junior in the right direction, only to have him swim back toward the shore. They tried the exercise until Lien's arms ached, and she was exhausted by the time a police cruiser arrived. With it was a truckful of men and women in wet suits.

"Reinforcements," Mr. Manning groaned, thankfully. "About time, too."

Mr. Manning stayed back to talk with the volunteers, but the others waded to shore and huddled into blankets that the police had brought along. Lien took a paper cup of hot coffee in almost numb hands and went to sit on a rock nearest the sea. After a few moments, Shani joined her.

"I don't think I'll ever be warm again," Shani complained through chattering teeth, "and I ache everywhere."

"My arms and legs feel like they're going to fall off," Lien agreed. "How long were we in there with Junior, anyway?"

Shani shook her head. Then she asked, "What was all that weird stuff you were talking about back there?"

Lien felt embarrassed. "Grandpa says things like that all the time," she mumbled. "I guess I was thinking aloud, trying to psych Junior out."

"Poor guy. He just wants to go home." Shani sighed. "He just doesn't know how."

As she spoke, a van bearing a familiar logo drove onto the beach. Scientists from the New England Aquarium had arrived! When a veterinarian waded into the surf to check Junior's condition, Lien threw off her blanket and followed him.

She held her breath with the rest until the vet declared, "I think we can save this one. We'll take him back to the Aquarium's Animal Care Center."

"All *ri-ight!*" Shani exulted, while the others whooped aloud.

The veterinarian was beaming, too. "We got lucky this time. This whale is very young. If all goes well, we'll keep him till he matures and eventually release him."

Lien remembered Junior's mournful, frightened cries. "But will he be able to survive away from his pod?" she asked anxiously.

"We'll release him near another whale community that will take him in," the veterinarian explained. He then added, "It's a good thing you found him when you did and kept him from actually beaching and hurting himself."

"Lien was the one who spotted him," Mr. Manning said, and Lien felt a warm glow until she heard Curt's snort. That derisive sound reminded her that nothing had really changed.

As Junior's rescue swung into gear, Mr. Manning marched the soaked Biology Club to dry land. "It's going to take a while before they get Junior away," he said. "If we want to hang around, we have to get out of these wet clothes. The scuba divers brought along some extra sweats we can borrow. We can change in the rest rooms near the beach parking lot."

As they followed their adviser up the dunes, Lien turned back to look at the sea. She saw that Junior was being fitted into a harness that would lift him onto a bed in a waiting back-loader. He was lucky, she thought. It was apparently easy for a displaced whale to find acceptance with a new group of friends, whereas humans—

"Saying good-bye to your fishy friend, slope-head?" Curt sneered in one of his carrying whispers.

Lien froze—but then Shani snapped, "Shut up, Curt. You are *such* a jerk."

"Yeah, Curt," Mitch agreed, and one of the girls—Debby Olivera—added, "It's not funny. We all care about Junior."

Once more Lien's eye felt gritty, but these were happy tears. Through them, she smiled at her new friends.

Someday, she was sure, a strong Junior would return to the open sea and join his new pod. And as for her—wasn't she also a daughter of the sea?

Maureen Crane Wartski

A former teacher of English and social studies, Maureen Crane Wartski is a Eurasian writer who was born and grew up in Ashiya, Japan, has traveled throughout Europe, and lived for five years in Bangkok, Thailand. She and her husband now make their home near Cape Cod, Massachusetts, where whales quite frequently beach themselves, as one almost does in "A Daughter of the Sea." In creating this story, Maureen Wartski incorporated some of her feelings about prejudicial statements and activities that had been in the local news at that time.

Her first novel for young people was *My Brother Is Special*, the story of a mentally handicapped youngster and the Special Olympics. She is also the author of *The Lake Is on Fire*, an exciting tale about the efforts of a blind boy and a half-wild dog trying to survive a raging forest fire. Maureen Wartski is best known, however, for her novels about Vietnamese boat people: the prize-winning *A Boat to Nowhere* and *A Long Way from Home*, fictional accounts of a harrowing escape from war-torn Vietnam and then about the difficulties that fifteen-year-old Kien faces in his new American surroundings.

She has also published several short stories for young people, a number of them in *Boys' Life*. Her awards include the Child Study Children's Book Committee at Bank Street College Award, Notable Books in the field of Social Studies, and recently the Society of Children's Book Writers' Magazine Merit Award.

Her most recent novel—*My Name Is Nobody*—focuses on an abused child who finds solace in the sea and in the love of a retired policeman who is by no means perfect.

❑❍❍❍▲❍❍❍❍❑

Dilemmas

Maria wanted to be like the other girls, especially when it came to pleasing Frankie Galvan. But she had made a promise to her mother.

DEAD END
Rudolfo Anaya

Maria hurried down the noisy, crowded hallway to her locker. She was on her way to calculus class, and she had forgotten her notebook with yesterday's notes.

She paused when she saw Frankie Galvan and his friends standing in front of her locker. Maria's heart skipped a beat. He was handsome, and lately he had been watching her.

"Hi, Maria." He smiled and moved away.

"Hi," Maria replied, and fumbled as she opened her locker.

The other girls waited until Frankie was gone, then they teased Maria.

"Hi, Maria," Sandra said, imitating Frankie. "My, you look nice today." The girls laughed. They were sharp dressers, while Maria wore only plain skirts and blouses.

"If you want Frankie to notice you, put on some lipstick," Denise said. She finished doing her lips and held out the stick.

Maria shook her head. "Gotta go to class."

"The *cholos* like lips red as wine." Ana laughed.

"And get out of those rags," Sandra remarked sarcastically. She was dressed in skintight jeans and a low-cut tank top that revealed her full breasts. Her lips were bright red, her eyes purple with eye shadow.

As Maria walked away, she secretly wished she could be like those girls. They didn't spend time with homework. Each day after school they cruised around the *barrio*. On weekends they went to parties, drank, smoked dope, and climbed in the back-seats of cars with the homeboys.

Each morning they arrived late to school and sauntered into the bathroom to smoke, then when they were good and ready, they dragged themselves to class and sat. They did their nails and discussed the prior night's adventure. They were tough, and they were always getting suspended from school for one thing or another.

Maria wished she could belong to their gang. She wished she could be free and easy like them, but ever since she could re-member, her mother had impressed on her the importance of an education.

"I never had the chance," her mother said, "because an edu-cation was only for boys. A girl was supposed to get married, raise kids, take care of her family. But you're smart, Maria. You must study and become educated."

Two years ago, at her mother's deathbed, Maria had promised she would not give up her dream of getting a good education. Her mother had smiled and closed her eyes. Her life had been hard, and the promise had brought a smile to her lips. Her daughter would be someone important, a teacher or a doctor. She would help people, and her life would have meaning.

Now that promise weighed heavy on Maria. She had very little idea of what getting a good education entailed, even though she tried hard at school. There was no one to talk to; her father was seldom home after the death of her mother. Once a week he gave Maria enough money to buy food for her and her younger brother and sister; otherwise, he returned only late at night. On weekends he was always gone.

Maria remembered there had been love in the family, now there was only bitterness in her father's face, a sense of loss.

She sent her brother and sister to school each morning and prepared supper at night. In the evenings she helped them with their homework. She was a senior in high school; she had too much to do. But she had to be like a mother to them and still keep up her studies.

Many times at night when she couldn't sleep, she got up and stood looking out the window. Things seemed hopeless, and she wondered how she could keep going. Then she would remember the promise she had made her mother and she would feel better.

That night as Maria was helping her little sister with her homework, the gang from school parked in front of Maria's home. They honked their horn; their car radio blasted out the latest rap.

"Hey, Maria! Let's cruise!" Denise shouted.

"Let's have fun!" Ana yelled.

Maria looked through the window at the car parked outside. The kids were drinking beer and laughing wildly. The girls were dressed in low-cut blouses, shorts, and summer sandals. They snuggled against the boys and teased them.

Eduardo was driving, and Sandra had her arms wrapped around him. Next to them Frankie Galvan sat alone. He looked out the open window at Maria.

Maria saw him, and her heart melted. Frankie Galvan was about the most handsome guy in school. For the past few weeks he had been hanging around her locker, and the girls had begun to whisper that he had a crush on Maria. They wondered why Frankie was interested in Maria when he could have any girl.

"Who is it?" Maria's sister asked behind her.

"Frankie Galvan," her brother said, peering through the parted curtains. "He's the baddest dude in the *barrio*."

Maria looked out again.

Yes, he was sitting alone, his black hair was slicked back, his dark eyes staring ahead. A gold chain glittered around his neck. The kids said he took dope. A year ago, his girlfriend had died in a car accident, and it really affected Frankie. Sometimes he hung around with the gang, but usually he was alone.

He's lonely, Maria thought. Her heart went out to him. When she saw him at school, he smiled and she felt goose bumps. She daydreamed of him holding her in his arms. She had never had a boyfriend or made love in the backseat of a car. She was too busy trying to keep the family together.

"Don't go," her little sister whimpered. Maria looked at her and saw she was afraid. "Don't leave us alone," she said, her eyes full of tears.

Maria knew her sister still hadn't accepted their mother's death. Sometimes she had nightmares at night, and Maria had to sleep with her to calm her fears.

Maria looked at her brother. He was only thirteen, but already he was a leader in his own gang. "I wanna be like Frankie some-day. Nobody messes with him," he said, then he turned away and ran out the back door.

Maria started after him, because she knew that the *barrio* streets at night could be dangerous for a thirteen-year-old. Some of the boys smoked marijuana, some sniffed spray paint, and the door of the crack house on Delmar Street was always open.

Outside she could hear the kids yelling and singing. *"Hasta la vista,* baby!" Denise called.

Maria looked through the window and saw Frankie turn to look at her. His eyes were inviting. Then they were gone.

Maria slumped into the sofa. She felt anger inside, a terrible anger at the unfairness of it all. Why couldn't she be out there? Why couldn't she dress like the other girls and cruise at night? Why couldn't she sit in the backseat of Frankie's car and feel his strong arms around her, and his warm kisses?

Tears wet her cheeks. Her sister stood beside her and stroked Maria's long black hair. Maria looked at her and smiled. "Come on," she said. "Let's finish your homework."

Next day, the gang hung out around the entrance to the

school, taking last-minute drags on their cigarettes before they went in. Maria and her friend Sue Yonemoto were hurrying to calculus class.

Ana stopped Maria as she passed by. "Hey, Mary, why didn't you come with us last night?"

Maria looked at her but didn't answer.

"Frankie was lonely," Sandra said. The girls around her made swooning sounds and laughed.

"She don't have a chance with Frankie," Denise said.

Just then, Frankie came around the corner.

Suddenly there was a silence in the air, a chill. Everyone knew nobody messed with Frankie.

Frankie looked at Denise and scowled. She turned away in embarrassment. Then he looked at Maria and smiled. He knew she read books and that she was smart. She answered the teacher's questions in class. She wasn't like the other girls. She was different, and he wanted her.

That night, Frankie drove up in front of Maria's house. He was alone. He parked and waited. Maria finally went out and walked slowly to the car. She could smell the fresh air of the spring night, and a faint fragrance of blossoms. It was spring, and school was almost out, and Frankie had come to park in front of her house.

She felt she was floating in air. That morning, he had looked at her and she had known he would come.

"Hi," she said, smiling.

"Hey," Frankie answered. "Want to cruise?"

Me? Maria thought. *He could have any girl in school, but he asked me.* She looked back at the house where her sister and brother stood at the window.

"I can go for a while," she said, and waved at her brother and sister. "Be back in an hour!" she called, and got into the car.

Frankie drove off slowly. Maria looked at him in the dark, his handsome features outlined against the lights of the street. The car smelled of sweet smoke mixed with the fragrance of hair dressing. He offered her a cigarette.

"I don't smoke," Maria said.

"What do you do?" Frankie asked, a strange laughter in his voice.

Frankie headed toward the bridge. There he parked and finished his cigarette. The sounds of the city seemed distant and remote.

When he finished smoking, he took Maria in his arms and kissed her. The warmth of his kiss excited her. She had never been kissed like this. She kissed him back, but when his hands began to explore her body, she resisted.

"Why not?" he asked.

She didn't know why not. Making out was what most of the girls talked about in the school bathroom. Going all the way was expected; it just depended who you did it with. And how high you got.

"I'm just not ready," Maria answered, and she thought of the promise she had made to her mother. She knew the kids who cruised every night didn't keep up with their schoolwork.

Couldn't she do both? For a moment she thought the promise she had made to her mother was a foolish thing. Even if she got into a university, even if she got grants and loans, there was still more money needed on top of that. And where was it going to come from? Who was going to take care of her brother and sister? It was a crazy dream, and she might as well forget it.

"Maybe this will help," Frankie whispered, and he lit a joint. He inhaled deeply and passed it to Maria. "Go on, take a hit. Make you mellow."

Maria hesitated. She had heard the story a thousand times, especially from the girls:

"A little weed puts you in a loving mood."

"Mellow, mellow for your fellow."

A lot of those girls had dropped out, and some had gone on to be regulars at the crack house on Delmar.

"Go on," Frankie whispered in the dark. The glowing ember of the joint was bright in the dark, and the thin feather of smoke was like a snake that swayed as it rose.

Suck me in and hold me, the smoke said, *and watch the problems slip away.*

Maria reached out and took the joint. She had tried smoking a cigarette once, in the privacy of her bathroom. It had made her sick. But she had wondered what marijuana was like, why it was so widely used by the kids. She had thought of trying it. Now was her chance.

She paused. Was she doing it for herself, or for Frankie? Was she doing it just to belong?

Outside, near the looming shadow of the dark bridge, she saw a shadow move. She heard a moaning sound, like a woman crying.

"Look!"

Frankie looked as the shadow disappeared into the dark.

"Bag lady," he said. "Go on, take a hit."

"She was crying," Maria said.

"You're not getting scared, are you? Miss Wonder Woman who gets A's in all her tests, scared?" Frankie chuckled.

"Did you ever hear the story of La Llorona?" Maria asked.

"Yeah, the crazy woman who cries at night?" Frankie laughed. "Yeah, my mom used to tell it to me. It's just a story to scare kids."

"Maybe," Maria replied. "My mother told me the story really happened. The young woman fell in love with a man. He was a sharp dresser, always had women around him. He made his living playing cards. He promised to love her, got her pregnant, and then he wouldn't help her."

"Smart dude," Frankie said. "I figure if a woman wants to get pregnant, that's her problem."

Maria continued. "The girl's father said the family's honor had been soiled, so he kicked her out of the house. She had nowhere to go, no one to turn to. When the baby was born, she drowned it."

Frankie sat up straight. "It's not a real story, is it?"

Maria nodded. "She drowned the child here, beneath the bridge."

"You're kidding," Frankie said.

"She had no help," Maria continued. "She went crazy and drowned the baby. Now she cries at night, looking for her child."

"Damn," Frankie whispered. He looked out into the darkness. The night had grown cool. There was only silence in the night, strange sounds, the distant wail of a siren.

"I'm going to be different," Maria said softly.

Frankie looked puzzled.

She handed the marijuana cigarette back to him.

He took it. "Why not?"

"I don't want to drown my children," Maria answered.

Frankie didn't understand what she meant. He touched saliva to his fingertips and put out the joint. "What's the matter with you? You don't smoke, you don't dress like the other girls. You think you're too good?"

Maria shuddered. She had heard that accusation before. The girls whispered behind her back. "She thinks she's too good for us. Runs around with the Japanese girl. Calculus Club. Just too damned good!"

First, Maria had tried to explain. No, she didn't think she was too good for them. But she couldn't explain to them about the promise to her mother. She couldn't tell them she wanted to go to college, because few of the girls from that school had ever dared try. Most of them drifted off, got married, or just disappeared. Maria didn't want to just disappear. She wanted her life to have a meaning, and that meant keeping to her mother's dream.

"Take me home," Maria said. She knew that saying take me home meant she was saying good-bye to Frankie Galvan. It also meant not belonging to the gang.

"Yeah, okay," Frankie answered. He started the car, and they slowly drove back to Maria's.

As they drove, Maria felt the anguish of her choice. *Why,* she asked herself, *oh why, couldn't I just let go? Let go of my dream? Follow Frankie?* He was the only young man who had ever invited her out, held her in his arms, kissed her. She wanted to reach out and touch him and say she would stay with him.

She felt a longing for him, and she knew that she would always remember this night. But seeing the figure of the woman in the night had reminded her that life was a struggle, and she had to take care of herself. Frankie's life was headed toward a dead end. She just didn't want to wind up with him on that street.

He parked in front of her house and looked at her. "Hey, I like you. I'm sorry for what I said. So you're different. That's why I like you. Maybe I can call you later."

"School's almost over, and all the exams are coming up," Maria said.

"School isn't everything." Frankie smiled in the dark. "You gotta have some fun."

Yes, she thought. *School isn't everything.* When he kissed her, she had felt she really cared for him. Maybe she had put too much of her time and energy into schoolwork.

"Maybe after exams are over," she said.

"Yeah, maybe." He nodded.

"Good-bye." She smiled and leaned toward him. "Thank you." She kissed Frankie on the cheek.

She quickly got out of the car and ran into the house.

Rudolfo Anaya

Son of a farmer's daughter and a *vaquero,* Rudolfo Anaya was born in an adobe-walled house in the small village of Pastura, New Mexico. Since 1952 he has lived in Albuquerque, where he earned degrees from the University of New Mexico. He has been a professor of English at that university since 1974.

His first novel, *Bless Me, Ultima,* required seven years of writing, but its publication in 1972 won Anaya the Premio Quinto Sol Award and earned him a position of preeminence in the history of Chicano literature. Throughout the 1970s and 1980s he was the most widely read Chicano writer in the world, and *Bless Me, Ultima* has been the most widely taught Chicano novel in the American Southwest.

While *Ultima* reflects the author's childhood feelings and experiences, his second novel, *Heart of Aztlan,* explores the relationship between the people of New Mexico and the land they have inhabited for centuries, along with the effects of the social and political issues of the 1960s. That book was followed by *Tortuga* in 1979 and *Silence of the Llano* in 1982. He has also published two nonfiction books, *Lord of the Dawn: The Legend of Quetzalcoatl* and *A Chicano in China.* He has edited several anthologies of Chicano short stories and folktales, including *Cuentos Chicanos.*

In addition to his own writing, Rudolfo Anaya helped found The Rio Grande Writers group, and in the late 1970s, while he was on the board of the Coordinating Council of Literary Magazines, he was instrumental in helping small presses establish themselves as significant developers of many of the country's young writers who had not found acceptance by large New York publishing houses.

His most recent novel, published in 1992, is *Alburquerque,* a story of romance and political intrigue, blending the historic past and the challenging present of that vibrant Southwestern American city.

◻◊◦◦▲◦◦◦◦◻

In Cambodia, Sundara's family would have chosen her husband and established the price his family would have to pay to marry her. But American customs are different. How Americanized will Sundara's family allow her to be?

BRIDE PRICE
Linda   Crew

"Even if your aunt is mean to you," Moni said, "I still think you are lucky to have a family."

Sundara glanced across the field at her Aunt Soka, who squatted between the strawberry rows, snatching berries from the leafy green plants with her usual furious intensity. Sundara had not been feeling particularly lucky recently, but now, after an hour of working alongside this other Cambodian girl, she had to agree that, in comparison, she was fortunate. Living with her aunt and uncle was not the same as being with her own parents, but it was better than living with American sponsors as Moni, newly arrived and alone in Oregon, was forced to do.

"At least you will have someone to arrange your marriage," Moni went on.

"Oh, I don't even want to think about that," Sundara said. Somehow her Aunt Soka's matchmaking talk always made her feel more uneasy than secure, as if she were merely a token in a game Soka was determined to win—a game called Bride Price. "You are a pretty girl," Soka would say. "We will hold out for a high price on you." She talked about Sundara's long black hair and smooth skin as if these were lucky cards that had been dealt not to Sundara but to her, Soka.

"I think about marriage a lot," Moni said, "ever since they took Srey to southern California to be married. Even in the short time we knew each other here, we had become like sisters. I miss her."

Sundara remembered Srey as a ghost of a girl who would have been pretty had her dark eyes not lost all life. Clearly her spirit had been killed by the Khmer Rouge Communists long before her stick-thin legs carried her over the mountains into a Thai refugee camp.

Sundara pushed her low, single-wheeled berry cart a few feet down the row. "She seemed like a child. It's hard to imagine her married."

"Sixteen, though. Many of my village friends were married at that age." Moni herself had married young and was now, at twenty-one, already a widow.

"Maybe I've gotten used to the way things are here," Sundara said. "Somehow, Srey being married seems . . . shocking."

"Does it? Well, to be honest, I don't think she was happy about it. But then, after what she's been through, she probably cannot be happy about anything."

Could any of them? Sundara wasn't sure herself what happiness was anymore, and she'd been one of the so-called lucky ones. She had been visiting her aunt and uncle's fishing village on the gulf three years before when the Communists overran Cambodia. She and her aunt's family had been able to flee to a crowded freighter and escape, but her parents, her brother, and her little sister had been in Phnom Penh. Later, she heard the Khmer Rouge had marched the entire populace out into the countryside to work as slaves. She had no idea now if anyone in her family was even alive anymore. Would it be right to feel happiness for herself, not knowing about them?

Moni popped another strawberry into her mouth. "How do you keep from eating these? I want to just eat and eat."

"Oh, they're good, I know," Sundara said, "but I'd rather take them home to wash first."

"Oiee! When you've been eating insects and leaves to stay alive, these berries would seem like food for kings even if I dipped them in mud."

A berry flew past Sundara. A squeal from a girl a couple of rows over, a bark of laughter from the boy who'd thrown it.

"Okay, Gabe!" It was Mr. Bonner, the farmer boss. "Any more berry throwing, and you're outta here."

"They throw the berries?" Moni whispered.

"Yes. The mushy, rotten ones. But Moni, you don't have to whisper. They don't understand Khmer."

Moni shook her head. "These American children . . ."

"Some of them work hard," Sundara said. "But others—their parents drop them off in big fancy cars."

"They put their children to work in the fields even though they're rich? Why?"

Sundara laughed. "They call it 'learning work ethic.' "

Another flying berry. More laughter.

"I don't think they're learning," Moni said.

A berry arced over them in the other direction.

Alarmed, Moni looked toward Mr. Bonner's truck. "He's going to be mad now."

Sundara squinted. "No, he didn't even see."

Moni let out her breath. "It's hard to get used to it here. The Khmer Rouge . . ." Her voice trailed off.

Sundara's stomach clenched. The name alone made her shiver, and she could guess what Moni was thinking. The Khmer Rouge probably dragged people from the fields and killed them for less.

She forced herself to speak lightly. "I've heard Mr. Bonner's wife threaten to charge these kids' parents for baby-sitting."

Moni's mouth fell open. "Can this be true?"

Sundara smiled. "It's a joke, Moni. But it makes sense. That boy throwing the berries? I heard that yesterday, for the whole morning, he picked only one flat."

"Now you *must* be joking!" Moni laughed. "I'm not that dumb. What do you think? I eat out of a coconut shell instead of from a plate? It's not possible to pick berries that slowly, even when you eat half of them like I do!"

Sundara shrugged. "Look around. No white parents to make sure they work."

"One flat? You're serious? Well, they'll all have plenty to eat tonight, whether they earn any money or not."

"That's right," Sundara said. "Maybe it's hard to work when you know it really doesn't matter."

"They don't know what hunger is," Moni said. "You should have seen me before—just bones, no meat. And so sick. The Khmer Rouge made me work anyway. I had to crawl down the row of potato plants, picking the bugs off the leaves."

Sundara listened, although she'd heard it all before. Lately stories like this were everywhere. People were escaping the Khmer Rouge regime and whispering of the horrors in tales that traveled across the ocean to friends already in America, in lines of a letter someone in Portland had received from a relative in a refugee camp, in a newspaper story passed on by somebody's cousin. Nothing Sundara heard ever gave reason for hope. Each story of starvation and senseless killing only made clear to Sundara that her previous worst imaginings had not been bad enough.

"Well, we're here now," Moni said. "I have new worries. As I was saying before, with no one to arrange it for me, I don't see how I'll ever be able to get married again."

Sundara let out her breath. Talk of marriage was an improvement, at least, over talk of killing. "Maybe you can be like an American and marry whoever you want."

"How you talk! You sound like an American yourself!"

Did she? At school, moving among the whites, she felt dark and foreign. But since she had been here three years, spoke English, wore jeans, and drove a car, she probably would seem American compared to Moni or her friend Srey.

"I wonder if I'll start to be American, too," Moni went on. "I cannot believe how my life has changed already. And do you know what seems so odd? I think of all the times I went to the fortune-teller—never once did he warn me that I would be such a young widow."

Sundara kept picking. Surely a fortune-teller with any wit at all could have watched all the men going off to war and predicted a legion of young widows.

Sundara no longer believed in fortune-tellers. Maybe Moni, too, would find herself giving up old superstitions here in the new land. How could you cling to old rules that no one else bothered following? *Never point at a rainbow*, Sundara had always been warned, *or you will cut your finger.* But you only had to risk it once, as a test. Then when nothing bad happened, you could boldly point at rainbows forever after. Maybe superstitions lasted longest when everyone agreed to fear the same thing and no one dared defy the rules.

Of course, the Americans had their own foolish ideas—never walking under ladders or stepping on sidewalk cracks. But she'd stepped on sidewalk cracks every time they'd gone shopping in Phnom Penh. Nothing bad had happened. Or more accurately, what had happened was so bad that only a fool would blame it all on sidewalk cracks.

Once, during an eclipse of the moon here, Soka had made them all stay awake all night, just to be safe. But when Sundara had nodded over her desk at school the next morning, noticing that her classmates seemed wide awake and none the worse for having enjoyed a good night's sleep, she vowed she'd never again sit up like that, no matter what her aunt said.

If only it were all this easy to figure out. But testing a silly superstition was one thing; testing a way of life was another. As far as finding which was the best way to marry, that would take years to prove. If you chose wrong, it might be too late to try the other. Maybe that's why the stories about other refugees seemed so important. The Khmers were always listening for patterns, clues about how to get along in America. Some people wanted to know how that Khmer family in Salem managed to buy a house, others how so-and-so got a job or filed income taxes. What Sundara always wanted to know was how the newest marriages were faring.

"Have you heard anything from Srey?" she asked Moni.

"Not a word," Moni said. "But then, I don't really know how to write letters myself." After a moment she said, "So. Is your aunt looking for a husband for you?"

"Oh, I think it's just talk right now. They want me to get a good education. They want me to be a doctor."

"A doctor! You, a girl?"

"Women can be doctors in America."

"Yes, I've heard of that, but—Cambodian women?"

"Why not?" This was said with more conviction than Sundara actually felt. "Once you're a citizen, it's not supposed to matter where you're from."

"Well," Moni said. "If your aunt thinks nothing of women becoming doctors, I would say she, too, is turning American."

"Maybe so. I think she doesn't know whether to be Khmer or American, either." One minute she'd be telling Grandmother she must learn English, the next she'd offer Sundara's little cousin Ravy a dollar if he'd speak Khmer all day long. She talked of Sundara being a doctor almost as often as she talked about the foolishness of spending money on education for girls. "I don't know what she wants," Sundara told Moni. "First she says I have to be matched with a Cambodian boy, then she turns around and warns me what scoundrels they all are. 'Take three Khmer men,' she says. 'One will be a gambler who loses all your gold, the next will spend it all on smoking and drinking, and the third will pay it out to sleep with strange women.' "

"But your uncle isn't like that, is he?"

"Ah, but Soka says that's because she knows how to make him behave." Guiltily she glanced toward Soka and lowered her voice. "I'm not joking about her fierce temper. One time I heard my parents saying she'd caught Uncle Naro with a young girl and got so mad, she attacked his motorcycle with an ax."

"Oiee! That takes a brave spirit. My husband would have beaten me."

"Yes, well, that's one thing Soka will admit to liking about America. Men don't beat their wives here."

"They don't?"

"Well, actually, some do. But the difference is, they're not supposed to, so you can complain about it. You can tell it to the police."

"Oh." Moni picked a berry with a rotten spot from her flat and tossed it aside. "Well, my husband didn't hit me very often. Only when I talked too sassy."

"Here they're not supposed to hit no matter how you talk."

"Really?"

"Yes. Don't hit. If they don't like you anymore, they get a divorce instead."

"They divorce a lot here, I think."

Sundara nodded. Neither system seemed quite right to her. She didn't like the Cambodian way, where a man could have as many wives as he could afford, but the American way of divorcing a wife when she got old so the man could have a new, younger wife didn't seem much better. At least with the Cambodian way, the first wife still had a place, a home. Here she'd heard stories of women working hard jobs so their husbands could become educated, only to find themselves thrown out when their paychecks were no longer needed. The man got richer and the woman was left to care for the children without any money.

So it wasn't as if one way were clearly better. Wasn't there something in between?

Sundara hardly ever dared argue any of this with her aunt, but once, when they'd been studying the American Civil War and slavery in school, she'd pointed out to Soka that buying and selling people was illegal in America. "So how can you sell a girl for a bride?"

"Selling as a bride is not the same as selling for a slave," Soka had replied.

Now *that* depended on the husband, Sundara thought. If your husband felt entitled to beat you, you might as well be a slave.

"Besides," Soka said, "we don't actually sell girls."

Sundara hesitated. "When you say 'bride price,' it sounds like it."

"Ah, but you must understand that the money the man gives is a show of respect for the girl's family. If they make him pay a lot, that shows they value her. And it's best for the girl, too, because the more he can pay, the better the man is."

Sundara pressed her lips tight, thinking, *No, the more he can pay, the richer he is.*

Not long after this, on the Sunday the Americans called Mother's Day, they'd been dutifully sitting in the back pew at the First Presbyterian Church when the minister read this passage: *"Who can find a virtuous woman? for her price is far above rubies."*

Soka had turned her eyes on Sundara as if to say, *There, you see? Even the Christian Bible understands about this.* She brought it up while they were driving home, smugly reminding Naro that a ruby or two had actually been included in her own bride price.

"Yes," Naro said. "Some days, I wish I had those rubies back."

"Oh, you!" Soka swatted him playfully. Everyone knew he was only joking.

Later, Sundara studied those passages in the Bible that the church people had given them. Maybe Soka had misunderstood. Maybe the old-fashioned English words meant that a truly valuable, virtuous woman could not be purchased with money or jewels at all.

"Smashing the motorcycle is not the only story about my aunt," Sundara told Moni now. "She's also very stubborn. One time when she got mad at my grandmother, she stopped talking and never said a word to anyone for a month!"

"Ah! So maybe being on my own is not so bad—is that what you're saying?"

Sundara only smiled. She had probably gone far enough with these disrespectful complaints.

When they carried their next full flats up to the truck, they saw a new Asian family gathered. Mr. Bonner was trying to show them that some of their berries weren't ripe enough. The mother didn't seem to understand. She spoke crossly to her daughters.

"Sundara," Mr. Bonner said, "could you explain it to them? I can't have these green spots, and the flats have got to be fuller."

Sundara put on the ever-useful smile of apology and spoke in English. "They speak Chinese, I think. Sorry, I'm not understanding."

"Oh." Mr. Bonner was taken aback.

These Americans! Where did they get the idea that all black-haired people spoke the same language? It bothered Sundara, too, the way the Americans seemed to assume that the dozen or so refugee families in Willamette Grove would of course be close friends. Did these whites imagine that if they were dropped into a town like Kompong Som, for example, with a few other white families, they would automatically get along? No matter that their backgrounds might be radically different? Didn't they un-

derstand that there was so much more to friendship than skin
color?

Sundara and Moni weighed in their berries. Then, back at the
end of their rows, they placed pint boxes in new flats. Behind
them, even at a distance, the Chinese woman's voice was as
annoying as whining mosquitoes. *Her poor daughters,* Sundara
thought.

Again Sundara glanced toward Soka. How she hated it, always
worrying about her aunt watching her. Had she noticed that
Sundara had gone up with only one flat instead of waiting to
carry a stack of two or three, the way Soka always said they
should?

It hadn't always been quite this bad. At first, Soka had seemed
proud of Sundara, bragging to people how she'd looked after
them all when they'd been seasick during the escape, how she'd
run around trading useless Cambodian riels for Malaysian money
when they'd landed there, how she'd washed everyone's clothes
in a bucket and brought them their rationed scoops of tuna and
rice on banana leaves. But after they'd been here a year or so,
Soka had decided that Sundara was turning into an American
brat.

"Oh, that daughter of Pok Sary!" she would start in. "They say
her parents talk to her, and it's like pouring water on a duck's
back. She is becoming far too American." Then she would stare
at Sundara with her black eyes, and Sundara would know they
weren't really discussing the daughter of Pok Sary at all.

But here in the strawberry field, Soka wasn't paying any attention to Sundara at the moment. Surprisingly, she wasn't
crouched over her row, either. Instead she stood in conversation
with another Khmer woman, Vuthy. *It must be an interesting
story,* Sundara thought, *if it could keep Soka from her work, from
earning money.*

Sundara and Moni bent back to their picking.

"Do you want to get married the American way?" Moni asked.

Sundara shrugged. Did Moni mean an American-style ceremony or an American-style marriage? No matter. Sundara wasn't sure about either.

Once, in the supermarket, she had stealthily thumbed through a thick, glossy magazine about being a bride. Imagine! A whole magazine about making a wedding party! As if being a bride would fill up the rest of your life. She marveled at the big, puffy skirts the ladies wore, a style that could not have been farther from the narrow Khmer skirts, wrapped tightly and cut short enough to reveal ankles bangled in gold. And all the white! How strange, to be married not in the golds and rich colors of celebration but in the white of mourning, the paleness of ghosts. The American brides did not always smile sweetly, either. Many of them seemed haughty; a few actually glared from the pages.

Back in Cambodia, she might have been married already, but here, people her age didn't seem to think of marriage at all. Even that girl in her class who'd had a baby. And she didn't seem one bit ashamed, either. Sundara had seen her in front of the 7-Eleven with her friends. She was turned away from the baby in the stroller, laughing, smoking a cigarette.

But Sundara *did* find herself thinking about being married, in spite of what she told Moni. Not that she was so anxious to have a husband to bicker with the way Aunt Soka bickered with Uncle Naro. But being a wife might be better than this role of dutiful niece where she was stuck now.

She let a handful of berries roll into her boxes. "The truth is, Moni, I don't know whether to keep to Khmer ways or try to be more American. Or maybe find something in between."

Moni didn't speak for a moment. Then she said shyly, "I'm very glad to have found another Khmer girl who can understand about this."

Sundara smiled.

When someone called lunch break, most of the pickers stood from their crouches and headed for the tree shade at the edge of the field.

"Didn't you bring food?" Moni said, seeing that Sundara was continuing to pick.

Sundara shook her head. "I'd like to, but my aunt thinks we should just keep working. She doesn't like the idea of eating in the fields. Besides, we only work until one o'clock or so. After that it gets too hot for the Americans."

"Too hot! I'll never be too hot here. I have been cold from the moment I stepped off that airplane, even when the sun shines."

"I know, but you'll get used to it."

They each picked a flat while the others ate, two more flats after that, and then Mr. Bonner was motioning everyone to stop and bring up what they had. It was time for him to make his deliveries.

At the truck, Sundara lingered in the fragrance of the harvested berries. The Chinese family straggled up, the mother still snapping at her daughters as if she had never stopped. Sundara noticed Soka giving the woman a respectful nod, almost as if she might have bowed, were they not surrounded by a lot of sassy white teenagers.

Moni unlocked her bicycle, which she'd parked behind Mr. Bonner's fruit stand.

"It's a long way on a bike," Sundara said. "Tomorrow we could give you a ride."

"Oh, I don't want to be any trouble."

"It's no trouble. I'll call you. You say your sponsors are the Millers?"

"Yes, on Sycamore Street."

"Niece!" Soka's voice was sharp. "Come now!"

Sundara slipped into the driver's seat of their new, American-made station wagon. Soka had insisted she get her license the day she turned sixteen. It was important to be able to drive cars in America.

"You seemed very friendly with that Moni."

"She's nice."

Soka made a little noise. "I hear her people were peasants."

Sundara held back, then blurted it out: "Does that mean I'm not supposed to talk to her?"

"I didn't say that. Just be careful you don't get pulled down to her level and start talking like a peasant yourself, that's all. I don't want to hear you rattling on with the know-nothing clank of an empty bucket."

Sundara clamped her jaw tight to keep from answering. When it suited her, Soka loved to point out that social class didn't matter in America. At times when the family of Pok Sary tried to act superior to them, for instance. "They cannot bear to let anyone forget they were so high up back home," she would say. "They've got to learn we are all equal here."

Soka seemed to forget this, however, when they met refugees with less affluent, less educated backgrounds. She would probably get worse, Sundara thought, now that Naro had his new job as an accountant and didn't have to wash dishes at the restaurant anymore.

"Did you see those new ones?" Soka said. "They're Chinese, from Vietnam. Just arrived."

"Yes," Sundara said. "Mr. Bonner is having trouble explaining things to them."

"Very rich before, I hear. They have a son who would be just right for you, Niece."

Heaven protect her! Sundara was thinking not of this unseen son as her husband but of the woman at the truck as her mother-in-law. Oiee! Better to put up with Soka's bossing than to be chained for life to a dragon lady like that!

"But, Younger Aunt," she said, "we don't even speak the same language."

"He's learning English, though. Every day he studies, they say. He's their only son, so while his sisters work in the fields, he must be the first to become educated."

Sundara stared straight ahead at the road over the bridge into town. Sons. Always the sons were so important. Would this have bothered her back home? Maybe she *was* becoming American.

Soka went on to the latest gossip about the family of Pok Sary. "I don't care how big their brick house in Phnom Penh was, they will never get a husband for that daughter of theirs if they cannot raise her right." She recounted with relish the recent sins of this daughter—wearing tight jeans, failing a school test.

But when Sundara thought of her, what came to mind was the way she sat in class, elegantly erect, serene. Unconsciously, it seemed, lost in a dream of dancing, she would continually force her fingers back, pushing them into the positions of the Cambodian Royal Ballet. This was a terrible American brat of a daughter?

"Oh, and here's another story for you," Soka went on. "Vuthy just told me. It's so shameful, I only repeat it because it's a good warning for you."

Sundara sighed. Was there any story that *wasn't* a warning for her?

Soka lowered her voice, as if whispered gossip might be more forgivable. "That foolish girl, Srey? Here she is, newly married to a very fine man with excellent prospects. Her parents went to a great deal of trouble to arrange that for her, and what does the silly girl do? Tries to kill herself."

Sundara sucked in her breath. Her eyes blurred. *Red light.* She slammed the car brakes.

Soka lurched forward. "Niece! What is this jerking of the car? Is this all the better they taught you in those driving classes?"

"Sorry," Sundara breathed, easing the car through the intersection on the green light.

Flustered, Soka settled herself again. After a moment, she once more lowered her voice. "About Srey? They say she tried to hang herself. Fortunately her poor husband found her right away. It was simply the hand of fate. He happened to come right back to their apartment."

"But . . . *why?*"

"He must have forgotten something."

"Yes, but I meant why would she do that?"

"Oh, I don't know. Clearly she's unhappy. But who *isn't?* Oh, what an awful thing! Now they say her mother cries all night long, every night." She shook her head. "Well, we won't speak of it again."

But stopping the talk about it couldn't clear Sundara's mind. She was thinking about being so unhappy that you would want to die. She was thinking about the dark mystery of surviving torture and starvation, only to want to kill yourself when you were finally safe. Or was Srey safe?

Soka was right: Srey's story was a good warning for her, but not in the way her aunt thought.

She would probably never know Srey's secrets, the torment that had brought her to such a place, but at this moment, driving home to their apartment, Sundara did realize something about her own fate.

Whatever choices the future held, she wanted to do the choosing.

She glanced at her aunt's profile, set and hard. Soka would not be pleased. But Sundara could be stubborn, too. She came by it honestly, as the Americans like to say. After all, was she not the niece of a woman who told her husband she didn't care what the custom was, he could forget the idea of a second wife? And then destroyed his motorcycle to prove she meant it?

For now, Sundara would pay her aunt the silence of a good Cambodian girl. No need to raise Soka's wrath when so much was still unclear. But to herself Sundara made a promise. For whatever happiness or misery came into her life, she would take the responsibility. When the time came, she would set her own bride price.

She did not think she would care to count it in rubies.

Linda Crew

Linda Crew, whose ancestors are German, English, and Welsh, owns and operates a small fruit and vegetable farm with her husband in Corvallis, Oregon. They have employed immigrants from various Southeast Asian countries and became friends with one family from Cambodia. "After hearing some of their stories," she says, "I began to wonder how we, as white Americans, looked to them. I then got the idea of turning their stories into a novel that would help us understand them." The result was *Children of the River,* a poignant story about a young girl who escapes from the horrors of war in her native country and then has to deal with the trauma of her past experiences as she learns to cope with a new life in an American high school.

Children of the River won numerous awards, including Honorable Mention in the Fifth Annual Delacorte Press Prize for an Outstanding First Young Adult Novel contest; the 1989 International Reading Association Children's Book Award, Older Reader Category; and a 1990 Golden Kite Honor Book Award from the Society of Children's Book Writers. It was named a Best Book for Young Adults by the American Library Association.

Readers familiar with that highly praised novel will recognize Sundara and her aunt in "Bride Price." Those who have not yet read it will surely want to read more about Sundara's life and what brought her to America.

Since *Children of the River,* Linda Crew has published *Someday I'll Laugh About This,* about a twelve-year-old girl coping with growth and change at the family beach cabin on the Oregon coast; *Nekomah Creek,* the story of a nine-year-old boy who begins to feel insecure about his slightly unconventional family (an ALA Notable Children's Book); and *Ordinary Miracles,* a novel for adults about life, death, marriage, and trying to have babies.

◻◊○○▲○○◊◊◻

Birthdays often are times for surprises. But this surprise was one that Monique hadn't ever imagined for herself.

MY SWEET SIXTEENTH
Brenda Wilkinson

"Who's that cute little girl?" Carla asked her roommate, Monique, who was busy placing on the wall at her side of the room a huge black-and-white photo.

"That's my goddaughter," Monique answered with wide-eyed admiration as she finished arranging the picture.

"She's some cutie!" Carla said, moving closer for a better look.

The two seventeen-year-olds had just moved into the dorm they would be sharing for the next eight weeks. They were attending a summer church camp at Jersey State College.

"You know," Carla raised her voice to say, "your goddaughter looks something like you!"

"You think so?" Monique responded, moving away from the picture.

"Uh-huh. Especially around the eyes."

"Maybe," Monique mumbled, walking over to her trunk to finish unpacking. She was trying hard to follow her mother's advice that she keep her business to herself, but she found it no easy task.

Already this girl can tell that the picture's the spitting image of me, she mused. *So how am I supposed to try to fool anybody here? The one person I ought to be able to level with is my roomie!*

"Why you looking so serious?" Carla asked, noticing the strange expression that had come over Monique's face.

"I was just thinking," she replied.

"You're not getting homesick for New York City already?" Carla asked, cuddling one of the stuffed animals on her bed.

"Anything but!" Monique was quick to say. "Church camp's about the last place I cared to spend my summer. But since it meant getting out from under my mother's thumb, I was down for it. My mother's stricter than the pope."

"Mine is strict, too," Carla noted. " 'Course, she says it's for my own good—which I guess she's right about, considering all the girls around my way who've gotten into trouble."

"Listen!" Monique said, walking to her bed to sit now. "There's something I think I should tell you before you go any further. Just promise me that you won't go blabbing."

"Blabbing what?"

"That little girl on the wall isn't my goddaughter. She's my baby."

"*Your* baby?"

"Yes," Monique confessed.

"So why didn't you just say so from the git-go?"

"Like, it was my mother's idea," Monique explained. "You know how church people can be sometimes."

"Do I?" Carla chanted, rolling her eyes toward the ceiling.

"My mother said that she didn't want people here looking down their noses at me," Monique continued.

"Oh, forget that!" Carla waved a hand of dismissal. "There's nothing so special about anybody at this place. Just a bunch of boring people from between here and New York City. This your first time coming?" she asked.

Monique answered that it was.

"Well you're lucky!" Carla intoned. "I've been coming here off and on since I was twelve and dying through every summer of it! 'Course, it's better here now than it used to be. At least they let us have dances. Not that you ever meet anybody worth writing home about. There are some okeydokey guys from this one church in Jersey City. They're all right, except for one or two who dance like somebody on *American Bandstand*."

"I didn't come here with great expectations!" Monique informed her. "Not when our preacher was the one who recommended coming here in the first place! But as I said—even this beats being home locked in the house. I never get out!"

"Well, you must have gotten out at least one time!" Carla cracked, her eyes dead on the picture.

"Yeah, well . . ." Monique uttered, smiling along with her, then pausing before adding, "That's not funny, you know."

"I'm sorry," Carla responded, "but I couldn't resist it! So who's keeping your baby? First, what's her name?"

"Maya. My grandmother, who lives with us, watches her most o' the time. Between going from my mother's arms to my father's to my grandmother's, Maya doesn't know what it is to sit on her own li'l rump!"

"So how old were you when you had her?"

"Sixteen on the dot! She was born on my birthday!"

"Almost like something somebody planned!" suggested Carla.

"But for sure this wasn't!" Monique declared. "I didn't *plan* to have a baby, period. And I sure didn't plan to have one on my birthday."

"Maya's a nice name," Carla said warmly.

"I named her that after Maya Angelou, the poet. That's my hobby—reading poetry, which I get a lot o' time to do, cooped up in the house unable to go anywhere."

"I see." Carla nodded, her eyes switching back and forth from the picture to Monique. *A baby?* she was thinking to herself. *A mother. Lord, I'm sure glad it's not me.* "So tell me more about it," she implored, folding her legs beneath her body, to get more comfortable.

"It's a long story," Monique began, "and kind of sad."

"What teenager having a baby isn't?" Carla snapped, wishing almost immediately that she could take the words back. For no sooner had she spoken than it occurred to her that she really hadn't known Monique long enough to be throwing her two cents' worth out on something so personal. She studied her roommate's expression for a moment, trying to see if indeed she'd rubbed the girl the wrong way. But Monique didn't appear fazed as she rattled on.

"After two or three months I knew that I had to definitely be expecting. In spite of praying night after night that I wasn't, I was crazy scared! And so was the guy I was going with. We've broken up now, and—"

"What happened?"

"My baby's father and I still halfway talk. But we broke up before I even had Maya. We disagreed about what to do. See, he was for. And I was against."

"I'm confused," said Carla. "He wanted you to have it. And you did. So why aren't you all together?"

"If you let me finish, I'll get to everything!" Monique responded with a bit of irritation. "I knew that I needed money to do what I had to. At least two hundred dollars! That is, if I was going to one of the nicer places I'd checked out. A few places were cheaper—but I didn't want to go to just any rinky-dink place! And I knew that the only time that I would be coming into that kind o' money would be at my sweet sixteenth birthday party. I was confident of getting close to five hundred for my birthday. So I figured I'd just have to hold off until then."

"Wait a minute! Weren't you worried about getting pregnanter and pregnanter? If I can make up such a word!" Carla cracked.

"Yeah. It was stupid on my part," Monique acknowledged. "But all I was thinking of at the time was that I didn't have any two hundred dollars! And my birthday party was the only time I would be getting that much at once. So I just had to wait!"

"You said you expected five hundred dollars?"

"Uh-huh."

"That's a whooole lotta bread!" gasped Carla.

"Normally I wouldn't get anywhere close to that for my birthday," she clarified. "But see, it was my sweet sixteenth—something my family's big on. We have these huge family celebrations. Everybody comes—cousins, aunts, and uncles. And the girl who's turning sixteen wears a special dress and is announced to the family members."

"Sounds sorta like a debutante thing," Carla suggested.

"Yeah, it is. Not quite as prissy, though—but very similar—the major difference being that instead of greeting high society it's only your lowly family," Monique kidded along.

Turning serious again, she said, "My parents were anxious for my birthday to come. Because having had to lay out money for so many of my cousins, they were ready to recoup! I was anxious, too, but clearly for a different reason. All I wanted was to get my hands on the money so I could get everything over with! I was tired of trying to sneak by my mother, my father, plus my grandmother without them paying too much attention to me. When we went to pick out my party dress, I'm sure my grandmother was kind of thinking something was up from the way she kept staring at me. My mother—I don't think she was ever suspicious. My father—definitely not! Come to think of it, he was probably glad that I was putting on weight, 'cause he never liked seeing me so skinny. And believe me, I *had* put it on! Trying like a dope—"

"*To wait for your birthday!*" Carla cut in, finishing Monique's sentence. Chuckling, she asked, "Didn't you ever stop to think that the longer you waited, the more dangerous it would be?"

"How was I to know?" she answered nonchalantly. "This never happened to me before!"

"Me, neither!" Carla was prompted to say. "Still, I know that the sooner the better, with what you were planning!"

"If I had been getting more allowance than a cheesy twenty-five dollars a week, maybe I *could* have done what I needed to earlier!" Monique complained.

"Twenty-five dollars a week?" exclaimed Carla. "Girl, that's more than double what I get!"

"Well, I don't know how you survive!" quipped Monique. "Then on the other hand, you aren't in the Apple."

"Oh, New York's not that much different from Jersey," Carla protested. "New York people are always acting like Jersey's the country. But just as much goes on here."

"Maybe," Monique conceded. "Anyhow—the day of my party finally came. I'd chosen something nice and loose—a kind of tent dress. And everything was all set. My mother and grandmother had cooked some of everything you could think of: fried chicken, curried goat, peas and rice, greens, yams. You name it—we had it! My father had decorated the basement. And one of my cousins had hooked up the music and was deejaying."

"So at what point did you change your mind about having the baby?"

"If you'd just wait and let me finish! Less than two hours after my party kicked off, I had more cash than I needed!"

"Lucky you!" chimed Carla.

"So I thought!" Monique countered. "But then midway through my party, I started feeling sick. I figured I was tired from all the excitement, and that if I could just sit at my throne for a while—"

"Throne?"

"Oh, yeah! I left out that part. The party person has this special chair, a crown, the whole works!"

"Oh, gross!" Carla squealed.

"I know," Monique said between laughs, "it's corny. But at least every girl in my family gets her chance to be royalty for a day. We don't have to go through this stage of life never once being made to feel special! Like happens to a lot of girls."

"You've got a point."

"I thought I'd feel better as I sat there, but I kept getting worse. Smelling a thousand different scents from all the food wasn't helping the situation. I was getting sicker and sicker. So I whispered to Verna that I had to go lie down for a few minutes."

"Who is Verna?"

"My number-one homegirl. Other than my baby's father, she's the only person who knew everything that was up with me at the time. She had come to my party prepared to spend the night. And the two of us planned to skip school the next day for me to do what I had to.

"So anyhow—after I started feeling so bad, I told Verna to go in the kitchen and tell my mother that I had a stomachache and had gone upstairs for a while. My plan was to come back to the festivities, but I never made it. I'm not sure just when the crowd thinned out, because I'm way up on the third floor of my house, just beneath the attic. It's a brownstone like the one on *Cosby*."

"Mmmmph, I'm impressed," Carla signified.

"Believe me. We're way from having Cosby money, honey," Monique sang out. "We just live in a similar house."

"I'm still impressed. Sharing a room with one person at summer camp is the most privacy I get all year. I'm stuck in a room with my two younger sisters!"

"I always had the peace of my own room," Monique stated. "Up until Maya came. Her crib's in there now. 'Course, she's in the room with my grandmother more than with me."

"You're jumping from the story again," said Carla.

"Oh, yeah—well, to get back. After I was upstairs in my room awhile, my mother came to check on me. I told her I didn't feel any better. She said I should try to go to sleep. When I asked if Verna could still stay, she frowned. Thinking quickly, I moaned how company would make me concentrate less on how bad I was feeling. My mother went along and told Verna to come on up. I had the hardest time getting her out my room, though!"

"Verna?"

"No! My mother. She finally left when I told her that I'd have Verna get her if I got worse. I had no such intentions, however. Soon as my mother split, I began tossing and turning all over the place! Verna was holding tightly on to one of my sweaty hands, while I clutched a pillow with the other, trying to muffle my groans. Oh, it hurt so bad!"

"Like bad cramps?" Carla interjected. "I know how that is because I get bad cramps."

"But nothing like what I went through," she declared. "Girrrl, I hate to scare you . . ."

"No. Tell me," Carla insisted.

"I can't even describe how awful it was! It was like—like— maybe lightning would feel ripping through your stomach! Then suddenly I feel this dampness—"

"Your water broke?"

"You *do* know all about it, don't you?" Monique registered surprise.

"What happens before a baby comes?" Carla hissed in reply. "Sure I know! Didn't you?"

"Not that part! But Verna did, thank goodness."

"Looord!" Carla groaned. "You obviously hadn't counted up your time right either, had you?"

"They said Maya was early. She had to be put in an incubator—"

"Slow down!" Carla ordered, determined to get every detail. "There has to be more before you get to that part."

"I don't know what would have happened if it hadn't been for Verna," Monique continued.

"You mean your friend sat there and didn't call your mother?"

"She tried to, but I kept begging her not to and holding her back."

"*Whaaat?*"

"Yeah. And then the baby started coming."

"Oh, I would have died!" cried Carla.

"I believe I would have too if I had been in Verna's place. But she hung tough. Cut the cord—"

"Cleaned the baby up and everything?" Carla asked, her eyes stretching wider and wider.

"Yeah. Did it all!" Monique recalled. "Then she had the nerve to go downstairs and ask my mother if she could have a little warm milk and water."

"What? She did what?" Carla leaned forward to make sure she was hearing correctly.

"Verna said we couldn't just let the baby starve all night. We'd decided we would take her to the hospital the next morning and say that we found her."

"That was real dumb!" Carla said without hesitation. "How wack can you get?" she fired boldly. "What a stupid idea!"

"I know," Monique accepted with embarrassment. "At least *now* I do. But I was desperate and couldn't think of anything better. And neither could Verna."

"For starters, you should have sent for your mother!" Carla said pointedly.

"Yeah, well—"

"How did you feed a baby without a bottle?"

"Verna just gave her little drops at a time. And we wrapped her in some towels."

"And then?"

"Verna told me to try to sleep a few minutes. I was so tired."

"I'm glad you didn't try anything like leaving the child somewhere mysteriously!" Carla said authoritatively.

"Girl, what kind of person do you think I am?" Monique shot back. "I was raised better than to do something that low."

"Yeah, well, having the baby in your room wasn't exactly highbrow," chided Carla. "You risked her life!"

"I don't need you reminding me," Monique said sadly. "I simply didn't know any better at the time. And Verna? She went along for my sake. I *do* have a conscience, though, and I could never have done anything crazy like you hear about on the news. Never! My plan was to get up early the next morning and take Maya to St. Luke's for adoption."

"Maaaaan!" Carla uttered, still shaking her head in disbelief over all she was hearing. *The blood. The gore! How could they have gone through with it?* "Weren't you and your friend worried about the baby crying out in the night?" she asked.

"I told you, I'm way upstairs. Still, Verna said she slept with one eye open."

"All I can say is that's one lucky little girl to have survived such an ordeal!" Carla surmised.

"It's like my grandmother said later," Monique shared. "Somebody upstairs was watching over."

"Wooord," Carla said in agreement, looking as pitifully at the photo as if it were alive.

"Thanks goodness everything turned out all right," Monique sighed wearily.

"Sure is. Because the two of you could have ended up in big trouble!" Carla mentioned.

"True. My mother explained that there's a law—"

"Endangering a baby at birth!" Carla blurted out.

"*Another* thing I wasn't aware of at the time!" Monique admitted. Then lowering her voice, she chanted, "My poor little baby. What I put her through! She almost didn't make it. I hate to even think about what I did," she ended tearfully, making Carla regret having come down on her so harshly.

"Don't cry," Carla said, leaping up to comfort her.

"I'm okay," Monique managed to get out between tears. "It's just hard when I think back," she said, still weeping softly as Carla stroked her shoulder. "I've talked to our minister about everything. And he tells me I'm forgiven. But I still feel so—so *guilty* sometimes!"

"Try to let it go," Carla suggested.

"I do," she said, "but it keeps haunting me. Letting Maya suffer like I did. We took her out of the house in a big shopping bag."

"A *shopping bag?*" gasped Carla.

"Yeah. At first I thought of my backpack, but I had to make sure she could breathe."

"And all the while she never cried out?"

"She whimpered a little—bless her heart." Monique shook her head as she remembered. "Poor thing was probably too weak."

"And what about you?" Carla questioned. "Weren't you about to drop?"

"I was. But I knew what I had to do. So the two of us eased on out the door with Maya and headed over to St. Luke's. It's close to where I live. When we got there, we walked up to the receptionist desk and said that we found the baby on our way to school."

"Thinking it was gonna be over just like that, huh?" said Carla.

"Yes! But they began to ask question after question. I got all confused and nervous, and before long, I passed out right there on the floor!"

"It's no wonder!" cried Carla.

"When I awoke, I was in a hospital bed. And it didn't take long for them to put two and two together. I have to give Verna credit though. Homegirl stuck with my story. They didn't get a thing out of her. I was the one who had to tell them the truth!"

"Then what?"

"They called my folks. My father didn't go too crazy. But my mother? Maaaan!"

"I can just imagine," said Carla.

"She was going to let me go ahead and give Maya up for

adoption like I wanted to, even though my father had some reservations. But then my friend Verna gets to school and tells Robert everything."

"Who?"

"Rob. My baby's father. And this was all he needed. His wish had come true: I had given birth to his baby! Which he goes flying around the whole neighborhood spreading! There was no way to go through with the adoption then. My mother said that people would have talked badly, not only about me but about her and my father if we gave the baby away after that."

"Sounds like your mother worries a lot about what other people think."

"She does," Monique concurred. "Too much! But beyond her concern about what the neighbors would say, Rob had come to the hospital acting like the baby was his already!"

"Well, she was, wasn't she?" Carla chuckled.

"Yeah. But I mean *his-his!* Like, his to take home! He was all worked up, claiming he would take care of her on his own if necessary."

"So because of this, and your mother's pride, you changed your mind about keeping her?"

"Well, actually, I had started getting attached to her myself. She was such a pretty baby."

"Still is," whispered Carla.

"I know," Monique said shamelessly, beaming now at her child's photo.

"Seems like you and the father ought to be able to work it all out now that she's here and everything," Carla suggested.

"Maybe someday," she responded. "But not right now. I just need to concentrate on getting myself out of high school. And I hope Robbie continues to do the same. I don't know about him, but I really haven't got much choice, the way my mother stays on my case. I can hardly breathe."

"You make her sound so cold," Carla commented.

"I guess I do exaggerate a little," Monique halfheartedly admitted. "I suppose my mother's no worse than anybody's mother whose daughter has a baby. She worries that it can happen to me twice. But there's no way!"

"So a lot of girls say!" Carla chimed. "Still, it *be's* that way sometimes."

"Well it won't *beeeez* happenin' here!" Monique declared.

"I guess not, since you claim you're such a prisoner!"

"Yeah. I do whine a lot," Monique fully confessed now. "But deep down I realize that I'm blessed to have the family I've got —one willing to take over raising my baby while I finish growing up."

"Because it's not that way for the average girl in your situation," Carla wasted no time saying.

"Wooord," Monique agreed. "There're few happy endings for a girl in trouble."

"I still can't get over it happening on your birthday!"

"Yeah," Monique ended, her head dropped slightly. "My sweet sixteenth."

Brenda Wilkinson

The second of eight children, Brenda Wilkinson grew up in Waycross, Georgia, in the 1950s. She was prohibited from using the modern library, which was reserved for the town's white people, and she was too poor to have any books at home except a Bible. In spite of the restrictions on her learning, she developed a love for reading and writing. When she later moved to New York City, where she now lives, she enrolled in a writers' workshop. There, under the guidance of John O. Killens and Sonia Sanchez, she was able to develop her writing talents, learning the craft as well as the social responsibilities of the writer.

Writing during her spare time—she is currently an executive with the United Methodist Church—Brenda Wilkinson has produced four novels and a biography of Jesse Jackson for young people. Most important among her writings is *Ludell*, the story of a poor Black girl growing up before the civil rights era in Waycross, Georgia, and its sequels: *Ludell and Willie* and *Ludell's New York Times*.

The story Wilkinson tells in "My Sweet Sixteenth" is based on a real incident that a young mother had described to one of the author's two grown daughters—the names and places changed here, of course.

Brenda Wilkinson is currently working on a novel about a group of teenagers growing up in a housing project where she once lived.

ꕔꔅꔅꔅꕔꔅꔅꔅꕔ

When you are no one special and the cutest boy you've ever known comes into your life, he can make you feel soooo good. But then what?

THE CHILD
Julius Lester

Gently, Karen went down the steps to the subway, flashed her student pass at the attendant in the token booth, and walked through the gate onto the platform. It was morning, though one did not know that beneath the ground. But Karen had not paid much attention to the day before descending the steps stained by traces of urine, wine, soda, cigarette butts and wrappers torn from candy bars. She looked up the track even though she knew the vibrations of the train would be felt and heard before seeing the light from its far-reaching beam. It was something to do, and she needed something to do this morning.

She was small and looked younger than her seventeen years. Being neither prettier nor uglier than any girl that age, there was nothing memorable about her. If anyone standing in the subway station had thought to focus attention upon her (and no one did), they might have noticed that she was standing dangerously close to the edge, as if she would not have minded if a breeze or hand had pushed her onto the tracks. They also would have noticed that, unlike the other teenagers waiting for the train, no book bag hung lazily from her shoulder giving a sense of purposefulness. In her jeans and white blouse and with her empty hands, Karen seemed to be without destination or function. But no one noticed.

"I used to be a fighter. Ha! Ha! That's the truth! I fought Muhammad Ali and beat'im! I whupped him so bad they made me quit the ring! Ha! Ha! Ha!"

She turned and stared at the drunk man who had just staggered through the turnstile, spit dribbling from a corner of his mouth and down his chin. His brown face was caked with dirt mixed with dried blood. His clothes reminded her of the subway station steps, and she moved even closer to the edge and peered up the track again. She wondered why she cared if the train ever came. Where was she going to go?

She hadn't really expected her mother to believe she was just putting on weight, not she who was as thin as sorrow.

"Girl, what is the matter with you? You think I be working two jobs and praying all the time, for you to go get yourself knocked up the first time a boy look at you and say hi? Help me, Jesus! Help me!"

"Ain't nothing he can do, Mama."

"How would you know? If you had had your mind on Jesus, you wouldn't be in this condition. How could you let something like this happen?"

"You see, Mama, it was like this. You go up on the roof on a warm night and you see the cutest boy that has ever walked the earth and somebody has a radio and you get to talking and somebody else has a little smoke and somewhere between the sweet words and the sweet music and the sweet smoke, he touches you, and, Mama, I never felt a feeling like that feeling when a boy touches you here and there, and there and here. Mama, I would do anything to feel like that all the time. You understand me, Mama. I would do anything to feel like that *all the time.* But it got even better than that. Yes, it did, Mama. But I don't be having to explain none of this to you, now do I, Mama? Wasn't you about seventeen when you had me?"

That was when her mother slapped her.

Karen slapped her back.

Now she got ready to board the subway as she felt the push of hot air through the tunnel signaling its coming even before the light shone down the track or the walls trembled.

"Hold that door! If you don't, I'll kick your behind like I done Ali!"

When the train rumbled into the station, the doors slid open and people pushed their way off and on at the same time. Karen waited, afraid someone would brush against her, afraid they would hurt the first thing in her life she could call her own.

She was surprised when no one offered her a seat. Couldn't they tell? She was different now. She wasn't like them. Couldn't they tell she was going to be a mother?

The train lurched forward, and she leaned against the door between the cars. She wanted to shout and tell everyone to look at her. She was going to be a mother! But she was afraid that if she yelled, no one would hear. All her life she had felt like something happened to the words between the time they left her lips and went toward other people's ears. Was there an invisible thief who stole words from the mouths of girls, leaving them to wonder if they had spoken, leaving them to wonder if they really existed? She had lived for seventeen years and never seen anybody's eyes come alive when she walked into a room. She had lived for seventeen years, and her existence had never put a smile on anybody's face. She had lived for seventeen years, and no one had noticed.

Then Philip had looked at her, and suddenly it mattered to someone that she was alive and not dead. He made her feel that the sun rose over her head and set at her feet. When he looked at her, she felt pretty. She wasn't and she knew it, but what did that have to do with anything? He held her; he touched her; he made her feel so good that she didn't know what she wanted the most —to live or to die.

When she told him she thought she was pregnant, he was happy. He laughed and strutted up and down like he had just won the lottery. She was relieved he wasn't going to make her get rid of it like Darlene's boyfriend had done her. But when she asked him to go with her to the hospital for the test, he said just because he got her pregnant didn't mean he was going to be a daddy, and he wasn't about to be nobody's husband. He laughed again, and she understood that what was growing inside of her wasn't anything to him but proof of his manhood.

"Anybody want to fight? Huh? Anybody want to fight?"

There was that ol' drunk man, hanging on to a strap for dear life as the train swayed from side to side. The least he could do was wipe the spit from his chin and stop disgracing every black person on the subway car.

Karen didn't want her child exposed to someone like him, not even while it was in the womb. Not her baby! She turned her eyes away and noticed a white girl seated in the middle of the car. She had long dark hair that spilled over her shoulders like silk threads. A book was open on her lap. Karen wished she could have hated her. Instead, she wanted to ask her what she was reading and what it was about. She wanted to smooth her hair and see if it was as soft as it looked. She wanted to go home with her and see the pictures on her walls and the color of the spread on her bed. Most of all, she wanted to hear her dreams. Not the ones that came in the night, unbidden and unwanted, but the ones that came when you were standing in the shower or walking along a street with nothing on your mind, or when you were sitting on the subway trying hard not to look at anybody.

"Y'all scared, ain't ya? You better be. I'll whup yo' head for you."

Karen could not imagine dreams stretching from one side of the sky to the other, dreams that spun themselves because that was what dreams were supposed to do like waves were supposed to arch and curl and fall. She wondered if you needed clean, quiet streets and big rooms and two parents who you knew in order to dream. She wondered if you needed white skin.

None of that mattered now. It would be a while before she read another schoolbook, what with the baby due in March. She wanted to believe she would go back and finish after the baby came, but none of her friends who'd had babies had done that. But that was okay. Seventeen years from next spring, her baby would finish school for both of them.

Her child wasn't going to have nothing to do with winos and junkies and dirty streets and loud music. It would stay inside and read big books and be real smart, and when it got grown, it would say, "Mama, let's go. I'm going to move you out of here. I'm going to take you away from all these drunk people and junkies."

Karen started to smile. Then she stopped, wondering suddenly if this new dream of hers had been her own mother's dream for the past seventeen years. *Oh, Mama!* she exclaimed to herself. *I'm so sorry.* She wanted to cry, but what good would it do?

Her mother shouldn't have had dreams for her, just like she shouldn't be having dreams for her baby. Everybody had to find their own dreams.

Her mother had been happier than Karen was when she had been accepted at the High School for Fashion and Design. "My daughter is going to be somebody!" her mother had exclaimed.

Be who? Karen wondered. Be what? Just because she could draw clothes didn't mean she was going to be a big fashion designer. If she had been white, like that girl, if her hair had been as smooth as a cloudless sky, then she would have dreamed. But it didn't pay to be black and to dream. It didn't pay. What happened to you when the dream didn't come true? What did you do then?

She looked at the white girl robed in her straight hair. That girl was somebody just because. That was the same reason Karen wasn't.

Karen touched her stomach lightly. It didn't feel any different. It was hard to believe a person was inside. Well, maybe not a person like she was, but it would be.

The train stopped. Before Karen could get a seat, a group of white boys yelled and shouted their way onto the coach, pushing each other playfully for the few empty seats.

"You kids watch whar you goin'. I do you like I done Ali."

"Yeah! That's right, old man!"
"You tell us about it!"
"Ha! Ha! Ha!"

Those kids didn't have no right to be making fun of him like that. Couldn't they tell there was something wrong with him? Whatever made him like that wasn't all his fault. Yet Karen said nothing aloud and wished that ol' drunk fool would get off the train and stop embarrassing her. Didn't he know that white people judged all black people by how each of them behaved? Somebody in his life must have told him that. Didn't he have any pride in himself and his race?

You think cause you white you can mess with me. Let me tell you one thing. One of these days you gon' be sorry."

"We'll be sorry as you! Right? HaHaHa!"

Her child was going to be a credit to the race. Like her, she added glumly. Well, having a baby wasn't the end of the world. People had babies every day. It wasn't no big deal. Not really. At least she had something to do with herself now. She was going to be the best mama anybody had ever seen. She was going to love this baby until it begged for mercy.

"Make fun of me if you want to, but I know what I'm talkin' 'bout. You think I'm drunk. I ain't as much drunk as you is 'sleep."

Karen looked at the white girl. Through all the yelling between the old man and the boys, she had not raised her head from her book. Karen doubted that she had heard—and why should she have? It wasn't like the old man could've been her father or grandfather. He was just an old black man to her. Maybe not even that.

Was that what it was like to be white? That you didn't have to care about anybody except yourself? You didn't even have to think about anybody else. You could sit on the subway and not even notice other white people and what they did. You didn't have to worry about what people might be thinking about you because somebody white was drunk or passed out from drugs. She shook her head, unable to imagine what it would be like to be free of other people's thoughts and opinions and ideas about you.

Karen gazed enviously at the white girl, wondering what her boyfriend was like and if he made her feel good. But her boyfriend would not have laughed at her if she was going to have his baby.

She touched her stomach again. *Everything will be all right,* she said silently to it. *It'll take a while, but everything will work out. I'll go back to school next fall and finish up and design clothes for little babies like you. And one day I'll go see Mama, and I'll be*

*driving a big car and I'll say, " 'Bye, Mama," and I'll drive over
the George Washington Bridge. I'll turn on the radio, and it'll be
on all the news: "Miss Karen Bridges left New York City today on
her way to Hollywood where she will become the dress designer
for the stars."*

That was how it would be. One day.

And she turned her back because she didn't want the girl to
look up from the book and see her crying.

Julius   Lester

Among Julius Lester's best-known books is the Newbery Honor Book *To Be a Slave,* a collection of true accounts of the lives of men and women who lived through slavery in America. He is also the author of *This Strange New Feeling,* three stories about love and freedom based on true accounts of three slave couples. Along with his popular *Black Folktales* and *How Many Spots Does a Leopard Have? And Other Tales* (an American Library Association Notable Children's Book), he has recently completed a rewriting of *Tales of Uncle Remus* in four volumes. First collected by Joel Chandler Harris in the nineteenth century, these famous tales about Brer Rabbit and his companions have been retold by Lester in the language of today. All of the first three volumes were ALA Best Books for Young Adults.

In addition to being a writer, Julius Lester is a professor at the University of Massachusetts at Amherst, where he teaches English, history, and Judaic studies.

Along with the Newbery Honor Book Award, two of Julius Lester's books have been named Coretta Scott King Honor Books; he has twice received the Lewis Carroll Shelf Award; and in 1972 he was a National Book Award Finalist for *Long Journey Home.* For his teaching, he received the University of Massachusetts Distinguished Teacher Award and was named Massachusetts State Professor of the Year.

Julius Lester says he wrote the first draft of his timely story "The Child" almost thirty years ago, out of his experiences as a welfare worker in Harlem in the early 1960s, and rewrote it for this collection. Readers can find out more about Julius Lester's life in *Lovesong: Becoming a Jew.*

◻◊○○◮○◊○◊◻

Connections

Rima vaguely knows about the fighting in Lebanon. But even though she is Lebanese American, that war is all in another place, another time. She's too busy with her music to get involved.

RIMA'S SONG
Elsa Marston

It was *awful* that last week of August in upstate New York, and even in Scott's air-conditioned basement Rima felt her tank top clinging to her like seaweed. But humidity wasn't her only problem. What dragged her down even more was that long-awaited, now imminent, arrival—that guy coming, in just a few hours.

Cranky and distracted, she struggled to focus on the music. At last, to her relief, Scott suggested they take a break.

"Look," he said, limbering his long, knobby fingers, "what we need now is an identity. A name, something nobody ever heard of before."

Rima propped her guitar against a massive speaker. "Killer Tomatoes?" she said gloomily.

"Naw, that was a movie," Wayland objected, chewing reflectively on a strand of long blond hair. "Killer *something* is good, though. Makes a statement. Killer Zucchini?"

"Killer Shish-kebab," said Jamal, twisting lazily on his stool amid the drums and cymbals.

"Too ethnic," said Wayland. "We want an image of—primeval violence. How about . . . Killer Slugs? Cabbage Worms?"

"Yish!" Rima stood, yanked down her hiked-up cutoffs, and

flicked the heavy black curls off her moist neck. "Killer Butter-flies. Bunnies! Killer *Kitties*!"

Scott, prodding a piece of ominously blinking equipment, turned to her with interest. "You're kinda jumpy today, Rima. What's the matter? Aunt Afifi getting on your case again?"

"Well, you might say—"

"Killer Caterpillars," Jamal broke in. Then, with a drum roll and clash of brass, "Catakillers!"

"That's deep," said Wayland approvingly. "Hey, like Cata-comb Killers, Cataleptic Killers—"

"Cataclysmic," muttered Rima, "catastrophic—"

"*Catakilla*—an existential statement!" said Scott.

An ironic grin came to Rima's face. "It'd kill Aunt Afifi, all right. She thinks we should be the—the Melody Masters. Or something Arabic. Like Scheherazade and the Three Sultans."

"Explain to her," said Jamal in mock seriousness, large hazel eyes peering through a wavy black fringe, "that a socially revolu-tionary musical group such as ours needs a name that makes you *think*."

"Aunt Afifi think? She'd have to stop talking."

"Hey, why's her nifty Lebanese restaurant closed?" asked Scott. "I was wanting a *shawarma* sandwich the other day, and it was closed."

Rima perched on her stool again, grimacing at the tacky feel of the vinyl seat. "Just for two weeks, before the students come back. We were hoping she'd go visit some relatives in Peoria, but she says she—ahem—has to watch her purse these days. And get things ready. For *him*."

"Who?"

"That dear nephew Fuad who she hasn't seen since she left Beirut in 'seventy-nine. He's arriving *today*."

"Oh, yeah, I remember," said Scott. "So how old is he? And why's he coming?"

"I guess about nineteen. And he's coming, obviously, to go to school. His education got all screwed up 'cause of the fighting. His mother had to keep taking him out of school, and the schools would shut down and—anyway, a total mess. Plus, his father got killed in the war somehow." Rima took a breath. "And in spite of all that, he's the smartest guy in Lebanon and Aunt Afifi wants him here so—"

"He can set a shining example for you," said Scott.

"Right. Among other things."

"So what's her problem with you?" asked Wayland. "You get good marks, and you got a real high rating at that big guitar competition—"

Rima lifted her smooth, rounded arms in a melodramatic shrug. "She says I'm wasting the beautiful brains God was so nice as to give me. She says I should go to MIT or Michigan and be a nuclear physicist or a doctor and get rich and famous. And when she heard I wanted to apply to Berklee, to a *music* school of all things—wow, I thought she'd burst a fuse."

"It's your life," said Wayland philosophically. He groped in his shirt pocket for a pack of cigarettes, then remembered he had quit. "Just tell her to get off it."

Jamal glanced at him balefully. "You don't know Arab aunts."

"And she's over at our house all the time these days," Rima went on, her voice rising, "'cause she gets lonely in her little dinky house. And she eats like a horse and stays thin as a breadstick. Burns it all off talking. At *me*."

"Well, now she'll have somebody else to talk at," said Scott comfortingly.

"Oh no, she won't have to nag Cousin Fuad. He'll be just perfect and will go to Harvard and save the Awad family honor. And in the meantime I have to take him under my wing and show him around and all that. But I don't know how to talk to him or where he's coming from—what do I know about Lebanon? Except that's where my folks came from and they've had a big war over there. And the way Aunt Afifi talks about this kid all the time, I just know he's a creep, with a pale skinny face and big scared eyes and a hollow chest from hunching over his books—"

"Unlike your *true* Arab, your authentic Palestinian terrorist-in-residence here!" proclaimed Jamal, brandishing his drumsticks like weapons.

Rima had to giggle in spite of herself. "Oh, don't I wish he could be a brute like you, man!" Then she glanced at her watch, and her shoulders drooped again. "Well, I'll try to be nice to him. But I won't like it. And now I gotta go home and change and go to the airport."

"Strength, O Scheherazade," said Jamal. "Or is it Queen Cat-akilla?"

The Awad family arrived at the airport only to find that Fuad's plane was delayed for a couple of hours. While Mr. Awad, nervous about being late for a meeting with his accountant, paced in the observation area, Rima sat in the small coffee shop with the two women. Silver, she noted, was starting to glimmer along the parting of Aunt Afifi's raven hair; but it would vanish soon, of course.

Afifi, sharp elbows flanking a second cup of coffee, turned to Rima. "Well, we still got time to kill. So how's that band of yours goin', Rima? You kids got a name yet?"

"Yup. Catakilla."

A moment's silence. Then, "*What?* What does that mean? *Cat* killers? You call yourselves *killers*, and you think I want you come play at my restaurant with a name like that?"

"Aunt Afifi," said Rima carefully, "we're just *starting*. We can talk about gigs later."

"Why don't you choose a *nice* name? Maybe somethin' Arabic. Like—like Oriental—"

"Orifice," muttered Rima.

"What's that? Well, whatever it means, it don't sound nice. You young people, what's the matter with you, you want to be so ugly all the time? For that matter, what's the matter with you, Rima, you want to spend your time just makin' ugly noise with those boys? Who are they, anyway? What do we know about them?"

"Oh, Lord, Aunt Afifi," Rima said wearily. "Okay. Scott Talbot is in National Honor Society, and his dad's a prof at the university. Wayland's kind of a dope in some ways but not a dope in other ways, and he has a great voice. He's really good at . . . like—"

"Screaming obscenities?" offered her mother.

"Right. And Jamal—"

"Jamal?" Afifi broke in. "Is he Arab? What's his last name?"

"Sakakini. He plays drums, and he may go to Cornell on a Trivial Pursuit scholarship." Rima had to conceal a grin at that. But it was no lie that Jamal was supersmart.

Afifi's carefully trimmed eyebrows drew together. "Sakakini? That's a Palestinian name. Is he Palestinian? Is he Muslim? Why couldn't you get a nice Lebanese boy to be in your band?"

At this Rima made no attempt to hide the exasperated roll of her eyes. "*Because*, Aunt Afifi, all the nice Lebanese boys are going out for football and ice hockey this year, and they don't want to hurt their fingers on those nasty strings, and—honestly, Aunt Afifi, what the hell does it matter? We're friends, we're musicians, for God's sake!"

"Now, Rima," said her mother, touching her arm. Georgette Awad usually played the role of mediator, a skill finely honed on her job in the county prosecutor's office. Turning to the other, she sprinkled a little more oil on the waters. "Don't worry, Afifi, Rima hasn't lost her common sense."

Afifi slapped the table. "Such a waste of good brains! Well—all right," she continued, though hardly pacified. "I don't want to force myself in other people's business. God knows, I got troubles enough of my own."

"Really, Afifi," Mrs. Awad said, "you must let us help more

with Fuad. Let Rima show him around—she'll be glad to. And I told you, he can stay with us for a while, since Mariam's and Ghassan's rooms are both empty."

And oh, how Rima wished they weren't! Especially that of Ghassan, her brother and one of her best friends. But he was in Cameroon, teaching English in the Peace Corps.

Now Afifi protested so vigorously that her heavy gold earrings wobbled. "Oh, no, we won't bother you! Fuad's room is all ready, and I can do everything. It's all goin' to work out just perfect."

Her thin face softened into a blissful smile. "My God, I been countin' the minutes! Havin' somebody in that hole of a house with me—it'll be a *home* now. And little Fuad—oh, the angel, he was so sweet. And smart! You can't imagine that child, how cute and gentle—not a mean bone in his body. And now at last, after all these years of me slavin' away to make that restaurant a success, savin' every penny so's I could bring that child here and give him a chance in life, make up for all what he suffered. . . ." She paused to shake a maroon fingernail at the other two. "He will go places, you'll see! He will be a doctor someday, I swear he will. I'll make it happen!"

"Yes, Afifi," Mrs. Awad said gently.

Rima glanced at her mother, frumpy but always comfortable, and then at her aunt, who met the public in shimmery fabrics and gobbets of gold—but she had gotten them, Rima knew for a very well-guarded-secret fact, at a thrift shop in Albany. Georgette, who allowed others the space they needed—and Afifi, whose strong hands grabbed others' space and tried to shape it like a stuffed vine leaf.

"Rima," said her mother, "what about taking Fuad to your band practice?"

With a tiny sigh, Rima answered, "Well—okay, sure. If he's interested in such low-life pastimes." She avoided her mother's eyes.

"That's nice," Mrs. Awad said lightly. "Oh, one thing. I know you and your friends will be kind of curious about what it was like over there, growing up in the midst of the war, but maybe you'd better not ask him about it. He's very sensitive, Afifi says. It may be too painful for him."

Afifi broke in, deep-set eyes fierce once more. "Absolutely. We don't want to talk about it. Not one word. We're closin' the door on all that and throwin' away the key. Fuad's startin' a brand-new life over here."

Such a sensitive boy. It just confirmed for Rima the way she had imagined him earlier, the skinny body and the fearful eyes. She thought, too, of Afifi's savings that would rescue this delicate boy for a brilliant future. Savings that, not too long ago, she had actually thought might help launch *her* toward Boston and the Berklee Conservatory of Music.

The plane landed, and Fuad Abillama disembarked. It didn't take Rima long to notice that his chest was anything but cavernous. Coffee-brown eyes gleamed through thick black lashes under strongly arched brows. Rima could not say what she saw in those eyes, but it definitely was not timidity.

With a pleasant smile Fuad greeted each person in turn, self-assured as a crown prince. Not the slightest tremor betrayed him as he endured Afifi's embraces. He was obviously a very well-brought-up young man, in addition to being such a gorgeous guy and unbelievably cool for someone who'd just spent thirty hours in planes and airports. Rima could see that her role as much-put-upon hostess would be more complex than she had thought.

But then and there she made up her mind about one thing: She would not let herself be bowled over by the externals. Even though he wasn't the boring, brainbound creep she had imagined from Aunt Afifi's gushing, he would have to prove himself to her, prove that he was a really good person, solid and deep and worthy of her friendship.

Nothing of Fuad's initial charm had faltered a few days later, when Rima conducted him to the basement in Scott's house and introduced him to the rest of Catakilla. There was another guest, Rima's friend Jessica, whose mouth dropped open at the sight of the newcomer as if a trapdoor had let her wits fall through. Fuad graciously shook hands all around, as the other boys untangled themselves from their instruments and struggled partway to their feet.

"*Tante* Afifi told me zat your band has an unusual name," said Fuad with polite interest.

"Oh," said Scott, "yeh. Catakilla."

"Killer? Cat killer?"

"Forget it, just a play on words. You into music?"

The slight frown on Fuad's face lingered for a moment longer, then vanished. "No," he said, "I like music but I don't know how to play an instrument. Please, I sink you were performing when Rima and I arrived. Please continue, I like to hear."

He sat quietly as they played, though the intent look on his face revealed little. One loud, rackety number after another ricocheted off every surface in the room, while Wayland, in fine voice, screamed. Finally the music stopped, and in the reverberating silence, Fuad spoke.

"It is very nice. But it seems zat your music is always angry. I don't understand why you are so angry."

A quick look passed among the musicians. Then Scott explained in tones that barely hinted impatience, "We believe there are many things to be angry about in our society. We want to—to make people *feel*, and to *think*. That's the role of an artist in society."

"I see," said Fuad.

Turning to Rima, Scott went on. "Hey, why don't you give us that song you played the other day—the one you're working on. It might go over a little better. Um, try the acoustic."

Rima squeaked in protest, only partly pretend. Then, clumsily, she put aside her electric guitar, picked up her old acoustic, and

tuned it while the others sat in silence. At last she started to play
—a gentle, quiet piece with a flowing melodic line, sweet but
melancholy, like the leaves of September drifting down one by
one and reminding the heart that there is not much time left.
Unsure of her song's appeal, she kept her head low over the
frets.

When the last notes had faded, Fuad said, "It is beautiful,
Rima. I sink it is very beautiful. Can you—sing words for it?"

"No," she mumbled, "I don't know what it's about. Not yet."

"I hope I hear it again someday," he said.

"Yes, it's nice, Rima," said Jessica, running a hand through the
moussed rivulets of her light brown hair. "But too kind of sad.
Listen, anybody want something to drink? Soda in the fridge,
Scottie? Come on, Rima, help me."

As Rima set down her guitar, Jessica tugged at her other hand
and led the way upstairs. In the kitchen, she turned to Rima,
glowing.

"He is a *hunk*! How do you get to have a cousin like that?"

"Actually, he's not a very close cousin."

"Well, whatever! How do you say his name? I want to get it
right. *Fou*-ad, or—"

"More like Fwad. It means 'heart.' "

"Heart! Wowee, tell me more! How does he like it here?"

Rima opened the door of the fridge and started rummaging
around for soft drinks. "Okay, I guess," came her reply. "He's
going to the community college to perfect his English—he went
to French-language schools—"

"So that explains the cute accent!"

"—and is making up some deficiencies so he can start at the
university next year. Or next month. Or Harvard, Yale, or Prince-
ton." She emerged with several icy cans of soda in her grip.
"Anything he wants, so far as Aunt Afifi is concerned."

"I think that's just great, her doing this for him," said Jessica.

"Yep. At least she's really happy these days. Now she has

somebody with a future, somebody who'll be spectacular all through college and have a terrific career and make piles of money. Not like the Awad kids."

"Oh, come on! Anyway," Jessica continued, "Fuad doesn't look *too* perfect, not in an obnoxious way. And I adore the way he shakes everybody's hand."

"It's the custom over there." Rima looked around for a tray. "The adults all think he's the best thing since Robert Redford. He jumps up whenever anyone comes into the room—and there've been mobs of visitors, I can tell you—and always says the right thing—man, he even takes the coffee cups out to the kitchen! And he's always cool and nice—"

"With that gorgeous smile!"

"Yeah. But—but sometimes it seems to me . . . maybe he's a little—hmm—*too* smooth."

"*Too?* How do you mean?"

"Oh, I wish he'd kind of open up. I'd like to know what's behind it all, what he's *really* like. And growing up during that war . . . looks to me like he came through just fine."

"Well, I'm glad he did," said Jessica firmly. "Hey, maybe we better get back down there with these drinks."

A sudden, uncomfortable silence greeted them in the music room, as if poisoned molecules were still bouncing in the unnaturally still air. Wayland started picking softly at his guitar, while Scott fiddled awkwardly with the amplifying equipment.

"About time," Wayland said, glancing up at the girls. "Things're a little warm down here."

"Forget it," said Scott. "Did you find enough diet stuff?" He peered intently at the tray of sweating aluminum cans.

"What's going on here?" asked Jessica. "Hey, guys?"

For a moment no one answered. Then Jamal spoke, and Rima, cold apprehension sneaking through her, saw that his eyes were locked with Fuad's.

"Okay, Fuad *amigo,* so you made your point. You Christians

clobbered us Palestinians, and we clobbered you. But that was over there, the old country, Lebanon. This is here. That's old dead stuff, and I don't want any of it. Just chill out."

Now warm with embarrassment, Rima said nothing. Nor did Fuad do any explaining, as they walked home together, swathed in politeness.

With the beginning of school, the next few weeks passed briskly. Rima worked hard. She wasn't aiming for MIT, and now Berklee seemed a hopeless cause; but she had her standards. So did Fuad. He devoted himself to his courses and made no demands on Rima. She began to wonder if she ever would get to know the other side of that smooth, attractive face.

Anyway, Afifi kept the family informed of Fuad's progress. If she didn't drop by after the restaurant closed at night, she would manage to phone almost daily.

"He got another A on his English composition, Georgette. All A's, everything is A! I think he should apply to the university for second semester. Premed, of course. . . . Yes, he even washes dishes for me—I come home to a clean house. Let me tell you, he is an *angel.* No, Georgette," she would sometimes confide, "he don't say nothin' about the family there. Just, his mother is fine, thanks God. Poor Emilie, now she can breathe, she won't have to worry about him gettin' the education he needs. Thanks God."

Sometimes Rima listened in on the other phone, and once, to her surprise, Fuad asked to talk with her.

"How is your band, Rima?" he asked. "I'm sorry I didn't hear you play again, but I am very busy."

Tell me about it, she thought. To him she replied, "Oh, not bad, not bad. I think we're getting somewhere. Anytime you want to drop by—"

"Sank—thank you," Fuad said. "I like to. I want to understand American—the things zat young Americans like."

That interested Rima mildly. But she did not really suppose he would make the effort to hear Catakilla play again, when he had so many more important matters on his mind. He was studying intensely, and Rima could sense the tension when he and Afifi came over on Monday evenings. Though he was as poised as ever, there were glimpses of something else, a vague anxiety and fatigue. The result of Aunt Afifi's overzealous attention? Well, that was the price of aiming for Harvard, after all.

So it was something of a surprise, one mellow afternoon before the first snap of autumn, when Fuad did turn up at Scott's front door. Wearing a meticulously ironed, high-fashion Beirut shirt and his usual unruffled expression, he asked if he might listen to the band practice. "I need to understand American music better," he explained.

Again Fuad sat intent and motionless, listening soberly to the raging passions of Catakilla. At last, somewhat ill at ease, Scott suggested they call it enough and go out, throw a football around or something.

The street was quiet, free of traffic and parked cars, and Jessica soon appeared as if summoned by magic. They divided into teams and started cheerfully heaving the football around. Fuad had never thrown an American football before, he said apologetically, but he caught on quickly. He had a sure arm and big hands.

The afternoon might have worn away happily if, at the moment Fuad let fly a short, hard pass, Jamal had not tried for an interception. He leaped, came down on a piece of broken asphalt, stumbled—and received the ball in the face. Clutching his nose, he let out a muffled howl.

"God, 'dja have to throw it so dab hard? Whatta ya think, it's a war zode arou'd here?"

Jessica ran to him. "Let me see, Jamal—oh, wow, you're bleeding! It's pouring out!"

Jamal glanced down at his sweatshirt, already spattered with crimson. "Oh, by God, I habn't gott'n a dosebleed like this since—"

"It isn't broken, is it? Scott, take him in and get some ice!"

"Come on, ol' buddy," said Scott, "we'll fix that nose up good as new."

But as the pain lessened slightly, Jamal's temper subsided as he saw the dramatic potential in his crisis. Clutching at his gut, eyes rolling and bloodrimmed mouth twisted, he staggered in small-boy imitation of violent death. The others had to laugh, and Rima joined in.

Until she turned and saw Fuad.

Fuad stood paralyzed, staring at Jamal. His face was drained of the ruddy color that had filled his cheeks a moment earlier. "I'm sorry, sorry," he whispered. "I'm sorry, I didn't mean it."

"Of course you didn't," said Rima.

Scott took a step toward Fuad. "Hey, man, take it easy. Jamal used to get a nosebleed every time you looked at him."

"No brobleb, bloodlettin's good for ya—" blubbered Jamal as the crimson continued to dribble down his front. Grabbing him by the arm, Scott pulled him toward the house.

Fuad remained motionless a moment longer, his eyes following them. And now Rima saw something in those eyes that she had not seen before—an anguish that quite baffled her. Even Fuad's body seemed to hollow slightly, mirroring the contortions of the dying-man act.

"I'm sorry," he whispered once more, and then an Arabic phrase in the same tone. Abruptly, without another word or glance, he turned and hurried away.

Rima stared, astonished. As she watched him, the surprise changed to scorn. She regretted it, but there it was. The veneer of this superman's charm and manners had cracked, and what she saw underneath looked puny and childish. *So he wants to be a doctor,* she thought. *He wants to be a doctor, and he comes totally unglued at the sight of a little blood.*

"What's with him?" asked Wayland. "Why's he have to take everything so hard?"

"I'm sure I don't know," said Rima. She went to pick up a pile of music and the guitar that she had left propped against the lamppost by Scott's front walk. "But maybe I better . . ."

"Maybe he wants to be left alone," said Jessica, kindly. "He's probably a little embarrassed."

Rima considered. "Well, maybe." Juggling her guitar and loose sheets of music, she flopped a hand in a farewell gesture. "Anyway, it sort of shoots the football game, doesn't it. I'll see you guys tomorrow."

As she headed down the street in the same direction that Fuad had taken, Rima pondered the incident. It was so out of character! She would have expected him to show some consternation, make his apologies gracefully, and help in any way he could. But this? It was really embarrassing! What was the matter with the guy?

Then another inner voice answered, quiet yet persuasive. It led her, however hesitantly, to Aunt Afifi's house, where the lawn was now mowed regularly and the walk swept free of pine needles. Finding the front door open, Rima walked in. No sign of Fuad, though the door to his room stood slightly ajar.

Rima hovered in the hallway, then said, "Fuad?"

No answer. He was there, though; she could hear his ragged breathing. "Fuad? Can I come in?" Still no response. Hands full of guitar and music, she nudged the door open and entered.

From his facedown position on the bed, Fuad immediately pushed himself up, swung his legs over the other side, and sat turned away from Rima.

She stood there awkwardly. "I just wondered—like, if you wanted to talk. . . ."

"You don't have to be kind."

It was almost like being shoved. Rima recoiled, then gaining some emotional balance, she asked the obvious question. "Why not?"

Fuad seemed to be caught off guard by her candor. He half turned, revealing a strangely disorganized face. A long moment passed before he muttered a reply. "Because I don't deserve it."

Oh, poor baby. Rima didn't try to keep the annoyance out of her voice. "Everyone deserves kindness. What makes you think you're any different? Don't be silly." She looked around the untidy room—books, loose papers, clothes everywhere—and set down her guitar case against the one chair. "Well, *why* don't you? If you're so set on that idea."

Slowly, Fuad got to his feet and took a step over to the window. He kept his back to Rima, but he did not tell her to leave.

"It was the blood," he muttered at last.

Well, that was obvious. "But you want to be a doctor," said Rima relentlessly. "How can you—"

This seemed to touch a spark in him. Though he did not move, suddenly he spoke with passion.

"Wait—wait, Rima!" A moment passed before he continued. "You don't know what it's like—and give thanks to God that you don't. It was like—like a disease, a contagion that creeps everywhere and infects everyone. I was too young—but I felt it. And . . . I came to want it. Yes, I did. Like an alcoholic wants what ruins him, like a martyr wants death."

"What on earth," said Rima, "are you talking about?"

"I'm . . . trying to tell you." He started to turn but abruptly averted his face. "Do you want me to? If you don't, it's okay."

"Sure. Go on." She didn't want to hear any self-pitying justification, but her curiosity had certainly been aroused by that last speech. And with it came the uncomfortable realization that she seemed to have forgotten one basic fact about Fuad, that he had lived all his life in the midst of a vicious war.

Slowly he resumed speaking. "Well, I got my chance, in the end. My mother had to stay in Beirut with my grandmother. But she knew it was coming—everyone did. So she sent me to stay with relatives in the mountains, to be safely out of it. She never knew what I did. Everything was so upset—roadblocks, no telephone—and everyone had to move around to get out of the way. When it was over, people were happy only to find their family still alive. And my family were happy to believe whatever I told them. No one ever knew the truth. Until now."

Aimlessly, Fuad pushed the limp curtain to one side, then let it fall. In contrast, his voice took on a new urgency. "You must understand, I thought I had to! I'd heard enough to make up my own mind. It was the right thing to do, I thought, a matter of life or death, the last chance to save my people, to save Lebanon! So at last I joined them. And they trained me, as much as they could before everything broke out."

He paused again, as if each step in his story required a flow of strength. Silently, Rima pushed a pile of books farther back in the chair and eased herself down on the edge. A lump of cold was growing deep inside her.

"It was the last of the fighting," Fuad went on. "The last big battle, everywhere in the Christian sector, the city, the suburbs, the mountain. Maybe you remember. And it was some of the most bitter, because . . . we were fighting brother against brother. But we were sure of our cause, sure the people were all with us.

"So I was glad when the command sent us to Antelias—that's a town at the foot of the mountain—where the enemy were strong. We had to infiltrate. We took a building, and my officer told me to go up to the top floor, and do what I could there. I was good, he said. Very good."

Fuad let out a sigh, a fleeting release of tension. "So, it seems, I have one natural talent. I can hit a target."

The last words sent a new chill of confusion through Rima. Had he really meant to hit Jamal? No, he couldn't have! Then what target was he talking about? She wondered whether it was time to break the mood—but his next words cut off any escape.

"Yes, I was a good shot. And that day I shot three. I saw them crumple and fall and lie there spread out in the sunny street, like piles of rags fallen off a wagon, while their blood crept through the dust. And I knew—even though I was on some drug—we all were—I knew I had put an end to those boys' lives. I knew they would never go home to their families. Boys like me."

Again his story lapsed for a moment. "But that," he then said softly, "was not the worst."

Rima sat frozen, her eyes focused on the blankness of his back against the light. She waited with the eagerness of dread.

"It was one of those early spring mornings in Lebanon when the air is light and full of flowers. But in the street all I could smell was smoke and the rot of garbage—and death. I had to make my way down an alley. There was firing all around, every nerve in my body was screaming. And suddenly—a guy came around a corner toward me, running. He looked scared, terrified. He didn't have a weapon, but I knew he was one of them. When he saw me he stopped short and let out a yell of fear. But he was the enemy, and I felt suddenly he was right on top of me—and so I—shot him. I saw his face, I saw the hole in his chest. I saw him as close as I saw Jamal."

Fuad's body, rigid throughout this rush of memory, now sagged. "I lost my reason at that moment," he said. "And when it was over, I knew I had lost my heart. I did not want any more, I didn't care for anything anymore. Inside me was dead and empty. Finally they had to let me go back to my home."

His voice dropped to a whisper. "So Aunt Afifi brought me here to be a doctor. Doctor Fuad Abillama. Fuad Abillama the killer."

Rima let out her breath, with a sobbing sound. Her mind went numb, and there was nothing she could think of to say. Her fingers clutched each other, as if for comfort. Then, as her gaze shifted from Fuad's form and wandered at random around the cluttered room, it fell on her scuffed black guitar case. Barely conscious of what she was doing, she opened it and lifted out the instrument.

At the first notes, a jolt went through Fuad and he spun around.

"Yes, oh yes!" he said, his voice suddenly harsh and sneering. "Play me a song. Play me a song to show it doesn't matter. Or maybe one of your angry, angry songs about the rotten world— this rotten world that you know so much about, you and your friends!"

But Rima did not speak or look at him. She went on plucking at the strings, and however diffident her touch at first, the painfully sweet melody of her song began to grow, like a fragile yet protective curtain. Then gradually, though she was hardly aware of any intention, words came to her mind. She played the piece once more, the words silently taking shape.

Only as she drew near the end did Rima notice that Fuad had left the window and was sitting on the bed. When she stopped, he turned slowly and for the first time met her eyes. She held his gaze until at last he spoke. The anguish had not left his eyes, nor the roughness his voice.

"You still have no words for that song."

Rima lifted the guitar again. "Yes, I do," she said, and as her fingers moved over the frets, the words found their way.

I sing for a boy with blood on his hands,
Blood in his eyes,
Blood in his brain,
The blood of young hearts pumped out warm in the dust.
I sing for a boy who is crying in blood. . . .
But his heart is still beating, his heart is still good.
Yes, his heart I know. . . .
And that heart is still good.

Fuad's back was turned to her once more, his head low. Rima saw the tremble start in his shoulders and spread, no longer controllable, throughout his body. Quietly she placed the guitar on the floor, made her way around to the other side of the bed, and sat down beside him.

Elsa Marston

Although Elsa Marston's ethnic roots are Anglo-Saxon, she has had a strong interest in Lebanon since her first visit there in 1957. In that country, she met a Lebanese man who later became her husband. Together they have lived for varying periods of time in Egypt, Tunisia, England, and Morocco as well as in Lebanon. They currently make their home in Bloomington, Indiana.

Her interests in art and archaeology as well as her travels have provided Marston with valuable material for many of her publications, most of which are nonfiction. They include *Mysteries in American Archaeology; Art in Your Home Town; Some Artists, Their Lives, Loves, and Luck;* and *The Lebanese in America.*

For teenagers, she has published a novel called *The Cliffs of Cairo,* and she has produced two picture books for children: *Cynthia and the Runaway Gazebo* and *A Griffin in the Garden.* Recently she won the *Highlights for Children* fiction contest for "The Olive Tree," a story set in Lebanon that reflects the war there.

"One aspect of the long Lebanese war that has always particularly concerned me," Elsa Marston says, "is the role of the young militiamen: their reasons for joining and fighting, their mentality, the effects of their experiences." "Rima's Song" grew out of that concern. For this story, the inspiration for Aunt Afifi came from Marston's sister-in-law, who ran a Lebanese restaurant in Bloomington for many years. And two of her three half-Lebanese sons have been rock guitarists since their middle teens, providing more than enough background on that aspect of her story.

◻◗○○▲○○○◗◻

Willa is the daughter Aunt Beverly never had. But why does Aunt Beverly act so possessively toward Willa?

GODMOTHER
Sharon Bell Mathis

Although Willa had never met her godmother, she recognized the woman immediately. "Your Aunt Beverly's got a headful of soft white hair, the plumpest cutest face, and the deepest dimples in Washington, D.C.," her mother had said, laughing. "Bev had a few strands of gray in her hair when we weren't but two little girls in Baltimore. We used to call her 'old lady' for fun. Our families lived side by side, and she was my best double-Dutch partner. Bev was fat—but she could jump in and out of a rope faster than anybody else on the block."

Now, Aunt Beverly, looking much older than the pictures she regularly sent to Willa, was lumbering across the black-and-white marble floors of Union Station.

Willa bolted up from the worn suitcase she was sitting on and met the woman halfway. "Hi, Aunt Beverly," Willa said, and hugged the short heavyset woman, her face framed by two thick, silver-colored braids pinned close to her head.

Aunt Beverly, dressed in an old-fashioned dark green linen suit, with matching dark green linen pumps, stepped back and stared at Willa. "My," she said, "I didn't realize you had grown so."

"I'm fourteen, Aunt Beverly," Willa said, hugging the woman again.

"Fourteen—and you're so tall."

"Uh-huh," Willa fussed, grabbing her suitcase. "And I'm trying not to think of how much taller I'll be tomorrow morning!"

"That valise has seen a better day," Aunt Beverly said, irritated. "We'll have to get you another."

"This is Mama's suitcase—"

"We'll have to get you another."

"I don't need a new suitcase, Aunt Beverly. This one is fine. I take it whenever I spend the night somewhere. I don't need a new one."

" 'Godmother,' " Aunt Beverly said. "I'm your godmother, and that is what you will call me." There wasn't even a hint of a smile on her face.

"Mama said to call you 'Aunt Beverly.' I always call you 'Aunt Beverly,' " Willa said, feeling the first nervous tic in her stomach, knowing that if she ever said "Aunt Beverly" again, there would be trouble. Willa watched silently as a Union Station redcap placed her scratched suitcase in the trunk of a taxicab. In the cab, Willa sat as far away from Godmother as she could.

"No more 'Aunt Beverly,' and I can't imagine why Angela wouldn't have you call me 'Godmother' from the beginning. I am not your aunt. Say 'Godmother,' I don't think it's very difficult to pronounce."

"Godmother," Willa managed, leaning away more.

Godmother moved close to Willa and hugged the quiet girl tightly. "Look at me," she said to Willa. Willa did. She saw that Godmother's dimples were the deepest she had ever seen.

"Doesn't saying 'Godmother' sound better?"

Willa didn't answer.

"You're my godchild," Godmother continued. "You're like my own child—you *are* my child. In fact, your father noticed me before he ever noticed your mother. I don't suppose Angela mentioned that. I was really quite surprised when they married. I was away in college, you know. Your mother and I graduated high school together, but she and Thomas fell in love and married and had all those babies. I went on to college and became a teacher."

All those babies!

"Life was hard, and I had to struggle. I was on my own—I know Angela had to tell you that. My mother died when I was young. I had it hard, but it made me strong. I learned early what I was made of."

My father didn't want you. He loved my mother!

"I thank God for everything that ever happened to me because I learned lessons I could never have learned in any other way."

Well, I'm glad you learned them. Big deal.

"Your mother, Angela, had both her mother and her father and her sisters and her brothers. I didn't have any of that. I had my daddy, and that was all." Godmother leaned forward and stared at Willa. "Honey," she asked, "is that lipstick you're wearing—at fourteen?"

"It's just lip gloss."

" 'Godmother.' "

"Godmother, it's just lip gloss."

"You have features just like your mother—the exact same lips, a little full. We—the kids, you know—would call her 'Libba Lips.' Oh, I remember that."

"That was mean, Godmother," Willa said with as much evil in her voice as she could summon.

"It wasn't mean—and Angela didn't mind."

"She did mind. Mama told me when people called her 'Libba Lips,' it meant that they were ignorant and stupid to call her names and hurt her." Willa's mother had never said such a thing to Willa—but Godmother didn't know that. "My mother knows there's nothing wrong with her lips! She has beautiful lips!"

"If she didn't think anything was wrong with her lips—why was she hurt?" Godmother asked, smiling.

You're the meanest godmother on earth.

"But why are we talking about Angela's lips? There are so many other things to talk about. Angela sent your report card to me. Straight A's. She was very proud. So was I."

"Mama's very smart, too," Willa said, quickly adding, "and she's kind to people. Everybody loves my mother. My brother and my sisters are smart, too. My brother was on television because he designed and built a model house—and he can sing and play a piano. Mama's never mean to people." *Like you!*

The cab felt stuffy to Willa, her cornrowed braids felt prickly at her neck, her body shiny with sweat, her stomach uneasy. Willa wanted to go back home.

"Yes, your mother's smart, but she didn't do anything with it—just got married and had those babies. Of course, she was very lucky to have children—and smart children at that. She has everything. I just have you."

You don't have me.

"I have many lovely activities planned for you this summer. I told Angela I don't want you to leave until Labor Day. I asked if you could stay the whole summer, and she agreed. That sweet letter you sent to me a few weeks ago mentioned that you would be happy to spend the summer with me."

I didn't know you were mean!

"We're going to have a wonderful summer. My child is here at last."

Godmother was still talking about the fun they would have when the taxi pulled up in front of a large red brick house with a vividly blooming flower garden—in a circular-patterned bed, edged with weathered railroad ties. Willa thought the house was beautiful, like a picture in a magazine.

The cab driver set Willa's suitcase on the front porch, took the money Godmother held out to him, and walked rapidly down the wide brick steps.

Willa wanted to run down the steps behind him, climb back into the cab, get on another train, and go back home to her mother—Angela. Angela, who was so proud of her lifelong friend Beverly who had become a teacher and who lived in such a lovely house with such a lovely flower garden on Kalmia Road. Angela, a poet and an artist, but who hadn't done anything except "get married and have all those babies." Willa, Deanna, Marlena, her brother Tommy, and her deceased father, Thomas, all reduced to zero by a fat woman who had once called her mother "Libba Lips."

"Mama can draw flowers that look more real than these," Willa said without a second glance at the brilliant, profuse colors.

"Now, that she could do," Godmother said. "She was drawing all the time. Drawing, reading poems, writing poems—and sewing. That was Angela. I can see her now—in those big plaits she used to wear, ribbons tied on and all. My mother was dead, and there was nobody to put ribbons in my hair. Certainly not my father—although he did the best he could. My hair just fell loose most of the time. I didn't know what to do with it myself. Thank God it was curly."

Just then, a tall girl—even taller than Willa—ran across the heavily treelined street and up onto the porch just as Godmother opened the door to the house. "Hi, Ms. Beverly," she said and reached for Willa's arm. "I'm Debby. I live right across the street in that house," she said, pointing to what looked like a mansion to Willa. Debby put her arms around Willa. "I've been counting the days until you got here," she said. "We're the only teenagers on this street!"

Willa looked at Debby's warm dark face, framed by closely cropped hair decorated with a single clip of African trade beads, and she smiled a real smile. "Hi," Willa said.

"Debby," Godmother said impatiently, "Willa's just arrived,

and she's tired and wants to rest. You run back home now. We'll see you later."

"Why does she have to go, Godmother? I'm not tired."

"I'll be back!" Debby yelled, already running back across the street. It was then that Willa noticed the scalloped edge on the bottom of the girl's denim shorts; white eyelet lace was showing through the scalloped edges. Willa wanted a pair of shorts exactly like them.

Godmother's house was totally white throughout. The furniture was upholstered in a white silk brocade fabric. There was a huge white baby grand piano—just like Duke Ellington's. Willa stopped breathing when she saw it. If only her brother, Tommy, could have a chance to play it. If only her brother could *see* it!

There were tiny figurines of white men and women—dressed like those in the movie *Gone With the Wind*—all over the mantel. In what Godmother called a curio cabinet, there were glass shelves filled with miniature birds in birds' nests, and miniature white children—boys in fancy pantaloons and girls in pale smocked dresses. There were lead crystal cups and saucers and dishes of every sort. Godmother told Willa the names of each one of the formal, smiling youngsters. "These are my children," she said. Godmother touched one ballerina dressed in a delicately shaded costume, balanced on one toe, her arms outstretched. "This one is my dancer," she announced with obvious pride.

Willa looked around the large living room and saw more white people, once again dressed in elaborate costumes, in ornate, heavy gold wooden frames. Willa thought of her own home with framed posters of The Dance Theatre of Harlem—signed by six of the dancers, a Romare Bearden print commemorating Brown *vs.* the Board of Education, Tom Feelings's *Bed-Stuy on a Saturday Afternoon,* prints of Charles White's muscular African Americans, and the photographs of Gordon Parks, Van der Zee, Roland Freeman, and Moneta Sleet.

Willa thought of the bedroom she shared with her sisters

Marlena and Deanna, where there was a framed book jacket of John Steptoe's *Mufaro's Beautiful Daughters,* signed by the author/illustrator. Willa's mother had had to stand in line for two hours, heart disease and all, to have the book jacket signed by the young author and illustrator of children's books. It had been Angela's Christmas present to her daughters. Willa's brother, Tommy, had received an autographed book, *Fallen Angels,* by Walter Dean Myers. Tommy's room was decorated with pictures of Herbie Hancock and Van Cliburn.

But now Willa was standing in a room filled with "expensive" figurines, John Steptoe was dead, and a beloved signed photograph of Herbie Hancock seated at a piano, lovingly placed atop a plain maple bureau, seemed a hundred million miles away.

"Is it all right if I take my suitcase to my room now?" Willa asked, hoping to get away by herself for a moment. Of course, it would be better if Debby came back over right now, this minute, today.

"Let me show you where your room is," Godmother answered, "and tell you a bit about where to find a few things you may need."

When Willa saw her room, she loved it immediately. It was decorated in several shades of pale lavender. The bedspread was an exact match for the wallpaper—tiny sprays of purple flowers caught up with lovely white ribbons and bows. The window shades matched the bedspread and wallpaper! The curtains were edged in white organdy. The furniture was mahogany—dark and shiny. But the best thing of all was the bed—with four posts almost to the ceiling. Stretched across the top, anchored by the four posts, was a canopy of the same fabric, more of the tiny flowers.

"Your mother said you loved purple, so I had the room done over for you."

Willa couldn't believe this beautiful room was all hers. If only her sisters could see it!

"Personally, it's a bit too fussy for me. I'd never be able to sleep in a room this busy-looking."

Willa was still staring at the fancy room.

"The decorators assured me that you'd be pleased."

"I love it!"

"Good," Godmother said, and began to open dresser drawers, pointing out slips and bras and panties and socks and stockings. In the closet were three new dresses, some skirts, and a few blouses. "Your mother sent your sizes, as I asked her to do. I wasn't sure if Angela had enough money to buy your summer clothes, and I didn't want you to look any different from the other girls around here. Shoes we'll buy tomorrow. A pair for dress-up, and some sandals. We'll get a bathing suit as well. Debby has a lovely pool in her yard."

A pool!

"I know your mother makes most of your clothes."

That was true, but Willa was mighty glad to see all this new stuff. Besides that, Marlena and Deanna—almost as tall as she was—could certainly share all this bounty.

There was even a purplish plaid dress with the back out.

"Debby picked that one," Godmother said, sounding annoyed. "It's a bit too much, I think. Rather naked. You certainly can't wear it to church."

"Is there a Catholic church near here?"

"I wouldn't know. You'll go to church with me. Episcopalian, just like a Catholic church. You'll feel right at home."

Episcopalian?

"Take a bath and take a nap, child. When you get up, dinner will be ready, and we'll have an opportunity to talk to one another."

"Can I call my mother?"

" '*May* I call my mother?' "

"May I call my mother? Please."

"Of course."

While Willa was dialing the telephone, she heard Godmother walking quickly down the steps. As soon as Willa heard her mother's voice on the telephone, she also heard Godmother pick up the downstairs extension.

"Hi, Ma," Willa said, and tried to keep her voice light. "Godmother's on the phone, too, and we just wanted to let you know that I got here safely."

"That's great, sweetheart! Have a good time, and don't *worry* about anything. She's my worrier, Bev. I told you that." Willa wanted to go through the telephone wires and get back to her mother, back to her home, back to her family—leave the purple-flowered room behind.

"I don't know why she would be worried. I was at that train station an hour ahead of time." Godmother sounded angry, and Willa didn't know why. "I was going to call you myself later, but Willa wanted to do it now. She's been talking about you since the moment she arrived. She really is a 'Mama's girl.'"

"She loves you, too, Bev," Willa heard her mother say quietly. "She's been looking forward to visiting you for a long time now."

"Well, I'm only the godmother—but she's mine while she's here. She's safe, and she has a lovely room to sleep in and good food to eat, and as you know, I've loved her since the day she was born."

"I know that, Bev."

"As much as you love her."

"Bev—"

"So I hope she doesn't think she's going to call you night and day and every morning."

"She knows what to do, Bev."

"I remember the night she was born—a snowy night. Didn't it snow, Ange?"

"Yes, it did, Bev."

"It was snowing here and in Baltimore. That's why I couldn't get to the hospital, couldn't get a train out. God knows, I tried.

When Tom called and told me you were ready to deliver, I just sat at the window looking out at the falling snow and praying. I never prayed so hard before, praying the baby would be a girl and praying that she would be all right. I prayed so hard."

"I know you did, Bev."

"You had promised me that I'd be the godmother to your first baby. I said to God: 'God, this one is mine—don't let anything happen to this child, and please, let it be a little girl.' And God did just that. He gave me that little baby girl."

"Yes, He did, Bev."

"I got there as soon as I could after that, didn't I?"

"Yes, you did."

"I was a college student. I didn't have much money, but I came to you anyway."

"Yes, you did."

Willa listened to Godmother talking about when she had first held Willa and how tightly Willa had held Godmother's finger. Finally, Willa spoke again. "See you, Mama," she said quietly into the telephone, and put the receiver down—disconnecting from her mother's quiet voice.

Willa rebraided her two long cornrows, folded back the beautiful bedspread and matching sheets, and flopped diagonally across the bed—her long feet hanging over. Willa listened to Godmother's voice, listened to her godmother mentioning all of the gifts she had sent to Willa over the years. "And now that little baby girl is here with her godmother—spending a summer, and I thank you, Ange." Willa listened until somehow she fell asleep.

She tried to make herself dream about home. It didn't work. Willa dreamed she was growing taller.

At dinner, Willa noticed that Godmother's speech seemed more pronounced, more deliberate, slower. Her voice became even more so throughout the evening, as Godmother sipped discolored milk from a crystal cocktail glass. "This is my brandy," she said.

"I didn't know you could drink brandy while you're a diabetic and have to give yourself insulin shots in your stomach."

"Don't be stupid, Willa!"

"Stupid?"

"Yes. I said brandy, not whiskey. Brandy. B-R-A-N-D-Y!"

"I didn't know you—"

"There's a lot you don't know, judging from the letters you write. Capital letters everywhere, and run-on sentences to boot. Your sentences stretch out and out, not a comma or a semicolon to be seen. In your two-page letters, you generally have one period, my dear. One period. Period!"

Willa felt her heart stop. In all of Godmother's return letters, she had never once mentioned commas, periods, and colons. And now here was Godmother laughing at letters Willa had written so very long ago. Making fun of them!

"Brandy is nothing but wine. My doctor—the only decent one I have—tells me that brandy is good for me. You don't know what's good for me. Unless I missed something in these years since you were born, you're not a doctor."

Willa tried to finish her dinner, but she couldn't.

"Your mother drinks."

"She does not."

"Well, she should."

Willa got up from the table and went back upstairs to her room and stood there in the near dark. The bright purple flowers looked black, the white organdy grayish.

"I could use some help down here in the kitchen with these dishes," Godmother called up the steps, her words slurred and cold. "If you come back down, I'd certainly appreciate it."

Willa went back down and entered the kitchen.

"Now, that's better," Godmother said, "and don't worry about my drinking brandy. I know more about diabetes than you'll ever know—and I *do* hope you *never* know. I'm happy you're young and healthy. When I was fourteen, I was healthy, too. When your mother was fourteen, she was healthy as well. Do you think she had a bad heart then? Well, I'm here to tell you that she certainly did not!"

While Willa was putting dishes into the dishwasher, Debby came over and Godmother let her stay. Godmother went to bed and the two girls giggled and laughed over many things. The purple flowers were bright again. Willa asked Debby where she had bought the denim shorts with the scalloped edges and white eyelet lace. Willa said she hoped they weren't expensive. "I've got fifty dollars, but it has to last me all summer."

"Heck," Debby said, "I made these. I can make them for you for about six dollars—including the zipper, if we can get the material on sale."

"You *made* those shorts?"

"Yep—and anything else you see me wear."

"You gotta be kidding, kiddo!"

"I started sewing when I was seven."

Willa was amazed. "Seven?"

"Yep! My mom and I were at a thrift store—she was taking her clothes to them so that the store can make some money—and I saw this old beat-up sewing machine and started hollering and screaming so that she would get frustrated and buy it for me. I was right. She bought it to shut me up. My mother learned to sew on that machine, trying to teach me how to sew. She kept saying, well, I'm certainly not going to buy a new one for you to play with. Both of us learned to sew, and then she got bored and stopped and I kept on going. The only thing better than sewing is kissing Denzel Washington."

"Juicy kiss," Willa said, squealing.

"A down-home, grits-cooking kiss."

"Do you get a chance to kiss anybody?" Willa asked.

"No," Debby said, suddenly serious. "Do you?"

"Nope!"

The two girls laughed harder about that than anything they had laughed at before. "Maybe one day," Willa said.

"Yep!"

"And please God, let it be Denzel Washington," the two girls said together.

"Guess what, Debby?"

"What?"

"My mother sews all the time, and I never even look at the machine!"

"Guess what, Willa?"

"What?"

"You're going to make your own shorts."

Willa stopped giggling then and begged Debby to reconsider. "I can't do it, I can't sew anything. I mean *nuthin'*!"

Debby insisted. "If you want them, you're gonna make them."

If Willa hadn't loved the scalloped shorts so much, she would have given up the idea right there and then. She knew Debby meant what she had said.

A short time later, Willa walked across the street with Debby, who was going home. It was ten o'clock at night. "I'm glad you exist," Willa said. "Godmother's kind of mean."

"She just gets real particular when she's drinking, that's all. She's so much fun—and real sweet to everybody. She talks about you all the time. 'My godchild this' and 'my godchild that.'"

"Does she drink a lot?"

Debby didn't answer for a few moments, standing there on her wide brick, three-level porch. "I don't know," she finally said. "I don't live there. All I know is that she wanted you to have a real good summer, made me promise to help you have a baaad D.C. good time. Do you say *baaad*—meaning great—in Chicago?"

"I really want to go back home."

"Willa, I can tell you what 'mean' is. I was looking forward to going to junior high school, couldn't wait. Mainly, I wanted to sign up for a sewing class. First I tried to get into an advanced sewing class. I couldn't do that because first you had to take something called Basic Sewing Techniques. First day, I was wearing a suit I made to show the teacher. She told me to take my seat, that the class was going to make aprons that day. She said she believed the sooner a student started sewing, the better. I made the apron. Perfectly. She hung up everybody's but mine. Then we had to make another apron. So—I bought a very difficult coat pattern—to impress her, so that maybe she could teach me some shortcuts or something. I cut out the coat and proceeded to sew. She kicked me out of class that day, just walked over to me and put me out—said I was undermining her authority. I wore the coat to school, and she passed me in the hall and didn't speak. Three times, I spoke to her. Now, that's *mean!*"

When Willa walked back into the house and locked the door for the night, she could hear Godmother's loud snoring. The sweetish smell of brandy seemed to fill the room, settling over her porcelain "children."

Willa walked quickly to the den, the room farthest away from her sleeping godmother, and called her mother in Chicago—collect. As soon as she heard her mother's voice, she started crying and telling her mother that she was homesick and that she wanted to come home. She didn't mention the brandy. Willa's mother told her that if she didn't feel any better about staying, then she could certainly come home—but "Give Bev a chance—you've been begging to go there for a long time."

"I met Debby."

"I see."

"She lives across the street."

"Good."

"She says 'yep' all the time. And, Mama, guess what?"

"What?"

"Debby sews. Debby makes everything she wears—even her slips!"

"Really?"

"Yep, for real. She sews like you."

"Great!"

"She's gonna teach me to sew some shorts."

"Uh-huh."

"For real, Mama."

"*You* want to sew, Willa Renee?"

"Yep! Just like Debby. I don't want anybody else to have clothes like me. I'm going to design my own—just like she does."

"Good for you."

"Mama, why did you let people call you 'Libba Lips' when you were a little girl? Godmother told me that's what they called you."

Willa's mother was silent on the phone for a while before she spoke. "That's just what people did then," she finally said.

"She wasn't your friend."

"Yes, she is."

"You don't have ugly lips!" Willa yelled, and didn't care if Godmother awoke and heard her. "Neither do I."

"We've got luscious African lips," Willa's mother said.

"We damned sure have," Willa said.

"Willa Renee!"

Willa and her mother were both laughing, and Willa felt better when she put the phone down. She had to be careful calling collect. Her mother did not have any money to waste on long-distance telephone calls.

After a long bath, Willa put on her favorite pajamas and lay down on the snazzy purple-flowered sheets. One long leg hung over the side of the bed and touched the woolen rug with the same purple-flowered design worked around the border. The soft rug felt good on her feet. The air conditioning was making her cold. Willa pulled the covers closer to her neck, but for some reason she kept her foot on the rug. *People who are real tall can do this,* Willa thought, and didn't really care if they could or not.

The only thing that really mattered was that Godmother's hard, ugly words had been made distant by her mother's soft voice. Willa felt better. She pulled her leg back into bed, wrapped her arms around her fluffy pillow, and fell asleep. Then she was awakened by the sound of movement in her room.

Godmother was sitting at the vanity table. She was smoking a cigarette in the early morning light. "Go back to sleep," she said quietly—the brandy-voice all gone now.

"What's the matter?" Willa asked sleepily.

"Not one thing," Godmother answered.

Willa put her head back down on the pillow and lay without moving. She turned her head away from the acrid cigarette smoke. Cigarette smoke made her eyes water. Her eyes were already stinging.

"I like sitting in a bedroom at night watching a child I love sleeping. I've often wondered what it was like." Godmother's voice seemed even quieter.

Willa lay still, said nothing. She was looking out the window, past the trees, at the sky showing off its dawn colors. She felt free and outside of this room.

"When you've never had children, these things are missed. I'm enjoying sitting here. You dangled those long skinny legs off the bed, once or twice. I lifted them back onto the bed, as best I could, so as not to disturb you. Such skinny arms. As skinny as your mother's used to be. Angela never got fat like the rest of us. She's kept her girlish figure."

"My mother never had a lot of money to buy food," Willa said, and hated herself for speaking.

Godmother lit another cigarette. "Maybe not," she said. "Maybe she was never meant to be fat. I was fat as an infant and all throughout my life. Even when I was hungry and struggling to go to school and eating someone else's leftovers, I was fat. How do you like Debby? What did you two talk about?"

"Nothing."

"Nothing?"

"We talked about sewing."

"Your mother could always sew. Oh, boy, could she sew. But she was always small and could buy clothes at any store."

Willa's eyes were watering badly.

"Angela was always drawing and reading and writing—poems. Sewing too—all the time. I can see her right now, seated at her mother's sewing machine, working the pedals. She would sit on the edge of the chair, those skinny legs just moving."

Willa listened.

"I lived with her family then. My mother was dead."

"Debby can make coats, Godmother."

"Would you like to make a coat?"

"No. She's going to teach me to make some denim shorts."

Willa turned over as Godmother put her cigarette out in an ashtray she held in her hand. Godmother left the room. "Go back to sleep," she said. "I didn't mean to wake you."

Later that morning, Willa helped Godmother work in her beautiful garden. They pulled weeds, trimmed some of the buds, cut flowers for the house, and watered the lawn. Willa was extra careful with her favorite flowers—the purple ones.

"Let's go," Godmother announced, as soon as the lawn was watered and lunch had been eaten and they had each taken another shower.

"May Debby go?" Willa had almost said "can" again.

"She may not. This is our time."

Willa was very surprised when Godmother opened the garage door and used her keys to get into a large station wagon. "I didn't know you could drive, Godmother. Why didn't you drive to the station to pick me up?"

"I detest that circle in front of Union Station. It confuses me. I never drive there."

"Oh."

" 'Oh' is right. I've spent a fortune picking up people and paying taxicabs."

At the White Flint mall, Godmother looked at a directory of stores and headed upstairs on the escalator. Moments later, they entered into a sewing machine shop.

"Why are we in here?" Willa asked, trying not to get excited, trying to stay calm.

"I haven't the slightest idea," Godmother said, sounding excited, too.

Godmother walked directly to a salesperson. "We want the nicest sewing machine, exactly what a fourteen-year-old would love to have."

Willa grabbed Godmother's arm. "Oh, my God!" she squealed. "Godmother, I was just going to use Debby's machine. Oh, my God! I can't sew!"

"You'll learn," Godmother said, "on your own machine. Your godmother's not a physician like Debby's daddy, but I think I can afford to buy my daughter a sewing machine."

Within an hour, Willa had a sewing machine with a zigzag stitch, a stretch stitch, an overlock stitch—and five other kinds of stitches. The salesperson taught Willa to thread the machine, fill a bobbin, select stitches, and adjust the tension—whatever tension was.

Willa sat in the back of the station wagon with her arm stretched over the top of the huge box containing what the salesperson called "a low-budget model." Willa thought her sewing machine was beautiful and fancy and just swell. Willa just kept thanking Godmother. Godmother laughed and kept driving. "I didn't want you to have to run over to Debby's house each time you felt like sewing."

As soon as the car stopped in front of the house, Willa jumped out of the car, leaving the huge box behind, and raced across the street to get Debby. Both girls ran back to the car yelling, excited. Mr. Jesse Lee, a neighbor, lifted the sewing machine out of the car and took it up to Willa's room. He set up the machine, attaching it to a matching worktable. The girls were winding a bobbin before he got the box broken down and into the trash.

That night, brandy glass in her hand, Godmother said. "Now, Debby can come to your home to sew."

And Debby did. Godmother prepared all kinds of nice dinners and let them put on fashion shows—complete with music—when it was time to model the clothes the two girls had sewn. Willa taught Debby how to crochet and attach granny squares. Godmother played the piano and taught them how to make chocolate chip cookies from scratch.

Godmother made them laugh when she told them about some of her boyfriends. She made them sad when she told them of how relatives had put her out when once she couldn't afford to pay her weekly rent of three dollars.

"I was going to school and working as a nanny at the same time for one of the most successful Black doctors in town. I had absolutely no money to waste. Most of the time, I ate crackers and drank glasses and glasses of water. That particular day, I came home and found a cardboard box with my few clothes—and all my books—on the front steps. I called up to the window, but there was no answer from anyone inside. They were distant relatives and struggling as well, I suppose.

"I gathered up that box and walked and cried. I got on the bus with it and rode back to my job. The folks I worked for let me back in, let me live there, paid me less money, let me sleep in the basement in a room of my own. I began to eat decent meals. I was glad to be in that basement. That basement was all I had. I told myself that when I became a teacher, all of that would be forgotten. I did become a teacher—realizing my dream, but I never forgot the things that happened to me."

By the end of summer, Willa could sew. She had sewn three pairs of shorts, a pair for herself and a pair each for Marlena and Deanna. Each pair had scalloped edges but with three different kinds of fabric showing through: white eyelet lace, red plaid, and ruffled denim. Willa made matching blouses for the shorts, plain sleeveless shells. She had sewn Tommy a stuffed pillow made in the shape of a grand piano.

Then there was a surprise. The sewing machine wasn't really hers. Godmother wouldn't let her ship it home.

"The sewing machine stays here so you'll come back," Godmother said. "I hope you want to come back—next summer. You already have Angela's machine at home—and I've asked her if she would let you spend Thanksgiving and Christmas with me."

No way! Willa thought to herself. Well, maybe *part* of Christmas.

Two days before Willa was to leave, Godmother sipped more brandy and milk than usual. "I hope you weren't unhappy here," she said, sitting once again in Willa's room. It was three in the morning.

"I read one of Angela's letters to you, and I could see that you had told her something. I hope it wasn't too disparaging. Probably about my brandy."

Willa lay still.

"It must be nice to be able to write to a mother and tell her things. I wished many a day that I had had a mother to whom I could send letters. Actually, I wrote quite a few letters to my mother. The trick was to mail them. I couldn't mail them. The destination 'Heaven' doesn't work. No zip code."

"It's late, Godmother. Why don't you go to sleep?"

"I can sleep when you're gone."

"I know you're tired."

"I asked Angela what you needed for school. She said you didn't need anything. I found that amazing."

"I don't. I wear a uniform."

"Don't you need a new uniform?"

"No, Godmother. I wish you would go to bed and get some rest."

"You sleep. I'll just sit here."

Godmother told a few more stories about what it was like while she was growing up—but mostly, they were fragments of stories. Willa fell asleep trying to listen.

Later that day, Willa and Debby went to the Adams Morgan area to eat at the West Indian restaurant Wings and T'ings. "I want to buy Godmother a gift, but she has everything," Willa said. "Plus, I don't have much money left."

"I told you we should have sewn something for her," Debby fussed.

"But you didn't have any ideas about what to sew—and neither did I!"

It was while they were looking in an African shop that Willa saw exactly the present she wished to give her Godmother. Willa prayed that she had enough money to buy the miniature figurine of an African woman dressed in kente cloth. There was another bit of cloth wrapped around a baby whose head was nestled against the woman's back.

Willa prayed harder.

"Do you love that?" the African merchant asked, his beautiful accent filling in the spaces around Willa, making her marvel.

"Yes," Willa said, and really meant it. "I hope it's not expensive."

"What is expensive?"

"Is it over five dollars?"

"Five dollar—exactly," the merchant said.

Both Willa and Debby stared at the doll. There was a small tag stating that the kente cloth was authentic. The name of the weaver was printed on the tag. The figures were so beautiful, and the faces were carved in an exquisite manner. The baby's face was no bigger than an eraser on a pencil. Both girls knew the cost had to be greater than five dollars. Willa picked up the tiny doll and held it close.

"Look at this," the merchant said, showing the wide-eyed girls a miniature box covered in the same kente cloth. "You must take them home in this."

Both girls asked in unison, "How much is that?"

"Since you have no more money," the merchant said, "it doesn't matter what the box costs. You cannot have one without the other."

On the way home, Willa and Debby worried about the package, didn't want to lose it. "Where's the package?" one or the other would ask whenever they stopped in a store to look at things.

"Suppose Godmother doesn't like it?" Willa asked Debby when they finally arrived home.

"We know she'll like it. Stop worrying."

"Godmother doesn't like Black books and art and stuff. She says 'a picture is a picture' and 'a book is a book.' "

Willa remembered the conversation.

"Your mother was always into Black this and Black that. It was Langston Hughes and Ann Petry and Henry Tanner. She knew them all. I liked Phillis Wheatley's poetry, but I was never into all that Black American–Black African stuff. I never started that sort of thing."

"My mother was always proud of being an African American. Daddy, too—that's what they taught us."

"Who said I'm not proud? And isn't it great that you had a mother and a father to teach you such things? I didn't."

Willa didn't feel like remembering. She felt like talking to Debby. "Thanks for seeing me through this summer," she said.

"There wasn't anything else to do," Debby said, grinning, "since neither of us knows Denzel Washington. Anyway, Ms. Beverly tells some wild stories, really weird. I like to hear them."

Willa stopped laughing. "Her stories are true," she said. "Not wild or weird."

"I would have run away if all that stuff happened to me," Debby insisted.

"If her mother hadn't died, all that 'stuff' wouldn't have happened to her. Besides, where would she run? She was already in the street."

"Time for me to go home," Debby said, and dashed across the street. "See you later, alligator."

"After while, crocodile," Willa said, and opened the door. There was the smell of brandy, and Godmother was snoring loudly from her bedroom. Willa went up to her beautiful bedroom and started packing her suitcase. In twenty-four hours she would be on her way to Chicago. Home.

Willa stopped packing and pulled out the miniature woman and baby. She placed the figures in the kente cloth box and wrapped the box in purple wrapping paper she had bought from the drugstore. Then she tied the box with purple ribbon and placed a purple bow on top.

Where would she hide the gift? She didn't want Godmother to see it until after she, Willa, was gone. Willa decided that she would place the box on Godmother's dresser, next to the pictures of her parents, just before they left for National Airport. Godmother was treating her to a ride home on an airplane!

On this last night in Washington, D.C., Willa finished packing her suitcase, walked into Godmother's room, and sat down watching. Willa smoothed the woman's wispy hair, straightened the covers, and ignored the smell of brandy. Willa pushed the dark squat bottle against the antique white legs of the chest of drawers.

The glow from the night-light allowed Willa to see the photographs of Godmother's parents on the dresser. There were pictures of Godmother as an infant—all the way through her twelfth year, but no pictures after that of her childhood. There was her graduation picture from Coppin State College. She was wearing her black cap and gown. Deep dimples, the widest smile. Somehow she must have saved enough money to have her hair done at a beauty shop. The curls were shiny and neat beneath the tasseled mortarboard.

She looked lovely.

Godmother stirred in the bed, opened her eyes, and moved fitfully to the other side of the bed. "What are you doing in here? Go to bed."

"Just felt like talking, Aunt Beverly."

Godmother sat up, reached into the night table drawer, fetched a cigarette, lighted the tip, and drew the smoke in deeply. "Don't start that 'Aunt Beverly' again. It's time for you to go home—so go home."

"I am going home."

"Good. Now you can tell Angela everything I did wrong—and you won't have to wait and send it in a letter—as if she's the only one who knows what to do with children."

"She knows."

"Good for her."

"And so do you."

"Thank you, ma'am."

"Don't let the kids in your class call one another 'Libba Lips,' Godmother."

"Why are you so fixed on that? It wasn't all 'Libba Lips.' Angela—the angel—is what we called her most of the time. Skinny Angela. Skinny and lovely. She would never hurt anybody's feelings. She was shy, too shy. I was the big mouth."

"Godmother—"

"You should have seen your mother's notebooks. Her pictures of frogs looked better than the frogs in the book."

"I've seen Mama's notebooks."

"Then you saw that she got A's in everything."

"I know that."

"But she fell in love and had all those—"

"Babies."

"Yes."

"And you became Godmother."

"Yes—but just to you."

"You would love my brother Tommy," Willa said. "He plays the piano, and he's good at it."

"Tell him to be a music professor in a great conservatory, to play the piano so that people learn something—not just bang on it for fun."

"He doesn't 'bang' on it."

"Marvelous."

"He could really play that piano downstairs."

"Tell him come play it."

"Deanna is ahead of her class in math and is a math tutor. She didn't want to be skipped. She hopes to be a physicist. She registered for summer calculus classes. When I spoke to her last week, she said the classes were fun. She was sorry they were ending. She can't wait for school to start."

"Let's hope she doesn't fall in love right after high school and get married and have baby after baby after baby."

"Marlena draws like Mama and writes poems like Mama does —all day long. She wants to sculpt and attend law school and specialize in artists' rights."

"What about you?" Godmother asked. "Do you know what you want?"

Willa didn't answer right away. She watched Godmother blowing smoke into the air. Her eyes were stinging, tears were running down her face. The harsh smoke had nothing to do with her tears. Willa didn't really know why she was crying.

"I suppose you plan to be a designer and sew a million pairs of shorts—all of them looking exactly the same. God knows who would buy them—other than me."

"I want to be a schoolteacher. Like you."

"You don't want to be a teacher 'like' me, you want to be a *better* teacher than I am."

"I'll try."

"Don't just *try,* do it!"

"I may never get married, either."

"Don't be stupid, Willa."

"You didn't marry."

"I had suitors."

"You might have had a daughter."

"And die and leave her to people to put her out in the street."

"Godmother—"

"I have a daughter. You."

"I know."

"You've been my daughter since the day you were born."

Willa sat there in the dark until Godmother put her cigarette out and turned over and stopped talking. Willa didn't leave the room until she heard Godmother snoring again.

Back in her own room, Willa opened her suitcase and took out her purple writing paper. *Dear Godmother,* she began, *this note is for you. I hope you like my gift.* Willa wrote and wrote and wrote. She thanked Godmother for everything, mostly for the fun the two of them had shared.

A few hours later, Willa was back home in Chicago—hugging her mother, couldn't stop hugging her mother. She hugged Tommy and Marlena and Deanna too hard—each one. They were all laughing and talking at the same time. Tommy was glad to hear about the piano. Marlena and Deanna put on their short sets right away. Mama's gift was a blouse Willa had made. Mama was so proud of it.

"Teach me to sew like you," Willa pleaded.

Her mother hugged her. "We can start today."

Godmother had given Willa one hundred dollars to help with school expenses. Tommy needed two new uniform shirts because he was growing so fast. Willa bought the new shirts and everybody's school supplies.

On the first day of school, Willa received a letter from Godmother.

Dearest Daughter:

Thank you for the lovely African mother and daughter (of course, it's a girl) you left on my dresser. I think of it as the two of us. It has a place of honor, at the center of my mantel.

The note you left did not have any unnecessary capital letters. I am proud of you.

Love always,
Godmother

P.S. Give my best to your family and thank God you have one.

Sharon Bell Mathis

Born in Atlantic City, New Jersey, and raised in the Bedford-Stuyvesant section of Brooklyn, New York, Sharon Bell Mathis is an African American mother of three grown daughters. Her own mother was a poet who could also draw, and young Sharon grew up in a home filled with books by Black authors—including Richard Wright, Frank Yerby, and Langston Hughes. That background is reflected in "Godmother," where Willa recalls the poster illustrations of books by John Steptoe, Walter Dean Myers, and others that made her home so different from her godmother's.

In the early 1970s, Sharon Mathis published several novels featuring Black teenagers, the most popular of which have been *Teacup Full of Roses* and *Listen for the Fig Tree*. In *Teacup Full of Roses*—a *New York Times* Outstanding Book of the Year—three young brothers are plunged into a tragic family crisis resulting from heroin addiction, while in *Listen for the Fig Tree*, Muffin, a blind teenager, finds the courage to survive through a recognition of her African heritage. In 1973, *Ray Charles*, Mathis's biography of the famous blind entertainer, won the Coretta Scott King Award. And *The Hundred Penny Box*, her book for younger readers, was selected as a Newbery Honor Book in 1975. Following those successes, she experienced a writer's block that lasted for more than ten years.

But Sharon Bell Mathis, as her story in this collection shows, is back writing and publishing. Most recently she published a collection of poems about peewee football (for seventy-pounders) called *Red Dog, Blue Fly: Football Poems*. And she has completed a new book of poems featuring one of the characters from the football poems, a little female running back. The working title of that novel is *Ebonee Rose: Running Girl*.

◻◇○○▲○○◇○◻

Playing blues guitar was the most important thing in Bobby's life. It seemed to be in his blood. But what would his grandfather know about that?

BLUES FOR BOB E. BROWN
T. Ernesto Bethancourt

I was just getting home from my after school delivery job at the Big Apple Market. It was about eight-thirty. I heard Mama and Papa going at it right through our apartment door. I stood outside in the hall of our second-floor walkup and tried to make out what was going on inside.

No sense in walking into an argument unless you already know whose side you're supposed to be on. That's the trouble when you're the last kid left at home. They always want you to take sides. Ever since my older brother, Lou, left to join the navy, it's been this way. My married sister, Margie, lives in Queens now. She's too far from West Eighty-eighth Street in Manhattan, where we live, for Mama to get her involved in her hassles with Papa.

"I don't care!" I heard Papa say. "I won't have him in my house."

"But Juanillo," I heard Mama counter, "he's your own father. Your flesh and blood . . ."

I knew Mama was trying the soft approach with Papa. When she's really pleased with him or wants something, she calls him Juanillo. Any other time, it's plain old Jack. But actually, my father's name *is* Juan—meaning "John"—and *Juanillo* means "Johnny" or "Johnny-boy."

All us kids have traditional Latino names, too. My brother Lou is really Luis Alfredo, my sister Margie is Margarita Dolores and I'm Roberto Ernesto, although everyone calls me Bobby. I couldn't imagine anyone calling me by my middle name. Or, worse yet, *Ernie!*

My dad speaks some Spanish; so does my mom. But us kids only know a few words—me least of all, being the youngest. To give you an idea how little, I almost failed Spanish in my junior year at Brandeis High School.

The hassle was still going on inside the apartment. "My mind's made up, Helen," I heard Papa say. "If he's so interested in seeing his grandchildren after all these years, that's tough. I want nothing to do with him."

Now I knew what was going on. We had heard from my grandfather. I didn't even know he was still alive. My dad never talks about him. Seeing as how my parents' fight wasn't about me, I put my key in the door and went inside.

The hall door opens right into the kitchen of our apartment. Then comes the living room and two bedrooms. But most of the time if we aren't watching TV in the living room, most of our family life is in the kitchen.

Mama was seated at the table with her ever-present cup of Cafe Bustelo coffee with milk. Papa, still wearing his Transit Authority uniform, was having one of his two daily bottles of Schaefer beer. I kissed Mama and got a hug from Papa. "Hi, guys," I said. "What's happening?" As if I didn't know.

"Nothing—nothing at all, Bobby," Papa said.

"Pretty loud nothing," I said. "I heard you two down the hall."

"Oh, *that,*" my dad said with a wave of a hand. "Just between your mama and me. A family matter."

"Jack!" said Mama. "You mean you aren't going to mention it?"

"Mention what?" I said, still not letting on.

My dad shook his head in a funny mix of disgust and dismay. "You might as well know, Bobby. Your grandfather has decided he's still part of our family. After all these years. We got a letter from him today."

"Grandpa's here in New York? Last time I heard you mention him, he was in California."

"He's still out there," Mama said. "But his letter says he's coming here this week. He says he wants to see us—*all* of us." Mama looked pointedly at Papa, who looked away.

"How did he even know where to find us?" I asked.

"It was your brother, Lou. He's stationed in Oakland now—"

"I know, but—?"

"Let me finish," put in Papa. "Your brother took it upon himself to track the old man down. He had some family records of my mother's that *someone* gave him." Papa looked angrily across the table at Mama. "So Lou found him—a man he'd never seen in his life—a man who didn't even come to his son's wedding."

"We know, Juanillo," Mama said softly.

"Then why should you care about a man you've never met?" my dad demanded of my mom.

"Because no matter what you say, he's your father. Yes, I know. He left when you were ten years old. But that was thirty-five years ago, Juanillo. In a way, *you* don't know him, either."

"I know all I need to know. My mother told me, God rest her soul."

I could see they were going to be at this for a while. I opened the fridge and took out a frozen dinner and popped it into the microwave. Then I walked down the hall to my bedroom.

I took my guitar off the chair and sat down to practice. I had an audition on Saturday night, downtown in the SoHo section of town.

I started with some simple blues changes and scales. That's my thing: traditional blues and jazz. No amplifiers—just straight acoustic. I was really getting into my solo on "Beale Street Mamma" when I heard the microwave beeping.

When I came into the kitchen, Mama and Papa weren't quite so upset. Papa looked at me and said, "Well, what about it, Bobby? Do you want to meet the old man?"

"We decided it's up to you kids," Mama said. "Your father has his mind made up. He won't see your grandpa. But if you want to meet him, that's okay with us."

"What does Margie say?" I asked.

"I'm going to call her in a little while and ask."

"That's not the point," my dad said. "It's what *you* say about meeting him."

I looked at both my parents. Here I was, on the hook again. If I said yes, probably Papa would feel I was letting him down. If I said no, Mama would think I was cold. After all, I see *her* father and mother every month when they come in from Long Island. And we always have Thanksgiving dinner at their place in Oceanside. Now what was I going to say? They were looking at me, expecting some answer.

"Can I think about it?" I asked.

"Sure, honey," Mama said, ignoring Papa's look. "Take your time. He won't be coming to town until next Monday."

I took my TV dinner out of the microwave and brought it to my room. While it was cooling, I put on an old album of blues artists that I had found in a secondhand store downtown. It was made in the 1960s. The record company doesn't even exist anymore. But there sure was some good stuff on it. That record was where I learned "Beale Street Mamma" from.

The guy who played and sang it was terrific. His name was Ivan Dark. I tried to find out more about him, but it seemed like this was the only recording the guy ever made. Too bad. They didn't even have a picture of him on the album cover. All it said about him was he came from New York.

But I kind of liked the idea. Almost all the great acoustic blues players came from down South, or from the South Side of Chicago. But here was a New York blues man. I had played his album track so many times, it was old and scratchy.

I ate my Budget Gourmet sirloin tips while I listened to Ivan Dark. Then I practiced until ten o'clock and went to bed. I had a full day of pedaling the delivery cart for Big Apple the next day —Saturday. And eleven-thirty that night, at Mary's Grill in SoHo, was my live audition.

Saturday at ten, I checked myself out in the bathroom mirror. I was wearing my all-black outfit: suit, shirt, tie, and shades. I debated with myself whether I should wear the black fedora hat. Then I decided I'd look too much like one of the Blues Brothers.

But I did want to look older than eighteen. My brother Lou is lucky that way. He was fifteen when he grew a moustache. I could get away with shaving twice a week. I think it's because Lou is like my dad: dark curly hair, medium complexion and build. Papa has always had a moustache, far as I can remember.

To look at me, you wouldn't think we were related. I'm tall and thin, with straight, light brown hair and hazel eyes. I took a lot of heat from kids in school about that. "Some Puerto Rican *you* are," they'd say. Called me *huero,* and a lot of other names not too choice. A lot of them just couldn't get next to a guy named Roberto Moreno who looks like I do. Mama says there's blondes on her side of the family. Maybe that's where I get my looks.

I looked at myself in the mirror and shrugged. "You are who you are, man," I told my reflection.

Then I went to my room and packed up my guitar. It's an old Gibson arch-top acoustic. The pawn shop guy I bought it from said it was made in the 1930s. I can believe it. But man, does that ax have a tone—a full bass and a treble that could cut glass. Just right for blues.

Mama and Papa were watching the ten o'clock news on Channel 5 as I left. We did the usual going-out-late stuff. *Yeah, I'll be*

careful, Mama. Yeah, Papa, I know it's dangerous out there. I'll
walk near the curb and away from dark doorways. Yeah, Mama,
I'll call if I'm gonna be late. . . . I finally got out the door. Jeez,
you'd think I was still a kid!

I hailed a cab at Amsterdam and Seventy-ninth Street. I'd
been saving my tips so I could cab it both ways. You get on the
subway at a late hour, and you're just asking for it. And if you're
wearing a suit and carrying an instrument—well, you might as
well wear a sign saying "Take me."

Mary's was in full cry when I got there. It had started out
years ago as a neighborhood place that served lunches and drinks
to the factory workers. But now all the factory lofts are full of
artists and sculptors. The little luncheonettes and neighborhood
bars changed with the times. Now they got sidewalk tables and
hanging plants inside, and they serve fancy food.

Mary's is a little different, though. They kept the old crummy
plastic-covered booths and the big, long bar. About all they
changed was, they put in a little stage and a sound system. And
behind the bar, they got a bunch of autographed pictures of jazz
and blues musicians who played there. Some names you might
know, if you're into my kind of music.

Brutus, the guy at the door, knew me and passed me in without checking any ID. Just as well. I was using Lou's old driver's
license. He gave it to me when he went into the navy.

The place was heavy with smoke and the smell of stale beer.
It's one of the few places in SoHo where they don't put the
cigarette smokers in some kind of sinner's jail room. But by the
late hours, the air gets so you can chew each lungful before you
inhale it.

The trio onstage was tearing up a jazz number I recognized—
an old Dave Brubeck tune called "Take Five," on account of it's
in 5/4 time. It's the house policy at Mary's that they don't play
anything there newer than bebop. I spotted Mary behind the
bar, right away.

She's hard to miss. Five four and easily two hundred pounds, with a flaming red wig that was probably new when the Beatles were big. She gave me a huge grin and waved me over. "Bob E. Brown, you rascal!" she hollered over the trio and the crowd noise. "I was wondering if you was gonna show. You're on in fifteen minutes."

Maybe I ought to explain about that Bob E. Brown. See, when I decided to be a blues man, Roberto Moreno didn't sound right for that line of work. I was already Bobby, and Moreno means brown in Spanish. And because there's already a rock singer named Bobby Brown, I came up with Bob E. Brown—the "E" being for Ernesto. It sounds the same as Bobby. It's just spelled different. It's no sin or anything to change your name. After all, Muddy Waters's real name was McKinley Morganfield.

I took the empty stool at the end of the long bar. Mary drew me a Coke with a piece of lime in it. "Try and act like it's a Cuba Libre, rascal," Mary said. "Don't want to give the customers the wrong idea." Mary knew I was underage, and I don't drink, anyway. But she's in the business of selling drinks.

She leaned across the bar, and a lot of Mary rested on the hardwood. "Best you tune up in the kitchen, rascal," she said. "The group will want the downstairs dressing room when they get off. You ready?"

"As I'll ever get." I didn't want to admit I felt shaky. Sure, I had played at neighborhood places and at assemblies in school. But this was different. This was *professional*.

Even when I had performed for Mary, it was in the daytime. And Mary's easy to be with and play for. It's like she's everyone's mama. I took a quick sip of my drink, then went into the kitchen to tune up.

When I came out, the trio was just finishing up. There was a light dusting of applause. It seemed like the crowd was more interested in each other than in what was happening onstage.

Mary got up and announced, "Let's have a nice hand for the Milt Lewis Trio, folks." A little more clapping was all that got her.

"Tonight," Mary went on, "we have a special treat for you. A young man who's making his first appearance here at Mary's, the home of good jazz and blues. Please welcome a new generation blues man—Bob E. Brown!"

I swallowed a lump in my throat the size of a baseball and got onstage to some indifferent applause. "Go get 'em, rascal," Mary whispered to me. I adjusted the mike in front of the chair on the stage—I work sitting down—and went right into a Bessie Smith tune, "Gimme a Pig's Foot."

Halfway through, I realized I was making as much impression as a snowball on a brick wall. I started to feel dribbles of sweat creep down my back. *What am I doing here?* I thought. *I must have been crazy to try this!* I finished the chorus and went into my vocal.

That was when it happened. Something clicked in my mind. If these people didn't want to listen, that was okay. What I was doing was between me and my guitar. If they liked it—swell. If they didn't, I still had my music.

I thought of what an old blues man said in an interview I once read: "Making music is like making love. Even when it's bad, it's good."

I threw back my head, not caring and sang, " 'Gimme a pig's foot and a bottle of beer. Send me gate, 'cause I don't care . . . ' " The damnedest thing happened. The house got quieter. Every now and then, when I looked up from the fingerboard of my ax, I could see heads turning and faces looking at me. The sweat on my back and on the palms of my hands started to dry out.

When I got to the last line, " 'Slay me 'cause I'm in my sin . . . ,' " they began clapping. They applauded all the way through the last four bars I played solo to finish the tune. I couldn't believe it. They liked me!

The next two tunes were a blur in my mind. Oh, I know what songs I did. I just don't remember paying attention to *how* I did them. All the hours and years of practice took over. I didn't watch my hands, like I usually do. I watched the faces of those people watching me. I sang *to* them, not at them.

The great blues man, Josh White, said that he didn't sing songs, he told stories. And every song is a story. I told those folks my story—but in the words of the blues I sang.

I glanced over and saw Mary. She had come out from behind the bar and was standing only a few feet away. She was smiling like it would bust her face. She waved and put one index finger across the tip of the other to form a letter T. That meant it was time for me to do my last number. I finished the tune I was playing, and the house really came apart.

For the first time, I spoke directly to the crowd. "Thank you very much," I said, my voice a little shaky. "I'd like to finish up with a tune I learned from a recording by a New York blues man, Ivan Dark. It's called 'Beale Street Mamma.'"

I went into the intro, and they were already clapping. I played the first chorus and went into the vocal: "'Beale Street Mamma, won't you come on home . . .'" As I did, I was startled by the sound of the upright bass from behind me. I almost missed a chord change. Out of the corner of my eye, I saw that the Milt Lewis Trio had come onstage behind me.

Then we really started to cook. Milt Lewis plays alto sax, and with the bass and a drummer added, we did I don't know how many choruses. I dropped into rhythm playing while everyone took his solo, then we all finished together.

In my entire life, I never felt anything like that. Nothing compared. Not even Angela Ruiz in the hall outside her folks' apartment. When we played the last note, there was a moment of silence, like the crowd wanted to make sure we were finished. Then the place blew up with clapping, hollers, and whistles.

Suddenly, Mary was at my side. "Let's hear it for Bob E. Brown!" she shouted over the din.

"Let's hear more!" somebody in the house hollered. "Yeah, more!" another voice said.

"We got all night, folks," Mary said. She put a huge meaty arm around my waist. "We gotta let this rascal get some rest. Don't worry. He'll be back. . . . Bob E. Brown, ladies and gentlemen. Remember that name!"

I got offstage on a cloud. As Mary led the way to the bar, people applauded as I went by. Some of them reached out and shook my hand. Lots of them said nice things as I went by.

Back at the bar, Mary drew a Coke with lime and set it in front of me. "Well, rascal, seems like you got the stuff," she said. "And if you want a gig, you got one here. Milt and the guys start a road tour in two more weeks.

"But I like the sound you made together. Can you pick up a trio to work with?"

I almost fell off the bar stool. "I don't know any other musicians," I admitted, my face feeling warm.

Mary frowned. "Bet you don't have a union card, either," she said. I shook my head. Then she smiled that five-hundred-watt grin. "Then you gotta get busy, rascal. You get your little butt up to the union hall. Tell them you got a contract here. They can call me to check it out.

"Pay them the fee. You'll have your card fast enough, if I know that local. And believe me, I know that local. You start in two weeks. I'll book a trio to back you."

It wasn't until I was in a cab headed home after one more show that Mary's words sank in. A fee? How much did it cost to join the musicians' union, anyway? But I was too tired and too happy to think about it that night. I was somebody. I was Bob E. Brown—a real blues man!

I nearly died when I found out on Monday what the union initiation fee was. I called Local 802 and spent about twenty minutes on the phone. If I drew every cent from my savings account, I was still five hundred dollars short. Half a thousand: all the money in the world!

I put down the phone and stared at the kitchen walls. Mama and Papa were still at work. I had thirty minutes to get over to the Big Apple market, and I still hadn't eaten a thing. I went to the fridge and saw the note from Mama on the door.

Bobby,
Your grandfather called. He wants you to call him at his hotel, the Waldorf-Astoria. He's in Room 1620. The decision is yours.

I took some spiced ham from the fridge and made myself a quick sandwich. There was no Pepsi left, so I got a glass of water to wash it down with. As I ate, I thought, *So he's in town, huh? Guess I gotta make up my mind.*

But to tell the truth, all that was on my mind was that five hundred bucks. How in the name of anything was I going to raise that in two weeks? I had finally gotten a professional gig, and now I was in danger of losing it. It was driving me nuts.

More to get my mind off it than anything else, I dialed the hotel. After two rings a woman's voice said, "Waldorf-Astoria Hotel. How may we help you?"

I couldn't believe it. I'd only walked past the Waldorf. My grandfather was actually staying there, at one of the ritziest places in town. I gave the switchboard operator the room number. It rang for a while before anyone picked up and a man's voice said hello.

"Mr. Moreno, please," I said.

"Which Mr. Moreno?"

All of a sudden, I had to think of what my grandfather's first name was. Then it came to me: same as Papa—Juan. That's who I asked for. "Just a moment," the voice said.

"This is Juan Moreno," a new voice said.

"This is Bobby, your grandson, I think. My mother left me a note to call you."

The voice warmed. "Bobby! How are you, kid? Yeah, this is your grandpa. Where are you? When can we get together?"

"Uh—I don't know. I'm home right now, but I got to go to work in a few minutes."

"I thought you were still in school, kid."

"I am. I work afterward."

"Until when?"

"Eight o'clock."

"Good enough. We'll have dinner. Get a cab. I'll leave money with the doorman. You know where I am?"

"The Waldorf-Astoria?"

"That's right. But I'm in the Waldorf *Towers*. That's the side entrance, not the Park Avenue one. Tell the cabbie; he'll know. See you about eight-thirty, okay?"

"I ought to clean up and change, right?"

"Okay, then. Nine o'clock. I'll be waiting, Bobby."

When I arrived at the hotel, I was wearing the same outfit I did at the Mary's audition, but with a white tie. I figured if I was going to have dinner at a place like this, I'd need one.

My grandfather had taken care of business. The doorman had money for my cab and even tipped the driver for me. And when he showed me into the lobby and what elevator to take, he called me Mister Moreno! I'd been having quite a different kind of life, lately. First I was Bob E. Brown, the blues man. Now I was *Mister* Moreno.

I rang the bell at my grandfather's door, and a guy about twenty opened it. He was my size and build, with dark hair and eyes. He was wearing a designer shirt and slacks, with a pair of shoes that would cost me a month's pay at the Big Apple. "Come in," the guy said, extending a hand for me to shake. "You must be Bobby. I'm your uncle Jim."

It wasn't a hotel room he led me into. It was an apartment like I never had seen, even in a movie. "Dad!" my "Uncle Jim" called out. "Bobby's here."

A man came out of the next room, and I went into shock. If someone had given me a magic mirror to show me what I'd look like in fifty-five years, here I was!

He had a full head of straight white hair. He was thin and over six feet tall and had a deep suntan that made his hair look silver. His eyes were the same color as mine, too. He was wearing a lightweight suit that screamed money, and a conservative tie.

As he extended his arms to give me an *abrazo,* I saw, from beneath the white cuff of his shirt, the glint of a gold Rolex. This was my grandpa?

He threw a bear hug around me, then stepped back and held me at arm's length. "So you're Bobby, huh?" he said. "I'd have known you anywhere, kid. Same as I'd know myself.

"Here, sit down," he said, waving me to a chair. "You want something to drink? Jimmy, get Bobby what he wants," he told my "uncle." "You've already met Jimmy, right?"

I just nodded. I was numb. Finally, I said, "He's my uncle?"

My grandpa laughed. "Yeah, he is. Not much older than you, though." He looked at me and laughed again. "I've been married a few times since your grandma, kid. Jimmy's from the latest edition. What can he give you?"

"A Coke would be fine, sir."

"Sir? What is that crap? Call me Grandpa. I kind of like it." Jimmy came over and handed me the soda. I thanked him.

"What about I leave you two alone, Dad?" Jimmy asked. "I have to get downtown, anyway."

"Have a good time, Jimmy," Grandpa said. "You got enough money?"

"I'm fine, Dad."

"And don't forget. If they won't let you tape the group, I want a full report on what you think."

Jimmy had put on a leather jacket from a closet near the door. I know guys on West Eighty-eighth that would kill for one like it. "Come on, Dad," he said. "If I don't know the business by now . . ."

" 'How do you run it when I step down,' " Grandpa finished. "Okay, boy. Have a good time."

Jimmy left, and Grandpa focused in on me. He sat down on the sofa facing my chair and leaned forward. "But tell me about yourself, kid," he said, "and about your family. I know a lot from your brother, Lou. Your sister isn't going to see me. And your mom has to side with your father. That I can understand. You're the only family I got here that's talking to me, it seems."

I thought I saw a far-off look of sadness in the old man's eyes. I don't know why, but I started to talk. He was a good listener. He didn't break in, and I could tell from the expression on his face that he was interested in what I had to say.

I told him everything: my dreams, the gig at Mary's coming up, my feeling about being a blues man. All except the money for the musicians' union. I could see the old man was rich, but I didn't want him to think that that was why I had come to see him.

When I'd finished talking, he went over to the bar in the corner and poured himself a tall glass of tonic water with ice. He saw me watching him and smiled. "I don't drink anymore," he said. "Not my idea. It's the doctors. I stopped smoking, drinking, and eating Caribbean cooking. I may not live a long time," he said, taking a sip of the tonic water, "but it sure as hell will *feel* like it." He set the glass down by the bar. "Stay here," he said. "I'll be right back." He went into the other room.

I sat there trying to digest all that had happened. My grandpa was something else. He had to be almost seventy—sixty-five at the youngest. Yet he was so *alive*. Not like my mama's dad, who really looks tired.

And what really knocked me out was that this guy didn't have a trace of an accent. My other grandpa talks like Ricky Ricardo on *I Love Lucy*. He didn't even have a New York accent like Mama and Papa. He came back into the room with a flat-top acoustic guitar, and I nearly fell off the chair.

It wasn't nylon strung, either. It was a Martin, model D-28. I knew it right away. That's how come I'd bought the Gibson. I couldn't afford one like this. He held it out to me and said, "It's already in tune, kid."

He went over to the bar and brought me one of the stools. "No straight-back chairs here," he said. "This will have to do. Okay, play for me."

"Play what?"

"Whatever you think I'd like best. Or better yet, what *you* like best. Please yourself enough, you'll please your audience." He sat down on the couch.

I played "Beale Street Mamma," naturally. I'd already told him how well it had gone down when I played at Mary's. When I finished, he reached inside his back pocket and took out a hankie that looked like it was silk. He blew his nose like a trumpet playing an A natural. He gave me a look that had no name on it and said, "You got the stuff, kid."

"That's what Mary said," I replied.

"She would. Mary and me go back thirty-five years. When her husband was still alive and ran the Jazz Stop on Hudson Street."

"How do you know Mary?"

"Give me the guitar, kid," he said. I handed the Martin over. And he played. "Beale Street Mamma."

A creepy feeling came over me. Every last lick I had practiced for hours just flowed from under his fingers. Then he sang the first chorus. The voice was deeper and darker, but the phrasing was there. I started to feel like I was in the middle of a *Twilight Zone*.

When he finished, I couldn't say a word. I just looked at him. My other grandpa is a retired garment worker. His idea of music runs to old-time stuff like you hear in the black-and-white musicals on Televisa, the Spanish-language network on UHF.

"You know the record, too!" I finally got out.

"Kid, I *made* the record," Grandpa said. "If your Spanish was better, you could have figured that out. Moreno doesn't mean brown, like you think. It means *dark*. In Russian, Juan is *Ivan.* That's how I became Ivan Dark. Who ever heard of a blues man from New York named Juan Moreno?"

"But how come you never made any more records?"

"I did. Lots of them. Just not as Ivan Dark. Got into Latino jazz. It's where I really belonged to begin with."

"But you were—are so good."

"Doesn't matter, Bobby. Sure I was good. I learned from the best. They were still alive in the late fifties and early sixties. Josh White, the Reverend Gary Davis, Mississippi John Hurt, Muddy Waters. I worked with all of them and learned by watching and listening.

"But good isn't great. And those men were great. There were other young guys who hung around and played blues. They're all gone, most of them.

"A guy I knew in 1957 is still at it. His name's Dave Van Ronk. He had his thirty-year anniversary in the music business this weekend. That's part of what brought me to town. They had a big blowout at the Village Gate. I was there on Sunday."

"But why did you stop playing blues?" I insisted.

"I finally figured it out, Bobby. Even though my folks learned their English from Black people—that's the neighborhoods we lived in after they came here from San Juan, and that's the first 'American' music I heard—it's not our culture.

"I could play rings around lots of Black kids my age. That didn't matter. I wasn't accepted, really.

"Dave Van Ronk is a white man from Astoria, Queens. I don't know if Dave was too dumb or too stubborn to quit. But I heard him last night. And he's a blues man down to his toenails."

"And so you quit?"

"I never quit!" said the old man, sitting up straight. "I went into my Latino roots. I found a way to meld Latino and jazz music. And I did well. I've got a club in Oakland, my own record label, and I do just fine."

"I'm sorry," I said. "I didn't mean to make you mad, Grandpa." But I knew I had said the wrong thing. I got up. "Well, I guess I have to go now."

"Why? We didn't even have dinner. I can call room service. Look, kid. I don't want to lose touch with you. We hardly started to know each other."

I came out and said what was on my mind. "Look, Grandpa. Maybe it was different when you were coming up. But there's lots of kids of all backgrounds who play blues, jazz, even soul.

"That's the great thing about music. It cuts across all lines today. The Milt Lewis Trio is Black; they never said anything but how much they liked what I did. Mary is Black, and she's gonna give me a job at her club. And are you gonna tell me that Joe Cocker, a white Englishman, has no soul?

"What brings us all together is the music. And it don't matter where you come from or where you're at. You're Juan Moreno. I'm gonna be Bob E. Brown."

The old man stood up and smiled. "Maybe your uncle Jimmy is right, kid," he said. "It's time for me to step down. Us old farts think we know it all. Maybe we can learn a lot from you kids. If we're smart enough to listen. I wish you well."

I got up and headed for the door. "It's getting late, Grandpa," I said. "And I got school tomorrow."

"I'll give you cab fare," he said.

"That's okay," I replied. "The subway's still running." I knew I was taking a chance wearing a suit, but I didn't want to ask the old man for anything more.

"You sure?" he asked.

"You already gave me 'Beale Street Mamma,' " I answered. "Thanks, *abuelo*." I took an *abrazo* from him and left.

I get regular letters from him now. I write when I can. The first letter I wrote was a thank-you. He got in touch with Mary the next day. He also paid my whole initiation fee to Local 802. When I got my union card, it was already made out. In the space that reads "Member's Name" it said Roberto Moreno. But there's another space on the card for the name you play under: your stage name. In that space, Grandpa had had the clerk put in *Ivan Dark II*.

I really was grateful for what Grandpa did. And I love the old man for it. But to hell with that *Ivan Dark II*. I'm Bob E. Brown, and I'll show the world I am.

T. Ernesto Bethancourt

Son of a Puerto Rican truck driver, T. Ernesto Bethancourt grew up in New York and Florida and now lives in southern California with his Japanese American wife. Long before he became a writer, Tomas Bethancourt, like Bobby in "Blues for Bob E. Brown," played blues guitar and sang in night clubs and coffee houses under the name Tom Paisley. Living on the periphery of all-Black neighborhoods in Brooklyn, he was more influenced by Black than by Latino music. The famous Josh White taught blues guitar to the young Tomas, who then went on to play with all the real-life blues players mentioned in this story. But back in the forties and fifties, only Black performers were taken seriously as blues musicians, a condition exemplified by Bobby's grandfather, and Tomas Bethancourt was forced to focus his attention elsewhere.

As a writer, Bethancourt began with an autobiographical novel that later was made into an NBC-TV movie with the title *New York City Too Far from Tampa Blues.* Among his other books for teenagers are *T.H.U.M.B.B.*, a hilarious story about a high school marching band; *The Mortal Instruments; Where the Deer and the Cantaloupe Play; The Tomorrow Connection;* and *The Me Inside of Me.* Several of his novels have been named Best Books for Young Adults, Notable Children's Books, and Young Adult Choices.

His most popular novels are the Doris Fein mysteries—the most recent of which is *Doris Fein: Legacy of Terror*—and *The Dog Days of Arthur Cane,* a clever look at life from a dog's perspective when a voodoo curse turns a teenage boy into a mutt. That story was made into a film for ABC television that is still shown on Nickelodeon.

T. Ernesto Bethancourt, who is working on a novel he has titled *Googie,* still plays and sings, though mostly for kids at the schools he visits.

◻◇◇◇▲◇◇◇◇◻

Confrontations

The alley between Seventy-fifth and Seventy-sixth streets holds a lot of memories for Cesar Rojas—friendships and conflicts, good times and bad. Today it offers one more challenge.

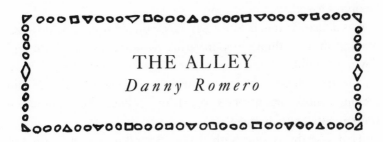

THE ALLEY
Danny Romero

The setting sun casts a growing shadow over the backs of the wooden houses lining the alley between Seventy-fifth and Seventy-sixth streets. From Bell Avenue it runs east to Crockett Boulevard, across it, then past the grammar school and the Catholic church to Lou Dillon Avenue, then Alameda and the railroad tracks where it dead-ends. The yards adjacent have either fences or walls surrounding them. Some are topped with strands of barbed wire; on others, shards of glass ward off would-be trespassers and felons.

A skinny young boy dressed in baggy khaki pants and an oversize Pendleton shirt scrambles desperately across the debris-strewn asphalt. In his frenzy he almost loses his dark glasses and the woman's purse he has stolen.

Behind him comes Cesar Rojas. Cesar has been walking home from the public library when he hears Mrs. Ramirez's high-pitched voice shrieking, *"Oye cabrón!?* What are you doing!?"* At that, Cesar looks over in her direction and sees the young *cholo* stumble for an instant, then regain his footing and head down the alley.

Cesar takes off in pursuit instinctively, not allowing himself time to doubt his actions. Later he will look back on it and see the real trouble he could have been in if he had been led into the alley where the rest of the gang had waited. He runs still carrying a book in his hand. It is a large, hardbound copy of *1984* by George Orwell.

Cesar uses it much as a relay-race runner uses a baton: legs moving in a rhythmic motion, arms pumping the book up and down, pistonlike. Two years earlier, as a sophomore, he had been on the track team, but his lackluster performance had left him feeling a more urgent need to get into college than running in track meets or relay-races.

That was the reason he had been spending so much time at the library. His English teacher, J. Smith, had given Cesar a list of books he should read, and *1984* was one of them. Now when Cesar read the newspapers and watched the television news closely, the resemblance between his world and that of the main characters in Orwell's novel grew more apparent and frightening. And he wondered what he could do to make this less true.

Cesar halts in his tracks for a moment. The boy in front of him now comes running back toward Cesar, carrying a long wooden stake. It is more than five feet long and had been used as a means of support for a young tree planted by the city. Cesar backs up. The stake, hurled through the air, flies end over end over end over end over end toward Cesar, then tangles in the electrical wires overhead and falls down, crashing loudly onto the hood of a rusted Volkswagen abandoned in the alley.

The pair cross Crockett Boulevard and pass the grammar school. Cesar still follows the khaki-clad figure.

When he was younger, Cesar and his friends walked this way home from school. Up ahead in the alley, he knows, there is a buzzer at the back door of a garage. As kids, they would press the button, then run off before anyone answered it. Now as he remembers it, he wonders if the buzzer really worked. He had never before waited to see who might answer it.

Plastic bags filled with garbage come flying back at Cesar. The younger boy grabs them as he passes by and flings them backward. Cesar steps over a large watermelon rind and a half-dozen used diapers. The khaki pants stops and picks up a bottle, turns, and throws it. Cesar stops just in time and moves behind a graffiti-covered wall. The glass splinters away from him. The chase continues.

It seems to Cesar like the summer he spent in this alley more than three years ago. It was during that summer before high school when things had changed for him. He was leaving the security of his *barrio* and would have to travel on the bus to another *barrio* for high school. In the beginning of that summer he had felt all alone. None of his old friends was around. And he began to wonder if it was only his family that never went on vacation. Then he met his friends in the alley.

They all walked a thin line between drugs, gangs, and the law. The boys made decisions about right and wrong, for better and for worse. The sheriffs, no matter, always held the boys under suspicion because of the color of their skin and the neighborhood they lived in. And more than once the boys had been lined up with their faces in the asphalt and broken glass. The boys were guilty in the sheriffs' eyes until proven innocent, and sometimes not even then.

Cesar and his friends had still been young enough to build go-carts with washing machine motors, and they raced them over the cracks and bumps in the asphalt of the alley straight away into the night.

After those few summer months Cesar never saw any of those boys again. Except for one whose name was Mando. Cesar had seen him a couple of times on the bus in the morning. They spoke to each other briefly, but they had never been very close among the bunch in the alley that summer. Cesar remembered that Mando once had blamed him for causing him to wreck and

flip over the go-cart and break his arm, but they both knew
Mando lied.

It had been Frank and his brother Clown who had caused the
accident. The brothers, fifteen- and sixteen-year-old gang members, were shot dead at the end of that summer by the sheriffs.
Cesar was the passenger on the go-cart that Mando drove, and
they both saw clearly the brothers at the far end of the alley,
sniffing paint. As Cesar and Mando had sped faster and faster
toward Lou Dillon Avenue, the brothers turned with slingshots
in their hands and, smiling, fired steel ball bearings. They hit
Mando, who lost control of the vehicle, veering closer and closer
to a wall on one side, then running into a trash can and flipping
over.

The pair crossed Lou Dillon Avenue.

Cesar already can smell the dog turd coming from the Lozano
family's yard near Alameda. The yard has been filled with a
dozen Chevrolet Impalas from the 1950s and 1960s, sitting along
the weeds for as long as Cesar can remember. Many people had
offered Mr. Lozano money for the vehicles so they could restore
them to their original splendor, but all had been refused.

The horrible smell comes from the chow-chow dogs that
guard the yard. There are three or four of them, Cesar does not
know for sure. He does know they are the meanest, oldest, and
ugliest dogs he has ever met, and he has wished never to see
them again. They begin a loud, rasping bark from the other side
of the sheet-metal siding that surrounds the yard these days.
Another bottle comes sailing past Cesar.

The thief has stopped and is hiding in some shrubbery near
the Lozanos' yard. Cesar proceeds with caution. He notices the
heavy traffic on Alameda, thousands of cars speeding north and
south. He tries to listen for the thief, the sound of his own heart
thumping in his ears.

The thief lunges at Cesar from the bushes, this time with a
piece of broken bottle in his hand. Cesar quickly raises his book

in front of him and deflects the blow. The glass sticks momentarily in the cover of the book, then is twisted free. Cesar slams the spine of the book into the face of the other boy with all his might. The dark glasses go flying. Blood splatters over both boys as Cesar grabs the hand holding the broken glass and turns the wrist until the weapon is dropped. The younger boy pulls Cesar's hair and head backward. Cesar backpedals, knocking both of them to the curb. Cesar turns the boy over.

It is his cousin.

Though it has been years since they have seen each other, Cesar remembers him. Cesar recalls that he is three years older and that their fathers had disowned each other as brothers years earlier after a drunken brawl at a family gathering.

The two boys had never been introduced. By the time they both had been born, the two men were firmly entrenched in their dispute, though it had overlooked the cousins. They knew each other only from those gatherings where the two families had sat on opposite sides of the room and never spoke to or acknowledged the existence of each other. Except for once, Cesar remembers, when at a funeral the two boys had seen each other from across the church and made eye contact, then nodded to each other. Quickly they recovered before anyone else noticed and never let their guard down again.

Lalo is his name, Cesar remembers. Cesar looks into the boy's eyes and sees the growing desperation and almost animallike look brought on by the pipe that never stops calling. Cesar has seen the same look on the faces of other boys, girls, men, and women in the *barrio* now addicted to rock cocaine. The rockheads, as they are known, always look worried and nervous: tense, as if their jaw were on a spring and wanted to snap right off their face at any moment. Cesar has noticed that at least with the PCP zombies they sometimes look as if they are having a good time.

Cesar unhands the boy and stands. He picks up the purse

from the ground nearby. No one has been hurt, he thinks, except for his cousin. He turns back toward the boy and sees the small figure dodging across the traffic on Alameda. Jail will not help the boy, thinks Cesar, though perhaps this chance he is given now might. Cesar can think of no other solution.

Danny Romero

The youngest of seven children, Danny Romero is a third-generation Chicano, born and raised in Los Angeles. He was educated in Catholic schools as well as on the streets of South L.A. "The Alley," like some of his other stories, takes place in his old neighborhood.

Once a problem student who was expelled from high school, Danny Romero has gone on to study literature and creative writing at the University of California at Berkeley and is currently a graduate student and future faculty fellow at Temple University in Philadelphia.

His short stories have been published in various literary journals and magazines, including *Konch, Occident,* and *Ploughshares.* His autobiographical essay "Saint Aloysius" can be found in the anthologies *West of the West: Imagining California* and *California Childhood: Recollections of the Golden State.* His short story "Fireworks" appears in *Mirrors Beneath the Earth: Short Fiction by Chicano Writers.*

ロ◔◦◦▲◦◦◦◦ロ

Part of growing up is learning that life is not fair. For Pochie and Nuncio, the lesson is even harsher.

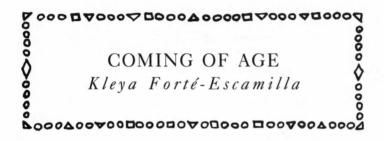

COMING OF AGE
Kleya Forté-Escamilla

It was mid-October, and strong winds from the northern mountains spun around the desert floor. Pochie had not found any coal on the tracks for a long time. She walked up and down, looking first into the hazy distance ahead, then back to where the telephone poles shrunk into toothpicks. There was nothing on the tracks anywhere, except this one water tank that made the trains stop. Pochie stood, brown hair in her face, thin, tense, as if waiting for what had already happened to her to reach her, waiting for the heat and smells and tastes, the pain to catch up to her. But she was too far away now. What had happened had settled into the hidden flesh of her body.

Shaking a little, tears drying undiscovered on her face, Pochie saw the railroad tracks, the spreading desert, and the eternally present sky that was filling up with huge round thunderheads. With stiff fingers she pulled her torn sweater closer around her, ignoring the pain deep in her stomach. She decided to keep walking south, toward the Mexican border. Maybe trains coming from there had dropped something worth picking up, something that would burn and make her warm. So she followed her intermittent shadow south.

———

When Nuncio was a small boy, he loved the desert so much, he would curl up in the dirt under a mesquite and lie there for hours. He watched the ants scurrying around, carrying scraps into their hole, which had dirt piled up at the entrance like a little mountain. He rested his head on his arms until he was eye level to the ants and could see everything: all kinds and colors of seeds, bits of plants, and the carcasses of insects. Caterpillar parts and flies' wings seemed to be favorites. When it was hot, Nuncio found coolness in the breezes under a mesquite. When it rained, he sheltered there, too, knees against his chest, arms wrapped around his legs. And he gazed out at the *lomitas,* dusted with raindrops, alive and moving under cloud shadows. The sparse branches of the mesquite were just enough to keep him from getting really wet. But perhaps in those moments, he was enough like the hills, enough like the sage bushes and cactus, that the rain only dusted him, too. His hair and skin shone, as though covered with a thin coat of oil. In those moments of perfection, he saw no reason to move, or walk, or eat. He hardly even breathed.

When Pochie couldn't walk anymore, she sat down on the edge of a rail, staring at the southern mountains. The blood had long ago dried on her fingers, but the pain came in big gulps that bent her in two. In a wave of nausea, she threw up on the few blades of grass that grew between the tracks. But nothing came out—only acid bubbles that burned her mouth. It was fitting because her spirit was like a sour *pozo* where water no longer flowed.

She found a clean piece of grass and stuck it between her teeth and chewed it. It made her forget the throwing up—and gave her something to do with her mouth, which felt strange, as if it belonged to another.

———

Only meanings that passed among cactus and mountains in those childhood days spoke to Nuncio. The distance between the top of a *saguaro* and the mountain peak behind it told him something. He saw the mountain grow more intensely violet, more than the yellow green of the cactus, and their relationship was revealed suddenly, starkly, bursting in his consciousness. And that was what moved him. Lifting himself from the earth that had nested around him, seeing how the mesquite placed him in space, he knew other things too. He saw creatures, the mourning dove, the gray mockingbird, the bobcat and *javelina*, the lizards, horned toads, tarantulas, and scorpions, all like himself, existing unattached to the earth, but contained in her embrace. And that was the only world he knew.

The place where Pochie sat was already a different place; the desert had changed from familiar to unknown. She no longer knew the mesquites by sight, nor the spaces between them leading to well-worn trails. Where she was now, the ironwood grew in thick gnarled trunks. Their knotted ancient bodies made shelter for gophers and pack rats, who lived in snug little burrows, hollowed-out pockets created by the living roots.

For an instant, the sun came out from the billowing clouds, warming her and releasing a covey of sparrows that flew, chirping sweetly, overhead. Pochie remembered she had almost been that happy, once. It was when Sophie LaRue, *la negra*, had gotten her pants on backward because the boys were peeking around the corner of the lockers in PE. Pochie thought that laughter, which sent delicious waves through her body and made her want to pee, must be happiness. But that seemed like a long time ago, before she was sixteen and Rocha made her quit school to take care of the house. He had to work—why shouldn't she? And he said she was too dumb to learn anything, just like her mother had been. But Pochie knew something was wrong, be-

cause Ester hadn't been dumb. She was smart enough to teach
herself how to read English from the newspaper. At night, when
Rocha was snoring and stinking of cheap tequila, Pochie remembered falling asleep in her mamá's lap, listening to her, sounding
out the strange words one by one, whispering in Pochie's ear, *"Ya
ves, m'ija, apprende tu también para que puedas hacer algo con tu
vida*—learn, Pochie, so you can be somebody in life." And
Pochie, staring at Mamá through half-closed lids, falling asleep
with her eyes open.

But this memory was spoiled by that other memory, of Rocha
lying there in his sweat-stained pants, the waist folded over under his greasy belly with the black hairs coming out of his navel.
And then, one time, the front of his pants had been open, and he
was watching her face when she saw him, over her mamá's
shoulder, and after that, every time he lay down, there by the
stove, he would grunt and reveal himself, even though she didn't
want to see. One time, just one time, Ester had seen him, and
then he pretended, *Ayi Dios,* what a big surprise, making a show
of turning his back to arrange himself, and Pochie just went
outside until she could stop shaking. She was older then and
knew what it was, knew she had to avoid getting near it, no
matter what. And then, for a few weeks after Ester died, he sat
by the cold stove, not eating, drinking, and begging Pochie to
come over so he could cry on her *pecho,* but she didn't. He
started making her stay home from school. "Your mama would
have wanted you to take care of me," he said. And then the worst
thing of all, he started watching her, watching her every move,
and finally—this morning . . . She started to retch with the
memory, down on her knees, trying to *basquear* the taste from
her mouth.

When she could, Pochie got up and walked a few feet into the
desert. She found some *yerba buena* growing out of the ribs of a
dead *saguaro,* and she rubbed it on her teeth and between her

hands, covering her face with it, breathing in the rich green smell, like rainwater on desert earth.

Where Nuncio lived, at the south end of the Mexican border town, pigs ran wild, splashing in the muddy gutters, occasionally chased and beaten by small children with big sticks. In a vast field on the other side of the road, tall wooden *barrancas* painted red surrounded the bull ring. Like the shell of an egg, the *barrancas* protected the soft center of the ring; the round, flat, yellow sand, cleaned and tended and swept every day, lying smooth and unbroken, until Sunday. And then, suddenly, strangely, unexpectedly, the shrieks of the gored horse, streaks of heavy dark blood flinging down lines against the pale yellow roundness, breaking it open. Nuncio felt fear pushing back the crazed, thundering mass of people screaming their heads off. Silence closed in upon the center of the ring, and when the moment became absolute, the way it had been in the desert, when he was like sage under raindrops, he fanned out the *muleta* a fraction of an inch away from his body and slid the *estoque* into the bull's spine. Then sound crashed over him again, and he almost fell, seeing what he had accomplished: the bull's legs crumpling as though they had been kicked out from under him, head extended, tongue hanging useless, blood melting into the sand. At the last moment before he turned away, Nuncio saw the pride, the fierce beautiful strength, the firm flesh of the animal, turn to water. Death drank the bull's life until nothing was left but a loose and shapeless mass. The bull was dragged away by a team of horses, as Nuncio, holding up the ears, circled the ring while the crowd praised him.

Later, *"Ahí qué hombre, qué macho eres ahora,"* the older men said, pressing on him *cojones con salsa picada* fried in butter. It was his due, they said, and would increase his manhood even more. The smile plastered on his face, he smeared the mess around on his plate, pretending to eat and swallow. The rest were too excited to notice his tenderness, his sensitivity, in the fingers holding the fork, picking up the shot glass. In those hours while Nuncio was drinking tequila and the others were celebrating, the brave bull's meat was cooking in the hovels past San Cristobal Street. There, where the dirt path became nameless, descending down into the misery of *El Oillo,* the bull had been partitioned and given to the poor, who gathered every Sunday at the rear gate, sweating, anxious to hear the roar of a kill that meant food in their stomachs.

What Nuncio was thinking about when he was tipping his glass was the sound of the bull's breathing, like a bellows, huge chest and rib cage rising and falling, blowing out the air, fanning it into a flame that came out of his eyes and reached into the razor-sharp tips of his horns. That sound, of life, ended by him, Nuncio. That life and death existed side by side, he thought, was terrible.

Nuncio's *primo,* who was also his *segundo,* had taken him home after that and placed him tenderly on the bed, turning his head, so he could vomit over the side of the bed, if he needed to, leaving him alone to sleep. But he had not slept; he had drowned in the bull's breath, been swathed and purified by the bull's rough skin, cradled in the bull's sweat and kissed by its horns. So he awakened and cried beneath the hot gush of water, standing in the shower stall in his clothes until he could bear to rip them from his body. He tore them into rags. He didn't want anything from that day. He didn't want his own life. He needed to be forgiven, but death could neither condemn nor forgive. Death was nothing.

That morning Nuncio followed the railroad tracks out into the desert. At last, he couldn't hear his thoughts, he couldn't remember or feel what it had been like, the shock to his own soul. Nuncio and the desert were alone.

———

"*Ahora sí, que eres mujer,*" Rocha had told her. "A girl does not become a woman until she bleeds for a man," he said, fixing his pants, as Pochie lay there, blood running down her legs.

"And get out of here and clean yourself," he'd said with disgust, and Pochie went, and kept on going, not thinking, not planning anything, until here she was, sitting by a dead *saguaro* in the middle of the desert.

It had not rained. The clouds had risen as far as possible into the sky, mushroomed and glowered gray and held. Now the mountain looked different, softer, *palo verde* branches smears of yellow-green brushstrokes everywhere on the slopes like the skirts of dancing girls at a *baile*. Then, suddenly, the clouds squeezed together, and thunder crashed and echoed, lightning sizzled on the hillsides, and rain reached down in a torrent, without curve, without delicacy, just definite flowing strength of sky falling to earth. Pochie held her nose as she sprawled on the ground, opened her mouth. She gulped and spat, chewing *yerba buena* leaves, spitting everything out. She took off her dress and stood naked to the wetness until her body opened again and released its sorrow. As if by agreement, the water yielded to a rush of wind and left her, moving north, fan to the ground. Pochie wrung out her dress and put it on, and with her sweater for a pillow, she lay down and closed her eyes. She was asleep in a moment, her breast faintly rising and falling like a child's.

When it first started raining, Nuncio ran for an ironwood tree, but thirsty and grateful, he, too, gave himself to the rain. The liquor that had bled from him in sweat and dried on his skin ran from his body in streams. When the rain had passed and the wind swept his face, he opened his eyes and saw her, Pochie, asleep on the ground. His body shook as if he had been struck. His stumbling on the rocks woke Pochie with a start, and she yelled the first words in her mind; "What are you looking at?" Nuncio, frozen where he stood, said, "I thought you were dead."

And Pochie cried, "I want to be dead! I want to be dead!" Nuncio walked over to her carefully and sat down near to her. "Me, too," he said quietly. But it was Pochie who asked him, "Why?"

"Because yesterday I killed something important to me, *algo sagrada como mi vida*," he said. And he told her about the kid he'd been, how smart and quick, doing anything he could to get near the matadors, until they had started training him. They loved his courage, oh, how they loved him; he was a reflection of their own desires to play with death and come out alive. When Nuncio was finished, Pochie said bitterly, "There is only one kind of man in the world."

"But I didn't want to be like that," Nuncio cried, and as he said those words, his heart broke completely, and he didn't even follow her when Pochie got up and walked into the face of the desert.

Kleya Forté-Escamilla

A resident of California, Kleya Forté-Escamilla has a mixture of Spanish, French, and Yaqui/Mexican blood. She grew up in Baja California, Mexico, as well as in the American Southwest. Her college education was in English and French. She won the first Best Short Story Award given by the University of Arizona, as well as in studio art and then in creative writing. She has worked as a neighborhood artist (in metal relief) in Oakland, California, as a professional musician (on the electric organ), and for more than ten years in social service agencies addressing the needs of women and children.

In talking about her story "Coming of Age," Kleya Forté-Escamilla says: "As a teenager I was aware of the pressures on young men and women—both from La Raza and society at large—to conform to identities prescribed: Women must enter the church, or belong to men, and produce children. Boys had to prove their manhood over and over again by engaging in dangerous activities, chief of which were fighting Brahma bulls and racing hotrods. Some of them died doing it." With that in mind, she wrote this story "to give Latino teenagers a chance to question the definitions of men and women that La Raza lives by, and to take courage in communicating and healing from difficult experiences."

"Coming of Age" is one of several stories that Kleya Forté-Escamilla has been writing for an as-yet-unpublished collection of her own that is entitled *Storyteller (with Nike Airs) & Other Barrio Stories.* Several of her stories have been published in journals and other anthologies, including *Chicano Stories,* edited by Gary Soto. She is also the author of *Daughter of the Mountain,* a novel about growing up in an Arizona *barrio* during the time when the old Spanish/Native way of life was being replaced by the new Anglo society and its values.

◻◗◗◗▲◗◗◗◗◻

Passing the driver's test is an important event for most teenagers. But there's a lot more riding on that experience for Saeng.

THE WINTER HIBISCUS
Minfong Ho

Saeng stood in the open doorway and shivered as a gust of wind swept past, sending a swirl of red maple leaves rustling against her legs. Early October, and already the trees were being stripped bare. A leaf brushed against Saeng's sleeve, and she snatched at it, briefly admiring the web of dark veins against the fiery red, before letting it go again, to be carried off by the wind.

Last year she had so many maple leaves pressed between her thick algebra textbook that her teacher had suggested gently that she transfer the leaves to some other books at home. Instead, Saeng had simply taken the carefully pressed leaves out and left them in a pile in her room, where they moldered, turned smelly, and were eventually tossed out. Saeng had felt a vague regret, but no anger.

For a moment Saeng stood on the doorstep and watched the swirl of autumn leaves in the afternoon sunlight, thinking of the bleak winter ahead. She had lived through enough of them now to dread their grayness and silence and endless bone-chilling cold. She buttoned up her coat and walked down the worn path through their yard and toward the sidewalk.

"Bai sai?" her mother called to her, straightening up from neat

rows of hot peppers and snow peas that were growing in the vacant lot next door.

"To take my driving test," Saeng replied in English.

Saeng remembered enough Laotian to understand just about everything that her parents said to her, but she felt more comfortable now speaking in English. In the four years since they had migrated to America, they had evolved a kind of bilingual dialogue, where her parents would continue to address her brothers and her in Laotian, and they would reply in English, with each side sometimes slipping into the other's language to convey certain key words that seemed impossible to translate.

"*Luuke ji fao bai hed yang?*" her mother asked.

"There's no rush," Saeng conceded. "I just want to get there in plenty of time."

"You'll get there much too soon, and then what? You'll just stand around fretting and making yourself tense," Mrs. Panouvong continued in Laotian. "Better that you should help me harvest some of these melons."

Saeng hesitated. How could she explain to her mother that she wanted to just "hang out" with the other schoolmates who were scheduled to take the test that afternoon, and to savor the tingle of anticipation when David Lambert would drive up in his old blue Chevy and hand her the car keys?

"The last of the hot peppers should be picked, and the kale covered with a layer of mulch," Mrs. Panouvong added, wiping one hand across her shirt and leaving a streak of mud there.

Saeng glanced down at her own clean clothes. She had dressed carefully for the test—and for David. She had on a gray wool skirt and a Fair Isles sweater, both courtesy of David's mother from their last rummage sale at the church. And she had combed out her long black hair and left it hanging straight down her back the way she had seen the blond cheerleaders do theirs, instead of bunching it up with a rubber band.

"Come help your mother a little. *Mahteh, luuke*—Come on, child," her mother said gently.

There were certain words that held a strange resonance for Saeng, as if there were whispered echoes behind them. *Luuke*, or child, was one of these words. When her mother called her *luuke* in that soft, teasing way, Saeng could hear the voices of her grandmother, and her uncle, or her primary-school teachers behind it, as if there were an invisible chorus of smiling adults calling her, chiding her.

"Just for a while," Saeng said, and walked over to the melons, careful not to get her skirt tangled in any vines.

Together they worked in companionable silence for some time. The frost had already killed the snow peas and Chinese cabbage, and Saeng helped pluck out the limp brown stems and leaves. But the bitter melons, knobby and green, were still intact and ready to be harvested. Her mother had been insistent on planting only vegetables that weren't readily available at the local supermarkets, sending away for seeds from various Chinatowns as far away as New York and San Francisco. At first alone, then joined by the rest of her family, she had hoed the hard dirt of the vacant lot behind their dilapidated old house and planted the seeds in neat rows.

That first summer, their family had also gone smelting every night while the vast schools of fish were swimming upriver to spawn and had caught enough to fill their freezer full of smelt. And at dawn, when the dew was still thick on the grass, they had also combed the golf course at the country club for nightcrawlers, filling up large buckets with worms that they would sell later to the roadside grocery stores as fishbait. The money from selling the worms enabled them to buy a hundred-pound sack of the best long-grain fragrant rice, and that, together with the frozen smelt and homegrown vegetables, had lasted them through most of their first winter.

"America has opened her doors to us as guests," Saeng's

mother had said. "We don't want to sit around waiting for its handouts like beggars." She and Mr. Panouvong had swallowed their pride and gotten jobs as a dishwasher and a janitor, and they were taking English lessons at night under a state program that, to their amazement, actually paid them for studying!

By the end of their second year, they were off welfare and were saving up for a cheap secondhand car, something that they could never have been able to afford as grade school teachers back in Laos.

And Saeng, their oldest child, had been designated their family driver.

"So you will be taking the driving test in the Lambert car?" Mrs. Panouvong asked now, adeptly twisting tiny hot peppers from their stems.

Saeng nodded. "Not their big station wagon, but the small blue car—David's." There it was again, that flutter of excitement as she said David's name. And yet he had hardly spoken to her more than two or three times, and each time only at the specific request of his mother.

. Mrs. Lambert—their sponsor into the United States—was a large, genial woman with a ready smile and two brown braids wreathed around her head. The wife of the Lutheran minister in their town, she had already helped sponsor two Laotian refugee families and seemed to have enough energy and good will to sponsor several more. Four years ago, when they had first arrived, it was she who had taken the Panouvong family on their rounds of medical check-ups, social welfare interviews, school enrollments, and housing applications.

And it was Mrs. Lambert who had suggested, after Saeng had finished her driver education course, that she use David's car to take her driving test. Cheerfully, David—a senior on the school basketball team—had driven Saeng around and taken her for a few test runs in his car to familiarize her with it. Exciting times they might have been for Saeng—it was the closest she had ever come to being on a date—but for David it was just something he was doing out of deference to his mother. Saeng had no illusions about this. Nor did she really mind it. It was enough for her at this point just to vaguely pretend at dating. At sixteen, she did not really feel ready for some of the things most thirteen-year-olds in America seemed to be doing. Even watching MTV sometimes made her wince in embarrassment.

"He's a good boy, David is," Saeng's mother said, as if echoing Saeng's thoughts. "Listens to his mother and father." She poured the hot peppers from her cupped palm to a woven basket and looked at Saeng. "How are you going to thank him for letting you use his car and everything?"

Saeng considered this. "I'll say thank you, I guess. Isn't that enough?"

"I think not. Why don't you buy for him a Big Mac?" Big Mac was one of the few English words Mrs. Panouvong would say, pronouncing it *Bee-Maag.* Ever since her husband had taken them to a McDonald's as a treat after his first pay raise, she had thought of Big Macs as the epitome of everything American.

To her daughter's surprise, she fished out a twenty-dollar bill from her coat pocket now and held it out to Saeng. "You can buy yourself one too. A Bee-Maag."

Saeng did not know what to say. Here was a woman so frugal that she had insisted on taking home her containers after her McDonald's meal, suddenly handing out twenty dollars for two "children" to splurge on.

"Take it, child," Mrs. Panouvong said. "Now go—you don't want to be late for your test." She smiled. "How nice it'll be when you drive us to work. Think of all the time we'll save. And the bus fares."

The money, tucked safely away in her coat pocket, seemed to keep Saeng warm on her walk across town to the site of the driving test.

She reached it a few minutes early and stood on the corner, glancing around her. There were a few other teenagers waiting on the sidewalk or sitting on the hoods of their cars, but David was nowhere in sight. On the opposite side of the street was the McDonald's restaurant, and for a moment she imagined how it would be to have David and her sitting at one of the window seats, facing each other, in satisfyingly full view of all the passersby.

A light honk brought her back to reality. David cruised by, waving at her from his car window. He parallel parked the car, with an effortless swerve that Saeng admired, and got out.

"Ready?" David asked, eyebrow arched quizzically as he handed her his car keys.

Saeng nodded. Her mouth suddenly felt dry, and she licked her lips.

"Don't forget: Step on the gas real gently. You don't want to jerk the car forward the way you did last time," David said with a grin.

"I won't," Saeng said, and managed a smile.

Another car drove up, and the test instructor stepped out of it and onto the curb in front of them. He was a pale, overweight man whose thick lips jutted out from behind a bushy moustache. On his paunch was balanced a clipboard, which he was busy marking.

Finally he looked up and saw Saeng. "Miss Saeng Pa-nouvong?" he asked, slurring the name so much that Saeng did not recognize it as her own until she felt David nudge her slightly.

"Y—yes, sir," Saeng answered.

"Your turn. Get in."

Then Saeng was behind the wheel, the paunchy man seated next to her, clipboard on his lap.

"Drive to the end of the street and take a right," the test

instructor said. He spoke in a low, bored staccato that Saeng had to strain to understand.

Obediently, she started up the car, careful to step on the accelerator very slowly, and eased the car out into the middle of the street. *Check the rearview mirror, make the hand gestures, take a deep breath,* Saeng told herself.

So far, so good. At the intersection at the end of the street, she slowed down. Two cars were coming down the cross street toward her at quite a high speed. Instinctively, she stopped and waited for them both to drive past. Instead, they both stopped, as if waiting for her to proceed.

Saeng hesitated. Should she go ahead and take the turn before them or wait until they went past?

Better to be cautious, she decided, and waited, switching gears over to neutral.

For what seemed an interminable moment, nobody moved. Then the other cars went through the intersection, one after the other. Carefully, Saeng then took her turn (*turn signal, hand signal, look both ways*).

As she continued to drive down the street, out of the corner of her eye she saw the instructor mark down something on his clipboard.

A mistake, she thought. *He's writing down a mistake I just made. But what did I do wrong?* She stole a quick look at his face. It was stern but impassive. *Maybe I should ask him right now, what I did wrong,* Saeng wondered.

"Watch out!" he suddenly exclaimed. "That's a stop sign!"

Startled, Saeng jerked the car to a stop—but not soon enough. They were right in the middle of the crossroads.

The instructor shook his head. An almost imperceptible gesture, but Saeng noted it with a sinking feeling in her stomach.

"Back up," he snapped.

Her heart beating hard, Saeng managed to reverse the car and back up to the stop sign that she had just gone through.

"You might as well go back to where we started out," the instructor said. "Take a right here, and another right at the next intersection."

It's over, Saeng thought. *He doesn't even want to see me go up the hill or parallel park or anything. I've failed.*

Swallowing hard, she managed to drive the rest of the way back. In the distance she could see the big M archway outside the McDonald's restaurant, and as she approached, she noticed David standing on the opposite curb, hands on his hips, watching their approach.

With gratitude she noticed that he had somehow managed to stake out two parking spaces in a row so that she could have plenty of space to swerve into place.

She breathed a deep sigh of relief when the car was safely parked. Only after she had turned off the ignition did she dare look the instructor in the face.

"How—how did I do, sir?" she asked him, hating the quaver in her own voice.

"You'll get your results in the mail next week," he said in that bored monotone again, as if he had parroted the same sentence countless times. Then he must have seen the anxious, pleading look on Saeng's face, for he seemed to soften somewhat. "You stopped when you didn't need to—you had right of way at that first intersection," he said. "Then at the second intersection, when you should have stopped at the stop sign, you went right through it." He shrugged. "Too bad," he mumbled.

Then he was out of the car, clipboard and all, and strolling down the curb to the next car.

It had all happened so quickly. Saeng felt limp. So she had failed. She felt a burning shame sting her cheeks. She had never failed a test before. Not even when she had first arrived in school and had not understood a word the teacher had said, had she ever failed a test.

Tests, always tests—there had been so many tests in the last four years. Math tests, spelling tests, science tests. And for each one she had prepared herself, learned what was expected of her, steeled herself, taken the test, and somehow passed. She thought of the long evenings she had spent at the kitchen table after the dinner dishes had been cleared away, when she and her mother had used their battered English-Lao dictionary to look up virtually every single word in her textbooks and carefully written the Lao equivalent above the English word, so that there were faint spidery pencil marks filling up all the spaces between the lines of her textbooks.

All those tests behind her, and now she had failed. Failed the one test that might have enabled her to help her parents get to work more easily, save them some money, and earn her some status among her classmates.

David's face appeared at the window. "How'd it go?" he asked with his usual cheerful grin.

Saeng suppressed an urge to pass her hand over his mouth and wipe the grin off. "Not so good," she said. She started to explain, then gave it up. It wasn't worth the effort, and besides, he didn't really care anyway.

He was holding the car door open for her and seemed a little impatient for her to get out. Saeng squirmed out of the seat, then remembered the twenty-dollar bill her mother had given her.

"Eh . . . thanks," she murmured awkwardly as she got out of the car. "It was nice of you to come here. And letting me use your car."

"Don't mention it," he said, sliding into the driver's seat already and pushing it back several inches.

"Would you . . . I mean, if you'd like, I could buy . . ." Saeng faltered as she saw that David wasn't even listening to her. His attention had been distracted by someone waving to him from across the street. He was waving back and smiling. Saeng followed the direction of his glance and saw a tall girl in tight jeans and a flannel shirt standing just under the M archway.

Someone blond and vivacious, her dimpled smile revealing two rows of dazzling white, regimentally straight teeth. *Definitely a cheerleader,* Saeng decided.

"Hold on, I'll be right with you," David was calling over to her. Abruptly he pulled the car door shut, flashed Saeng a perfunctory smile, and started to drive off. "Better luck next time," he said as his car pulled away, leaving her standing in the middle of the road.

Saeng watched him make a fluid U-turn and pull up right next to the tall blond girl, who swung herself gracefully into the seat next to David. For a moment they sat there laughing and talking in the car. So carefree, so casual—so American. They reminded Saeng of the Ken and Barbie dolls that she had stared at with such curiosity and longing when she had first arrived in the country.

But it wasn't even longing or envy that she felt now, Saeng realized. This girl could have been David's twin sister, and Saeng would still have felt this stab of pain, this recognition that They Belonged, and she didn't.

Another car drove slowly past her, and she caught a glimpse of her reflection on its window. Her arms were hanging limply by her sides, and she looked short and frumpy. Her hair was disheveled and her clothes seemed drab and old-fashioned—exactly as if they had come out of a rummage sale. She looked wrong. Totally out of place.

"Hey, move it! You're blocking traffic!"

A car had pulled up alongside of her, and in the front passenger seat sat the test instructor scowling at her, his thick lips taut with irritation.

Saeng stood rooted to the spot. She stared at him, stared at those thick lips beneath the bushy moustache. And suddenly she was jolted back to another time, another place, another voice—it had all been so long ago and so far away, yet now she still found herself immobilized by the immediacy of the past.

Once, shortly after she had arrived in America, when she had been watching an absorbing ballet program on the PBS channel at Mrs. Lambert's house, someone had switched channels with a remote control, and it seemed as if the gracefully dying Giselle in *Swan Lake* had suddenly been riddled with bullets from a screeching getaway car. So jarring had it been that Saeng felt as if an electric shock had charged through her, jolting her from one reality into another.

It was like that now, as if someone had switched channels in her life. She was no longer standing on a quiet street in downtown Danby but in the midst of a jostling crowd of tired, dusty people under a blazing sun. And it was not the balding driving instructor yelling at her, but a thick-lipped man in a khaki uniform, waving at them imperiously with a submachine gun.

Ban Vinai, Thailand. 1978. Things clicked into place, but it was no use knowing the name and number of the channel. The fear and dread still suffused her. She still felt like the scared, bone-weary little girl she had been then, being herded into the barbed-wire fencing of the refugee camp after they had escaped across the Mekong River from Laos.

"What're you doing, standing in the middle of the road? Get out of the way!"

And click—the Thai soldier was the test instructor again. Saeng blinked, blinked away the fear and fatigue of that memory, and slowly that old reality receded. In a daze she turned and made her way over to the curb, stepped up onto it, and started walking away.

Breathe deep, don't break down, she told herself fiercely. She could imagine David and that cheerleader staring at her behind her back. *I am tough,* she thought, *I am strong, I can take it.*

The sidewalk was littered with little acorns, and she kicked at them viciously as she walked and walked.

Only when she had turned the corner and was safely out of sight of David and the others did she finally stop. She found herself standing under a huge tree whose widespread branches were now almost leafless. An acorn dropped down and hit her on the head, before bouncing off into the street.

It seemed like the final indignity. Angrily, Saeng reached up for the branch directly overhead and tore off some of the large brown leaves still left. They were dry and crisp as she crushed them in her hands. She threw them at the wind and watched the bits of brown being whipped away by the afternoon wind.

"Who cares about the test, anyway," she said in a tight, grim whisper, tearing up another fistful of oak leaves. "Stupid test, stupid David, stupid cars. Who needs a license, anyway? Who needs a test like that?" It would only get harder, too, she realized, with the winter approaching and the streets turning slippery with the slush and snow. She had barely felt safe walking on the sidewalks in the winter—how could she possibly hope to drive then? It was hopeless, useless to even try. *I won't, I just won't ever take that test again!* Saeng told herself.

That resolved, she felt somewhat better. She turned away from the oak tree and was about to leave, when she suddenly noticed the bush next to it.

There was something very familiar about it. Some of its leaves had already blown off, but those that remained were still green. She picked a leaf and examined it. It was vaguely heart-shaped, with deeply serrated edges. Where had she seen this kind of leaf before? Saeng wondered. And why, among all these foreign maples and oak leaves, did it seem so very familiar? She scrutinized the bush, but it was no help: If there had been any flowers on it, they had already fallen off.

Holding the leaf in her hand, Saeng left the park and started walking home.

Her pace was brisk and determined, and she had not planned to stop off anywhere. But along the way, she found herself pausing involuntarily before a florist shop window. On display were bright bunches of cut flowers in tall glass vases—the splashes of red roses, white carnations, and yellow chrysanthemums a vivid contrast to the gray October afternoon. In the shadows behind them were several potted plants, none of which she could identify.

On an impulse, Saeng swung open the door and entered.

An elderly woman behind the counter looked up and smiled at her. "Yes? Can I help you?" she asked.

Saeng hesitated. Then she thrust out the heart-shaped green leaf in her hand and stammered, "Do—do you have this plant? I —I don't know its name."

The woman took the leaf and studied it with interest. "Why, yes," she said. "That looks like a rose of Sharon. We have several in the nursery out back."

She kept up a steady stream of conversation as she escorted Saeng through a side door into an open courtyard, where various saplings and shrubs stood. "Of course, it's not the best time for planting, but at least the ground hasn't frozen solid yet, and if you dig a deep enough hole and put in some good compost, it should do just fine. Hardy plants, these roses of Sharon. Pretty blossoms, too, in the fall. In fact—look, there's still a flower or two left on this shrub. Nice shade of pink, isn't it?"

Saeng looked at the single blossom left on the shrub. It looked small and washed out. The leaves on the shrub were of the same distinct serrated heart shape, but its flower looked—wrong, somehow.

"Is there—I mean, can it have another kind of flower?" Saeng asked. "Another color, maybe?"

"Well, it also comes in a pale purplish shade," the woman said helpfully. "And white, too."

"I think—I think it was a deep color," she offered, then shook her head. "I don't remember. It doesn't matter." Discouraged and feeling more than a little foolish, she started to back away.

"Wait," the florist said. "I think I know what you're looking for." A slow smile deepened the wrinkles in her face. "Come this way. It's in our greenhouse."

At the far side of the courtyard stood a shed, the like of which Saeng had never seen before. It was made entirely of glass and seemed to be bathed in a soft white light.

As she led the way there, the florist started talking again. "Lucky we just got through moving in some of our tropical plants," she said, "or the frost last weekend would have killed them off. Anything in there now you'd have to leave indoors until next summer, of course. Next to a big south-facing window or under some strong neon lamps. Even so, some of the plants won't survive the long cold winters here. Hothouse flowers, that's what they are. Not hardy, like those roses of Sharon I just showed you."

Only half listening, Saeng wished that there were a polite way she could excuse herself and leave. It was late and she was starting to get hungry. Still, she dutifully followed the other woman through the greenhouse door and walked in.

She gasped.

It was like walking into another world. A hot, moist world exploding with greenery. Huge flat leaves, delicate wisps of tendrils, ferns and fronds and vines of all shades and shapes grew in seemingly random profusion.

"Over there, in the corner, the hibiscus. Is that what you mean?" The florist pointed at a leafy potted plant by the corner.

There, in a shaft of the wan afternoon sunlight, was a single bloodred blossom, its five petals splayed back to reveal a long stamen tipped with yellow pollen. Saeng felt a shock of recognition so intense, it was almost visceral.

"*Saebba*," Saeng whispered.

A *saebba* hedge, tall and lush, had surrounded their garden, its lush green leaves dotted with vermilion flowers. And sometimes after a monsoon rain, a blossom or two would have blown into the well, so that when she drew up the well water, she would find a red blossom floating in the bucket.

Slowly, Saeng walked down the narrow aisle toward the hibiscus. Orchids, lanna bushes, oleanders, elephant ear begonias, and bougainvillea vines surrounded her. Plants that she had not even realized she had known but had forgotten drew her back into her childhood world.

When she got to the hibiscus, she reached out and touched a petal gently. It felt smooth and cool, with a hint of velvet toward the center—just as she had known it would feel.

And beside it was yet another old friend, a small shrub with waxy leaves and dainty flowers with purplish petals and white centers. "Madagascar periwinkle," its tag announced. *How strange to see it in a pot,* Saeng thought. Back home it just grew wild, jutting out from the cracks in brick walls or between tiled roofs. There had been a patch of it by the little spirit house where she used to help her mother light the incense and candles to the spirit who guarded their home and their family. Sometimes she would casually pick a flower or two to leave on the offerings of fruit and rice left at the altar.

And that rich, sweet scent—that was familiar, too. Saeng scanned the greenery around her and found a tall, gangly plant with exquisite little white blossoms on it. *"Dok Malik,"* she said, savoring the feel of the word on her tongue, even as she silently noted the English name on its tag, "jasmine."

One of the blossoms had fallen off, and carefully Saeng picked it up and smelled it. She closed her eyes and breathed in, deeply. The familiar fragrance filled her lungs, and Saeng could almost feel the light strands of her grandmother's long gray hair, freshly washed, as she combed it out with the fine-toothed buffalo-horn comb. And when the sun had dried it, Saeng would help the gnarled old fingers knot the hair into a bun, then slip a *dok Malik* bud into it.

Saeng looked at the white bud in her hand now, small and

fragile. Gently, she closed her palm around it and held it tight. That, at least, she could hold on to. But where was the fine-toothed comb? The hibiscus hedge? The well? Her gentle grandmother?

A wave of loss so deep and strong that it stung Saeng's eyes now swept over her. A blink, a channel switch, a boat ride in the night, and it was all gone. Irretrievably, irrevocably gone.

And in the warm moist shelter of the greenhouse, Saeng broke down and wept.

It was already dusk when Saeng reached home. The wind was blowing harder, tearing off the last remnants of green in the chicory weeds that were growing out of the cracks in the sidewalk. As if oblivious to the cold, her mother was still out in the vegetable garden, digging up the last of the onions with a rusty trowel. She did not see Saeng until the girl had quietly knelt down next to her.

Her smile of welcome warmed Saeng. *"Ghup ma laio le?* You're back?" she said cheerfully. "Goodness, it's past five. What took you so long? How did it go? Did you—?" Then she noticed the potted plant that Saeng was holding, its leaves quivering in the wind.

Mrs. Panouvong uttered a small cry of surprise and delight. *"Dok faeng-noi!"* she said. "Where did you get it?"

"I bought it," Saeng answered, dreading her mother's next question.

"How much?"

For answer Saeng handed her mother some coins.

"That's all?" Mrs. Panouvong said, appalled. "Oh, but I forgot! You and the Lambert boy ate Bee-Maags. . . ."

"No, we didn't, Mother," Saeng said.

"Then what else—?"

"Nothing else. I paid over nineteen dollars for it."

"You what?" Her mother stared at her incredulously. "But

how could you? All the seeds for this vegetable garden didn't cost that much! You know how much we—" She paused, as she noticed the tearstains on her daughter's cheeks and her puffy eyes.

"What happened?" she asked, more gently.

"I—I failed the test," Saeng said.

For a long moment Mrs. Panouvong said nothing. Saeng did not dare to look her mother in the eye. Instead, she stared at the hibiscus plant and nervously tore off a leaf, shredding it to bits.

Her mother reached out and brushed the fragments of green off Saeng's hands. "It's a beautiful plant, this *dok faeng-noi,*" she finally said. "I'm glad you got it."

"It's—it's not a real one," Saeng mumbled. "I mean, not like the kind we had at—at—" She found that she was still too shaky to say the words *at home,* lest she burst into tears again. "Not like the kind we had before," she said.

"I know," her mother said quietly. "I've seen this kind blooming along the lake. Its flowers aren't as pretty, but it's strong enough to make it through the cold months here, this winter hibiscus. That's what matters."

She tipped the pot and deftly eased the ball of soil out, balancing the rest of the plant in her other hand. "Look how rootbound it is, poor thing," she said. "Let's plant it, right now."

She went over to the corner of the vegetable patch and started to dig a hole in the ground. The soil was cold and hard, and she had trouble thrusting the shovel into it. Wisps of her gray hair trailed out in the breeze, and her slight frown deepened the wrinkles around her eyes. There was a frail, wiry beauty to her that touched Saeng deeply.

"Here, let me help, Mother," she offered, getting up and taking the shovel away from her.

Mrs. Panouvong made no resistance. "I'll bring in the hot peppers and bitter melons, then, and start dinner. How would you like an omelet with slices of the bitter melon?"

"I'd love it," Saeng said.

Left alone in the garden, Saeng dug out a hole and carefully lowered the "winter hibiscus" into it. She could hear the sounds of cooking from the kitchen now, the beating of the eggs against a bowl, the sizzle of hot oil in the pan. The pungent smell of bitter melon wafted out, and Saeng's mouth watered. It was a cultivated taste, she had discovered—none of her classmates or friends, not even Mrs. Lambert, liked it—this sharp, bitter melon that left a golden aftertaste on the tongue. But she had grown up eating it and, she admitted to herself, much preferred it to a Big Mac.

The "winter hibiscus" was in the ground now, and Saeng tamped down the soil around it. Overhead, a flock of Canada geese flew by, their faint honks clear and—yes—familiar to Saeng now. Almost reluctantly, she realized that many of the things that she had thought of as strange before had become, through the quiet repetition of season upon season, almost familiar to her now. Like the geese. She lifted her head and watched as their distinctive V was etched against the evening sky, slowly fading into the distance.

When they come back, Saeng vowed silently to herself, *in the spring, when the snows melt and the geese return and this hibiscus is budding, then I will take that test again.*

Minfong Ho

Born of Chinese parents in Burma and raised on the outskirts of Bangkok, Thailand, Minfong Ho grew up in an airy house "next to a fishpond and in a big garden," she says, "with rice fields on the other side of the palm trees, where water buffaloes wallowed in mudholes." As a child, she spoke Thai and Cantonese, then learned English when she started primary school. At sixteen she left home and went to Tunghai University in Taiwan, where she mastered Mandarin, then continued her studies in English at Cornell University in Ithaca, New York. Since then, she has learned some basic Cambodian while working with refugees as a nutritionist and relief worker on the Thai-Cambodian border. Recently, she has picked up a smattering of French in Geneva, Switzerland, where she now lives with her American husband and their three young children.

Minfong Ho started writing while she was at college in the United States, to combat homesickness by weaving her own private, familiar world around herself. Her first book, *Sing to the Dawn,* was the result of notes and letters she wrote while sitting in the Cornell University greenhouse that was filled with lush tropical plants, like those Saeng sees in "The Winter Hibiscus." That book won first prize from the Council on Interracial Books for Children. Her next two novels, *Rice Without Rain,* based on her experiences teaching in northern Thailand, and *The Clay Marble,* the result of working with Cambodian refugee children on the Thai-Cambodian border, have garnered numerous awards, among them the Parents' Choice Award, *Booklist* Editor's Choice, and a Best Book for Young Adults from the American Library Association.

Currently, Minfong Ho is working on a nonfiction book about life in Vietnam, Laos, and Cambodia after the war, and is translating Chinese poetry from the T'ang dynasty.

◻◗◗◗▲◗◗◗◗◻

Donald R. Gallo

Professor of English at Central Connecticut State University, Donald Gallo grew up in Paterson, New Jersey, hearing stories from his mother's Dutch family and enjoying the warmth of his father's Italian relations, most of them having immigrated to America as children. This is Dr. Gallo's fifth collection of short stories written by outstanding young adult authors for Bantam Doubleday Dell, following the highly praised *Sixteen, Visions, Connections,* and *Short Circuits.* He is also the editor of *Authors' Insights: Turning Teenagers into Readers and Writers* and compiler and editor of two volumes of *Speaking for Ourselves: Autobiographical Sketches by Notable Authors of Books for Young Adults.* His most recent paperback publication for Bantam Doubleday Dell is *Presenting Richard Peck.* Dr. Gallo is the 1992 recipient of the ALAN Award for outstanding contributions to the field of adolescent literature. He lives in West Hartford, Connecticut.

◻◗◦◦▲◦◦◗◦◻